THE BILLIONAIRE'S WIFE

BILLIONAIRE NEXT DOOR
BOOK 6

ELIZABETH MADDREY

For my sister, Lynellen.
I know you're better in heaven,
but life without you here is hard.

1

TRISTAN

"Faith." I took a long look at the woman by my door. She'd changed. Of course she had. It had been fourteen years since I'd seen her in person. And she was good at keeping a low profile online. Even with the tools at my disposal as an attorney, I'd had a hard time keeping track of her. I cleared my throat and dug my keys out of my pocket, then closed the distance to the door.

Faith stepped out of the way.

My lips twitched up. She still smelled like watermelon bubble gum. I unlocked the door and pushed it open, then glanced over my shoulder. "I guess you should come in."

I paused just inside the door of my condo to take off my shoes and set down my bags. I didn't bother to see if she followed. I needed aspirin. And a minute to gather my wits. Why was she here?

I stalked to the kitchen and yanked open the drawer where I kept vitamins and first aid basics. I grabbed the pain reliever bottle and wrestled with the cap. When it finally came off, I shook two into my hand and tossed them into my mouth so I could swallow them dry.

"Bad day?" Faith leaned against the corner of the hallway wall where it ended at the kitchen.

"Just long." I closed the bottle and put it back in the drawer, then moved to the fridge. I grabbed a diet ginger ale and, after a moment, held it up. "Want?"

Faith's eyebrows lifted. She shrugged. "Sure. Why not?"

I could think of ten reasons why not just off the top of my head, but I reached into the fridge to grab a second can instead. I shut the door, set one of the cans on the island and pushed it toward her, then popped the tab on my drink and took several long swallows of the icy cold soda.

My headache didn't magically disappear, but I could pretend that I felt it easing. "Did you lock the door?"

"I did." Faith scooted a little closer and stretched to get the soda.

I headed into the living room and dropped into an armchair, then propped my feet on the coffee table. I didn't want to be the one to broach the topic. Silence was the best weapon of a lawyer. Most people felt the need to fill silence with noise. I learned a lot that way. So. I'd wait. And I'd see what I could learn from Faith.

Faith opened her soda and shuffled into the living room. She hovered at the edge a moment, like a nervous butterfly, before finally lighting on the sofa. But she stayed perched on the edge.

Purposefully casual, I lifted my drink and took a sip.

Faith cleared her throat. "So. Hi."

I tipped my head to the side.

"Right. Of course you're not going to make this easy." Faith set her soda on the coffee table. She reached up and pulled off the baseball cap, then gathered her long, brown hair and twisted it into a knot that she fastened with a band off her wrist.

"Am I supposed to?" I sat up, my feet dropping to the floor. "It's been a minute since you disappeared, Faith."

She swallowed visibly.

"I'm ordering Chinese." I dug my phone out of my pocket. "You still like pot stickers and pork fried rice?"

Surprise flashed across her face before she nodded.

Maybe I shouldn't remember her favorite meal. But I did. I remembered everything. No matter how much I tried to forget. I didn't bother to sigh as I opened the app for my favorite Chinese delivery, then I glanced up. "Feel free to keep talking."

"Should I start by saying I'm sorry?" Faith twisted her fingers together.

"Only if you are." I offered a tight smile then returned to ordering the food. I was being antagonistic. I could put the blame on my headache, but that wasn't the only reason. All the hurt I'd buried had resurfaced the minute she'd spoken in the hall. Fourteen years, and the gaping wound she'd made when she walked out was still bleeding.

"Tristan." Faith stopped and I heard her take a deep breath.

I looked up.

She blew out her breath. "I *am* sorry."

I nodded. I wanted to ask for more details. Was she sorry for leaving? Sorry for hurting me? Sorry for disappearing? Or was she simply sorry because I'd implied she should be?

"I need your help. Believe me, if there was any way to have done this without involving you, I would have gone that route."

I was suddenly glad I'd spent nearly every Friday of the last few years playing poker with the guys. That plus my courtroom experience meant I was able to keep my expression neutral. She didn't need to know she'd just sliced a new hole in my heart. "You should've made an appointment at the office."

"I wasn't sure you'd agree to see me."

I scoffed. "Please."

"Okay. You're right." Faith frowned and turned to look out the floor-to-ceiling windows that made up the end of my living room wall. "You have a nice view."

"It was a definite selling point." I followed her gaze and looked out at the rain slashing down from dark clouds to the Potomac River below.

"Will you help me?"

I felt her gaze on me.

I turned back and met it. I forced my brain to shift back into business mode. "Depends."

"On what?"

My eyebrows lifted. "On what sort of help you need. I'm not hurting for clients, and the people I'm already representing deserve to get the same time and attention they've been getting from me."

"But—" Faith broke off and pressed her lips together. Her eyes swam. "I don't know where else to turn."

"You said that. So, we'll eat dinner and you'll tell me what's going on. And if I think I can help within the time I have available, I'll take on your case. Otherwise, I should at least be able to make a referral to another lawyer. Someone I trust."

She shook her head. "No. If you can't help, I'll try to deal with it on my own. I'm not involving anyone else."

I clamped my teeth shut to keep from blurting out any of the retorts that sprang to mind. They weren't kind. They definitely weren't going to help the situation.

"There's one more thing."

"What's that?" Was she going to ask to stay here? Knowing Faith—although, ha ha, could I say I knew her anymore?—she was. She probably had no money. From the way she was acting, I gathered she was probably avoiding credit cards to keep off the grid.

"Is there any way I could stay here?"

My laugh had no mirth. Called that one. Technically, I had the room. But...

"I promise I'll stay out of your way. You'll hardly know I'm here. I just...really need to lie low." She fidgeted in her seat. "I know it's a lot to ask."

I heaved out a breath. I wanted to say no. I wanted to scream it from the rooftop. Everything in me said this was a bad, bad, bad idea. But it was Faith. And Faith was the one person in my life whom I'd never been able to say no to. I rubbed a hard circle in the center of my forehead with the knuckle of my thumb and tried to talk myself out of doing what I was, inevitably, going to do.

Then I caved. "Yeah. Fine. Let me show you the guest room."

I pushed to my feet and jerked my head for her to follow. I turned down the short hall that led to the guest bath and bedrooms. I pointed to my door. "This one is mine. It's off limits."

Faith nodded.

I reached in and flipped on the guest room light. "This is yours. Bathroom's in the hall."

"I appreciate this, Tristan. I know it's not easy for you."

I pinned her with a glare. "Let's be clear about one thing, okay? You don't know me. Not anymore."

She blinked.

I stepped into the room. I used this space primarily as a home office. There wasn't much in the way of files, but those that were here should definitely not be flipped through by random strangers. And that was how I was going to think of Faith from now on.

In a perfect world, at least.

I crossed to the desk and pulled open the file drawer. I scooted all the hanging folders close and scooped them into my arms. I turned.

She was watching me from the doorway.

"There shouldn't be anything sensitive left. But don't go snooping." I brushed past her. There was a lot more static electricity in the air than seemed reasonable for a stormy, wet evening. Of course, I knew it wasn't static. It was Faith. The chemistry between us—at least on my end—hadn't changed. "Why don't you get comfortable? I'll let you know when the food is here."

"Okay. I appreciate this."

I nodded once and took a few steps toward my room. Then I stopped and looked back. "Do you have luggage somewhere?"

"I have a bag in my car. I'm in one of the visitor spots."

That wasn't going to work long term. I had a second hanging tag for residents. "Get me your keys. I'll move you to a better spot and bring in your things."

"I can—"

"Just get me your keys." Exasperation leaked into my voice. "I'll be right back."

I went into my bedroom and stacked the files neatly in one of the corners. I took a moment to close my eyes and breathe. I could do this. I would hear her out. I would do my best to make the time to help with her legal problems. And then, when it was done, I'd give her the papers that I should have sent her years ago.

I crossed to my dresser and opened the top drawer. I grabbed the spare parking tag from the top pile of random things and then, after a moment, shifted some of the junk stashed in there to the side and pulled out the manila envelope that I'd buried in the drawer when I moved into the condo. I opened the flap and slid the top of the papers out. It was still a kick in the gut to read the words. Divorce. It wasn't something I wanted.

I never had.

But it was probably long past time to accept reality.

So. This was good. I tucked the papers back in the envelope and returned them to their place. This would be closure. And then I could move on and stop being the only one of our group of friends who wasn't in a relationship.

I snickered a little at that. I was married, sure. But a relationship? Faith and I definitely didn't have that. Not anymore.

I went back into the hallway. Faith didn't look as though she'd moved.

"Keys?"

She reached into her pocket and tossed them to me.

I snagged them out of the air. "Make? Model?"

"It's a dark blue Camry. Kind of old. Dinged." She hesitated. "Michigan plates."

"Okay. I'll be back. You can get settled."

"Could I grab a shower?"

"Sure." I squashed the flitting memory from the days when I'd believed our marriage could be real. "I'll leave your suitcase outside the bathroom door. There should be towels. Take your time."

I didn't wait for her response. I turned and headed toward the door. My thoughts were going close to two hundred miles an hour. Michigan. Last time I poked around to see what she was doing, she'd been in Illinois. It wasn't a big stretch to make the shift, but I didn't really understand why she moved around so much.

Maybe that would be part of her explanation.

I drummed my fingers on my leg as I waited for the elevator. When it finally arrived, I got in and selected the ground floor. Thankfully, none of the kids from the building had managed to get back in and push all the buttons again, so the trip down was short. I hurried through the lobby and out to the parking area.

Visitor spots were mostly grouped together near the main building entrance. I scanned the cars there for a Camry, then pushed the lock button on Faith's key fob. Lights blinked and a chirp came from the second row. I pushed the button again as I crossed toward the car.

I laughed.

"Dinged-up" was an understatement. How did this thing even drive? There were more dents and crumples in the body of the car than I'd seen outside of an accident report. And was that duct tape? I ran my finger over the long strip. It was indeed.

I sighed and unlocked the door, then lowered myself into the driver seat, pausing to scoot the seat back so there was a chance of my legs fitting. Faith had always liked to sit close to the steering wheel. She said it was better on her neck and back.

I started the car. It coughed several times before rattling to life. Had she driven this piece of junk from Michigan? She was either brave or crazy.

Maybe both.

Nothing bad happened when I shifted into Reverse and backed out of the spot. I drove around to where my car was parked and pulled hers into the numbered spot beside mine. After parking and turning the engine off again, I hung the parking tag on the rearview mirror. I didn't see the trunk release, so I pushed the button on the fob to pop it open.

I climbed out from behind the wheel, shut the door, and moved around to the back. There was only one suitcase. It looked like it was more tape than anything else at this point. I'd expected more. Boxes. A second case. Something.

I hauled out the bag. "Ooof."

Heavier than I anticipated. I closed the trunk. It popped right back up. I pushed it down harder. Same result. Frowning, I slammed it. This time it stuck. I clicked the lock button, grabbed the suitcase handle, and started back toward the lobby.

The wheels on the bag kind of worked. Or maybe it was safer to say they worked well enough that I wasn't tempted to just carry the thing. Not with as heavy as it was. I rolled the bag onto the elevator and held the door as another resident who I vaguely recognized dashed on.

She flashed a grin at me. "Thanks."

"Sure." I pushed the button for my floor and moved out of the way.

She pressed her floor—two below mine—and glanced at the bag. "Company in town?"

"Yeah."

"That's always nice. I'm hoping my parents can come out for Thanksgiving. Maybe if they do, I'll finally get around to driving out to Skyline to see the leaves. Have you done that?"

"No. I never seem to make the time."

"Right? That's why company is good." She laughed. "Hope you do something fun with yours while they're in town."

The elevator stopped at her floor and she got off before I could figure out what kind of response was appropriate. Thanks, probably. Or some kind of general and positive acknowledgment?

Didn't matter.

My stomach tightened as the elevator stopped on my floor. For all that my neighbor was excited about company, I wasn't. At least, not this particular guest.

I rolled the suitcase down the hall, unlocked my door, and went in. The water was running. So, good. That gave me a little time before I had to face Faith again and hear whatever story she had to share.

I moved the suitcase into the hallway and parked it by the bathroom door, then knocked. "Luggage delivery. I'll be in the kitchen. Take your time."

I didn't wait for an answer, I just turned and headed for the kitchen. I got down a glass and filled it with water from the dispenser in the fridge door. At least the rain had stopped. Looking out the windows at the clouds, I was certain it would be back—probably storm off and on all night—but for the moment there was a reprieve.

I sipped the water and worked to organize my thoughts. I needed to figure out how to treat her like any other client. If I was going to help her—and that was still a big, undecided question mark in my mind—I couldn't do it with all the hurt and anger currently frothing in my soul.

A knock startled me out of my thoughts. That was probably the food. A little faster than usual, but not outside the realm of possibility. I set my water down beside my unfinished ginger ale from earlier and padded to the front door. I checked through the peep before unlocking and opening the door.

"Evening." The kid who didn't look old enough to be driving deliveries around thrust the order at me.

"Thanks. Appreciate it."

He nodded. "Have a good night."

"You, too." I shifted the order to one arm, then stepped back and shut the door. I flipped the lock, then took the food back to the kitchen and set it on the counter.

I cocked my head to the side and listened. The water was off. Faith should be out and ready to eat soon, then.

I tugged open the stapled paper bag that sat inside a plastic bag and lifted out the various boxes and containers holding the food. The spicy scents teased my nose and made my stomach growl.

I got down two plates, then dug out some forks and wooden chopsticks. I didn't usually bother with the sticks. Forks were faster and less messy. But Faith had always been a purist. At least back when I knew her. So I'd give her the option.

I pried lids off the food and opened the paper containers, then dished some rice onto one of the plates. I went through adding little bits of this and that, then pulled out a stool at the island and sat. Normally, if I wasn't eating at my desk, I'd eat on the couch, but that seemed too informal and friendly for today.

"It smells good."

I glanced over. She had her hair wrapped in a towel on top of her head but had dressed in threadbare flannel pants and a long-sleeved T-shirt bearing the name of my college. "Is that my shirt?"

Faith looked down, then back up at me. Her cheeks were red. "You never noticed it was gone?"

I shrugged. I had. But I'd figured I'd lost it somewhere. It never occurred to me that Faith had taken it. "Why don't you fix a plate, have a seat, and fill me in?"

2

FAITH

The Chinese food smelled amazing, but my stomach was in so many knots, I had no idea if I'd be able to keep anything down. If I'd thought it was an option, I would've stayed in the shower, letting the hot water pound on me, until Tristan gave up and went to bed. But ignoring problems never made them go away. And Tristan wasn't likely to let me get out of spilling the details tonight.

I blew out a breath and reached for the empty plate. I put a couple of dumplings on it, then scooped some fried rice. It wasn't a lot, but hopefully it was enough to keep him from nagging me about eating more. I went the long way around the island to avoid brushing past him, and sat.

I hadn't missed the frisson of electricity that had passed between us earlier. And as much as I might love to explore that again, it was a bad idea for hundreds of reasons.

I reached for the chopsticks, a tiny tendril of warmth worming into my heart at their presence.

"Can I pray?"

I jolted, cleared my throat, and nodded. "Sure. Yes. Of course."

I looked away from Tristan's piercing gaze and bowed my head.

I didn't hear what he said when he prayed. It had been so long since I'd even gone through the motions of prayer that the whole sensation was strange.

"So." Tristan scooped a forkful of fried rice and held it over his plate while he spoke. "Start at the top."

I couldn't stop the quick, tight smile. It was so like him. Or at least like the Tristan I'd known all those years ago. Except, when I looked over at him, he was clearly not the same man. That was part of it—he was definitely a man now. Back then, he'd really been a boy. We'd both been children.

I cleared my throat and set down the chopsticks without eating anything. "I guess it goes all the way back. My dad, you know about him. Obviously. He traded information in return for a lighter sentence. It's why I left."

Tristan tipped his head to one side. "Because your dad went to jail?"

"No." I blew out a breath. Why couldn't he make this even a little easy? "Because some of the information he gave them made his bookies angry. They had threatened to use me as collateral before. I didn't want to risk them showing up and you getting sucked into the mess farther than you already had."

"You were my wife, Faith. I would have protected you."

"That's just it. I know you would have tried. But—" I cut myself off as Tristan's face turned stony. Maybe it was better not to go down that road. "Anyway. I stayed under the radar. I've always been good with computers, so it wasn't too hard. Moved around a lot. And I thought I was doing all right until six or seven months ago."

"What happened?"

I paused to pick up a dumpling with my chopsticks and dunk it into the sauce. I took a bite and chewed. Tristan was going to hate everything about what I had to say. But I couldn't gloss over it, either. I needed his help. And he needed the truth in order to help me.

I set the chopsticks down again. "So. I had to support myself. Right? And I couldn't get a regular job with all the tax reporting and so forth. But it turns out there's a pretty good living to be made with computers that isn't *technically* all aboveboard."

Tristan sighed and put down his fork. "Tell me you haven't been hacking for hire."

I couldn't meet his gaze. I kept my head down and scooped rice into my mouth. Maybe it wasn't all hacking, but I was pretty sure that qualification wasn't going to mean very much to him.

Tristan scooted back his stool and stood. He strode across the kitchen through the living room, and stood staring out the glass that made up the far wall of his condo. He raked his hands through his hair. "I knew you'd be trouble."

I winced. He probably hadn't intended to say it aloud. I could give him a break there. It still hurt. "I always am. Tried to warn you."

He turned and his gaze skewered me. "Do *not* make a mockery of what I felt for you. What I tried to do for you."

I hunched my shoulders. The past tense verbs shouldn't have been able to hurt me, but they did. "Sorry."

He rubbed the back of his neck and came to the kitchen island and sat. "So you became a hacker."

"Among other things. It wasn't all hacking. I made some IDs. Documents that weren't strictly original. That sort of thing." I hated how it sounded, even though I could explain to anyone— or, well, anyone but Tristan—why it had been my only option.

"Mmhmm."

I stabbed one chopstick into a dumpling and wiggled it in a circle, making a slowly widening hole in the dough. "I was careful. Did a lot of screening of potential clients. I mostly only took word-of-mouth referrals from people I'd already vetted and had been working with a while. But I screwed up."

He didn't speak.

I waited, but he just sat. I'd expected...something. Some kind of reaction. When it was clear none was coming, I continued. "I took on a new client. One of my repeats had vouched for them—admittedly not someone I'd known a long time, just a year. Ish. The job sounded interesting and the pay was more than I usually charged."

"That doesn't smell like a trap at all." Sarcasm dripped off Tristan's words.

"Yeah, well. I see it now. I was blinded by greed, I guess." And the idea that the money would have been enough for me to create the new identity for myself that I'd been designing. I'd been planning to get out—all the way out. And yeah, sure, I'd been considering touching base with Tristan to see if he wanted to come along. Somewhere in the back of my mind I couldn't shake the idea that we could be good together if he'd give us a chance. That part of the situation I probably didn't have to share though.

Tristan stood. He moved around the island and started scraping the food off his plate back into the takeout containers.

I guess his appetite wasn't very strong either right now. I nudged my plate toward him.

"You're finished?" He nodded toward the barely touched food.

I nodded. "I figured out the plan before it was completely too late, but not before they'd stolen back the money they'd paid up front plus about eighty percent of my cache. They had my location and the ID I was using. I took what I could that was untraceable and ran."

"Who was it?"

I hesitated. "If I tell you, it puts you at risk."

"You need my help, right?"

I nodded slowly. I still desperately wished for an alternative —any alternative.

"Then I need to know what we're up against."

I blew out a breath. He was right. "The Ortegas."

Tristan held up a single hand like a police officer stopping traffic. "You did *not* just say the Ortegas. As in the cartel Ortegas?"

I nodded, wincing.

"A cartel, Faith? Seriously?" He set the plate down on the counter with a smack so loud I was surprised it didn't split into two pieces.

"I didn't know." I frowned. "I didn't work with drug dealers. I was always really clear about that. I had no reason to think this client was setting me up, either."

Tristan just shook his head. He closed up the containers and turned to stick them in the fridge. "Are you sure they can't find you?"

"As sure as I can be." I twisted my fingers together in my lap. "I don't have a cell phone. The car down there is the third one I've had since I started running—all cash and trade transactions. None of them registered to an ID I've used before. I haven't used my own computers—they've been powered down in my suit-case. I stop at libraries and Apple stores when I need to find information. I'm not stupid. And I'm not taking chances with your safety."

He looked like he wanted to make a snarky comment, but I was grateful when he kept it to himself. Instead, he just nodded.

I sat and let the silence thicken between us. The sound-proofing on his condo was good. I didn't hear anyone in the hall or in the unit next door. Not even the quiet hum of someone's television.

Finally, I couldn't take it. I looked up an met his eyes. "Can you help me?"

"Depends. What do you want? What's your endgame here?"

That was a good question. When I'd finally settled on coming here and begging Tristan to bail me out one more time, I'd planned on figuring out how I could still just disappear. I could make that new ID, figure out the finances, and poof. And okay, yes, I'd figured on hitting Tristan up for the finances. He was a successful lawyer. He had to have a little extra, didn't he? Fifty or a hundred grand would do. Sure, more would be better, but there was no point in getting greedy.

But now—no. I should stick with the plan. Just because seeing Tristan again dragged up all the thoughts and feelings I'd had about him, didn't mean I should do anything about them.

Or that I could.

Being married to Tristan didn't change anything.

And still, I couldn't bring myself to say more than, "I don't know."

"Okay. Well, I guess that's step one. Figure that out, then we can talk some more."

I swallowed. I was glad he wasn't immediately kicking me out. He absolutely could. No one would blame him. I certainly wouldn't. "Thanks."

"Don't thank me yet." He sighed. "Do you want my opinion?"

"Of course."

He shook his head slightly. "There's no 'of course' about it. But I think you need to go to the authorities. The FBI, I guess? Or maybe the DEA. I can research that. Come clean. Find a way to start a real life, not one that's hidden in the shadows."

The mental picture his words painted was one I wanted to grab with both hands and pull into being. What would it be like to have a life like that? One where I didn't have to hide who I was. What I was. Where I was.

I honestly couldn't quite imagine it.

"I'm not sure I know how to live like that." The closest I'd ever gotten was the six or so months we'd lived together after we eloped. And we both knew how I'd handled that. "But it sounds like something I'd like to try."

His eyebrows lifted. "Is that your choice?"

I wanted to hunch into a ball. I wasn't in a place to make that big of a decision. Not right now. "Can I sleep on it?"

"Sure." He shrugged like it was no big deal, but I caught the flash of disappointment on his face.

That was Tristan. He defined the straight arrow. And me? I was the complete opposite.

Opposites might attract, but that didn't mean the relationships they ended up with were healthy for either of them.

3

TRISTAN

When the clock finally showed six a.m., I sat up. Six was a reasonable enough hour to get out of bed and give up on the ridiculous idea that I'd be getting sleep.

I'd spent the night alternating between fixation on the fact that Faith was here, in my condo, just a few steps away, and that she'd managed to get herself involved with the Ortegas. I didn't know a ton about cartels and crime families, but the *Ortegas*? They made headlines. Everyone who could read—and probably anyone who couldn't—knew about them.

It was so like her. Why get involved with a small, harmless cartel when she could find the biggest, bloodiest one instead?

Not that harmless and cartel went together, but the point stood regardless.

I pulled on workout clothes—not something I usually did on a Saturday morning—and then exited my room as quietly as possible. A quick glance showed Faith's door was still shut. I was going to bank on that meaning she was in there, asleep, and not waiting to ambush me in the kitchen.

I wasn't used to tiptoeing in my own place, but I made it

work. The kitchen was dark and empty. Just like it should be. Like every part of my condo should be. I squeezed my eyes shut. I needed to get out of my head and stop being so resentful. I could have sent divorce papers any time in the last fourteen years. With a few exceptions, I'd known where she was—or been able to find her with some digging. The fact that I hadn't explored how she was keeping herself afloat was on me. What would I have done about it? What *could* I have done about it?

She'd left me.

So really, what was I supposed to do? Run after her and beg?

I'd thought about it, sure. But at some point, wasn't I entitled to keep a shred of my pride? I'd loved her before we married. She'd seen me as a way out.

Even knowing that, I'd gone through with it.

Of course, I'd thought we had time. That she'd hang around and see that I was worth loving back. That the two of us could make something of our lives. Together.

I blew out a breath.

This was getting me nowhere.

I grabbed my keys off the hook, unlocked the door, and stepped into the hall. After a moment's thought, I relocked the door and headed for the stairs.

No point in taking the elevator when the whole point of working out was exercise.

My muscles were warm and limber by the time I reached the basement gym. The lights were off and no noise pumped out of the TVs on the wall. I flipped the switches to turn on the bright overheads, but opted for quiet.

My head was noisy enough without adding to it.

I chose the treadmill farthest from the door, stepped on, and hit the power. I scanned the program options and finally settled on a thirty-minute hilly run. Maybe the changing intensity would be enough to wear me out and stop all the obsessing.

I pushed start and fell into step on the conveyor belt. I focused on keeping my breathing deep and even. The only sound was the hum of the machine and light slaps of the soles of my shoes as I ran.

I didn't love running, but it was good for helping me focus. By the time the machine slowed to a stop, sweat ran in rivulets down my back and my muscles sang out in exhaustion. I swiped my forehead with my shoulder and blinked the sting of sweat from my eyes. I should have brought a towel down. While I worked to steady my breathing, I used alcohol wipes to clean the machine, then turned to face the free weights.

Normally, after a run, I'd spend another fifteen or twenty minutes with them. Ingrained habit had my feet moving that direction, but I stopped halfway across the mat. There was no way.

Not today.

I didn't even usually work out on the weekends, so I was ahead of the game. Besides, in addition to the usual tired-but-energized feeling that came from working out? I felt vaguely ill.

It was most likely the lack of sleep.

I pressed my lips together as I was hit with a wave of nausea. Definitely the lack of sleep. I remembered this feeling from law school the few times I'd been forced to pull all-nighters. Planning ahead was my preferred choice—it had been in school and it continued in life—but sometimes stuff came up.

And then I paid the price.

Shaking my head, I headed out of the gym, pausing to flip the lights back off. I had no idea what the usual crowd was like on weekends, but there was no point in running up the electric bill on a common area. The association was always looking for reasons to increase our condo fees.

I took the stairs to the main level and paused, a hand on the rail, then looked up.

Nope.

I pushed through the door into the lobby. My stomach growled. I hesitated. I had cereal upstairs. The coffee I usually made. Did I need to go out and get something fancier—better? —because I had a guest?

Mom would say yes. Dad called her "the hostess with the mostest" and it was probably true. But I wasn't trying to be the male version of that. I wasn't even sure I wanted to be a host. Actually, that was untrue. I *knew* I didn't want to be one.

I just didn't have a choice.

Dad was a big fan of "begin as you mean to go on." So today? I guess I was on team Dad. If Faith didn't like cereal and my locally roasted coffee beans, she was welcome to go out and find something else. Or order it up.

That would be her problem to handle. Not mine.

I was already on the hook to handle enough of her problems.

I strode across the lobby to the elevators and poked the call button. The doors slid open immediately and before long, I was letting myself inside my condo.

I closed the door, locked it, and stood with my head cocked, listening. It was still quiet. I could pretend it was empty. If I was any good at pretending, at least.

I hung the key back up and went to the kitchen. No Faith. I blew out a breath. Good. I'd get the coffee set up, go take a shower, and then, if everything worked out the way I hoped? Maybe I could even get a cup of coffee and some food into me before I had to face Faith.

I filled the bean grinder and winced slightly at the noise, but it was unavoidable. The taste was better—so much better—with fresh ground. Maybe I'd gotten spoiled, but usually there was no one to care what time I started things up in the kitchen.

When the machine was set with grounds and water, I hit the

button to start it brewing, then hurried down the hallway to my room. The door to the guest room remained closed. No light peeked out from under it. The hall bathroom was dark and empty.

I breathed a quick prayer of thanks for that seemingly small favor and slipped into my bedroom, taking extra care to lock my door, before shedding my sweaty workout clothes and heading into the bathroom to shower.

I think I got in and out of the hot water faster than ever before in my lifetime. There was a part of me that would have loved to stand under the hot spray and imagine my life was normal—or at least the normal I'd been fine with before yesterday—but also? I really wanted coffee without Faith.

I was going to need my brain firing on all cylinders in order to deal with her. There was too much at stake. I would help her as best I could, then I would give her the divorce papers, and then? Then I'd move on with my life.

At no time, and under no circumstances, was Faith ever going to find out that I loved her as much today as I had when we got married.

Really, that shouldn't be too hard, since I was reasonably sure she had no idea I'd been in love with her then, either.

I pulled on jeans and a thermal tee, then ran a comb through my hair and spent a few extra seconds mussing the front like the hairstylist always did after a cut. It wasn't something I usually bothered with, but I could admit it looked nice that way.

Which shouldn't matter.

Maybe I just liked looking nice for myself?

I blew out an exasperated breath and turned away from the mirror. I gave my room a quick once-over on my way through, then paused at the door and listened.

Still quiet.

I slowly opened the door just enough to squeeze through,

then closed it behind me and hurried down the hall to the kitchen.

The rich aroma of coffee filled the air. I breathed it in as I opened a cabinet and took down my favorite oversized mug. I filled it, added cream and sugar, and carried it into the living room. I took the first sip of the life-giving liquid standing at the floor-to-ceiling window. I stared out at the Potomac River as the first fingers of dawn began to lighten the sky.

I let my thoughts drift. Of course, they kept coming back to Faith and her little cartel problem. Hopefully she'd choose a real life going forward. I couldn't help her if she didn't. I knew most everyone classified lawyers as people with no moral compass, but it just wasn't true. And I couldn't—wouldn't—help someone continue to lead a life based on breaking laws.

Not even Faith.

"Good morning."

I turned. I hadn't heard her come in. A quick glance at her feet explained it. Her feet were bare save for the hot pink nail polish on her toes. Nothing about the baggy sweatpants and long-sleeved T-shirt should make my mouth water, but I had to stop myself from saying something idiotic.

"Morning. Sleep well?"

Faith lifted one shoulder. "Mostly. It's a comfortable room."

I drained the remainder of my coffee and skirted around her on my way to the kitchen for more. "I'm glad. You want coffee?"

"Only desperately."

I gestured to the machine and got down a second mug. "Help yourself. You need food?"

"I wouldn't say no." Faith filled her mug and doctored the coffee before crossing to the fridge and tugging it open. She hesitated briefly before removing one of the takeout containers from last night. "Okay if I eat this?"

"Sure." I'd forgotten her penchant for weird food in the

morning. The thought of Chinese for breakfast had my stomach clenching. I filled my mug halfway, doctored it, then got down a bowl. From another cabinet, I took down the box of granola and shook some into the bowl. I put the box back and went to the fridge for milk.

"You still like that?" Faith shook her head as she opened the takeout container. She sniffed it, smiled, and reached in with two fingers to extract a pot sticker. She bit it in half.

I poured milk on my cereal and carried the meal around the island so I could sit. "Apparently."

"I don't get it. You've got perfectly good Chinese food. Why would you eat twigs and berries?"

I chuckled. "It's oats, honey, and almonds. And it's filling and delicious. And healthier."

"Maybe. Maybe not." Faith popped the second half of the pot sticker into her mouth.

"Do you want a fork? Or chopsticks? Maybe a plate and the microwave?"

"I'm good." Faith licked her fingers. "Unless this bothers you."

It did, actually, but it didn't seem like something worth mentioning. "It's fine."

She leaned on the counter and dug another pot sticker out of the container. I looked down at my cereal, stirred it, and started to eat. I wanted to bring up the decision she needed to make. I had a list of questions brewing that I needed answered.

If I was going to help her, it was better to start now. Get it done. Move on. Dragging things out was only going to hurt more in the long run.

At the same time, I could tell it wasn't the right move. Not yet. For one, she needed to be awake. And properly attired. Surely she'd be less distracting in clothes that didn't look obviously slept in.

I finished my cereal and stood, then carried the bowl to the sink. I rinsed it and loaded it into the dishwasher.

Faith started laughing.

"What?" I turned, frowning.

"Nothing. I'm sorry. It's really nothing." She waved a hand in the air, seemingly oblivious to the half-eaten pot sticker still between her fingers.

Oookay?

I went back to the island and sat so I could finish my coffee.

"You're good at the silence thing."

"I'm not used to having someone in my space in the morning. And I try to avoid talking to myself."

She flashed a grin. "No girlfriend?"

"No. You might remember I'm married."

Red stained her cheeks. "On paper, sure. But you've dated, right? Come on, Tristan, no one expected you to be a monk for the last fourteen years."

My eyebrows lifted.

She cleared her throat and looked away. "Seriously?"

"Married. It matters."

"Well. Um." She blew out a breath. "Wow."

I took a drink of coffee even though it tasted like dust now. "I guess you have a boyfriend?"

"Not now. No. But, there have been a few guys...sometimes it's the easiest way to get a place to crash." Faith twisted her drink in her hands. "That sounds bad when you say it out loud."

I nodded.

She drank, then set the mug down on the counter. "I guess I owe you an apology?"

"Are you asking me?"

"Kind of? I'm lost here. I thought the whole marriage thing was your way of getting me out from under Dad's thumb and away from a situation that wasn't safe."

"It was." It was that and so much more. "It was a way for me to protect you."

"And I ruined it. Because of course I did." She pinched the bridge of her nose. "'I'm sorry' feels inadequate, but it's all I've got. Maybe...maybe once we figure out the whole cartel thing I can figure out some way to make it up to you."

I wasn't sure right now that I wanted to know how she thought she'd make up for fourteen years of absence. None of the ideas that popped into my head were in line with living for Jesus. "Don't worry about it. But since you brought it up, have you thought about what you want?"

Faith gave a curt nod. "I want out. All the way."

The weight on my shoulders eased marginally. "Okay. That's good."

"I'm not sure I believe it's the right choice. I'm not even sure I believe it's possible. But I know you'll do what you can, and I'll hate myself if I don't at least try."

4

FAITH

I looked around the front room of the tiny office suite that Tristan had for his business. I wasn't sure what I'd expected, but it wasn't this. There was no big conference room or pool of secretaries out front. No line of offices. Nothing like what was on TV when they showed law offices.

Although, to be fair, those were usually big firms, and Tristan was an office of one.

"How long have you been solo?" I followed Tristan into his office and dropped onto the sofa that lined one wall.

"Almost two years." He set his bag down on his desk and lowered into a big leather chair. That, at least, was like on TV.

"You like it? I thought your dream was to be partner in a fancy firm. Corner office. All that." Maybe I didn't remember as well as I thought I did, but that scenario sure sounded familiar.

"Dreams change." He closed his eyes and held up a hand as if he realized how gruff his voice had come out. "Sorry. You're right. That was where I'd been aiming. I was nearly there, too. Then...circumstances changed."

I tilted my head to the side. "You're not sick or something, right?"

He scoffed and a hint of a smile flirted with the corners of his lips. "No. You haven't kept tabs on me at all?"

I shrugged. "A little. Here and there. I've been kind of busy lately."

"Fair enough." He sighed and tented his fingers. "I've got enough money I could stop working. My friends and I played the stock market and won big."

Something about that was familiar. When it came to money, I kept my ear to the ground. It was always good to know who the players were. "Wait. You're one of the Billionaires Next Door?"

He winced. "I hate that they named us."

"Better than having your full name and photos splashed all over everything." I frowned. "Who are the others? Only two have really hit the news with any kind of big splash."

"Scott and Austin, yeah. There are actually six of us, not the five that they always hint at." He shook his head. "Can we talk about this later?"

"Why? Just spill now and then we can move on. You're a billionaire with your friends—wait. Scott? College Scott?"

He nodded. "The others are from school, too. You just didn't stick around long enough for them to meet you."

"Ouch."

"It's true."

"I guess. Any idea how many shots you're going to need to take before you can let it go? I'd like to prepare myself." I didn't even bother to keep the snark out of my voice. "I thought I was doing what was best for both of us, okay? Maybe you expected me to discuss every little thing with you because we were married, but we both know that marriage was you playing rescuer."

"Is."

"Huh?"

"Is. The marriage is. It's not as if it's over."

I blinked and tried to process his words. "On paper, I guess. We can probably fix that, too. Right?"

His face paled. It had to be a trick of the light though, right? Sure, I might have worked up some fantasies involving convincing Tristan to disappear with me, but I knew that was what they were. Tristan wasn't the kind of guy who tiptoed over the line of illegal. Disappearing with not-quite-legal-IDs definitely was a step or two beyond that line.

Even with my decision to try to fix this the right way, I was keeping my options open. The Ortegas had a long reach, and I wasn't convinced that anything we did was going to truly keep me safe from them.

"Sure. Of course. You want to do that first?" His voice was flat.

I shook my head. "I'm in no rush. But you've got to have someone waiting in the wings."

"There's never been anyone but you."

I opened my mouth to speak but couldn't figure out what words I was supposed to use. He couldn't mean it the way it sounded, could he? Why would he? Sure, we'd been friends in high school. Of a sort.

I'd been a project for his parents. I'd known that then. I'd been desperate enough to get away from home that hanging out with the Lees—even when they seemed to be at church more than at home—was better than any other available alternative. Mrs. Lee had been the mother I'd always craved. And Mr. Lee? A father who would never try a doorknob, let alone get angry when he found it locked, was a dream.

"How's your mom?" I blurted out the question without really thinking about how it would sound.

Tristan's whole face softened. "She's great. Dad, too. They're spending until Thanksgiving in Vietnam."

"Vietnam?" I laughed. "You know what? I can picture them there. Probably riding elephants or something."

"Or something." Tristan pulled out his phone and tapped at it. After a moment, he flipped it around and offered it.

I took the phone and looked down at a photo of his parents surrounded by a throng of children who all looked to be younger than eight or nine. If the genuine joy shining out of their eyes was anything to go by, they were having the time of their lives.

I handed him back his phone. "They look just the same."

Tristan glanced at the photo, smiled, then put the phone back in his pocket. "Pretty close, I guess."

"Do they know about us?" I'd always wondered. Back then, I'd never been sure what answer I wanted him to give me.

I still wasn't.

He shook his head.

"Oh." Disappointment stabbed my heart. Which was stupid. Why should he have said anything to them? I cleared my throat. "So. What do you need me to do?"

Tristan blinked. "Do?"

"You're the one who said I should come to the office with you today. I guess I thought that meant you needed me for something." Wishful thinking, I guess.

"Oh. I just didn't want to leave you cooped up at the condo."

I didn't buy it. "Scared I'd paw through your things?"

"No." He huffed out a breath. "Honestly? Scared you'd decide to take off again and take your chances instead of doing the right thing."

Ouch.

Not that he was wrong. It was a possibility. I really hadn't decided completely against it even now. We'd spent all weekend holed up in his condo, each of us pretending that the other didn't exist. I had come out of the guest room for meals, but otherwise it had seemed like keeping out of sight was the better choice.

Even if it meant I was stuck with his book selection for entertainment.

He read legal thrillers.

Because of course he did.

Those were better than the theology books and Bible commentaries though.

I sighed. "Do you at least have a tablet I could use? I can scroll the Internet. Or do a puzzle or something."

"I think staying off-line is better for you, all things being equal. But I can hook you up with a puzzle." Tristan stood and pushed away from his desk. He crossed to double doors that I'd assumed led to a closet and pulled them open.

I wasn't wrong. But I also wasn't right. It was a closet, but it was huge. Boxes took up a lot of the space—probably old case files that he wasn't ready or able to get rid of.

Tristan moved one stack of boxes aside and dragged out a small folded table. He leaned it against one of the doors, then shifted the boxes back into place before reaching to the upper shelf that ran along the whole back wall and bringing down a stack of smaller boxes.

Puzzles.

I smiled in spite of myself. "You still do jigsaws?"

"They help me think." He shrugged and pushed the boxes toward me. "Pick one."

I grabbed the stack and studied the picture on the top box. It was the castle in Germany everyone said was the inspiration for Sleeping Beauty. Or Cinderella. I could never remember. But it was mostly white, and the photo had been taken in winter with gray skies and snow on the ground.

I glanced up. "You never choose the easy ones."

"They're not as fun." He pulled the castle box off the top. "Is that one better?"

I wanted to groan. Where the castle had been mostly white, this was awash with color. The field of lavender and sunflowers was beautiful. But also not easy. "Maybe you could choose the one that took you the least amount of time to do. I imagine I'll still need at least twice as long."

Tristan smirked and took the sunflowers off the stack. He tapped the remaining box in my hand. "This one was pretty simple."

"Starry Night." It was my favorite painting. I glanced up at him, but his expression was blank. I swallowed and let the questions swirl around in my head like the glow of the stars on the box. "Perfect. Should I set up in the front room?"

He shook his head. "In here is better."

Tristan put the rejected puzzles back in the closet and shut the doors. He opened the table legs and flipped it up before positioning it in front of the couch. "That work?"

"Sure. Thanks." I hesitated. It suddenly occurred to me how big of an imposition I really was. "I appreciate this, Tristan."

He shot me a tight smile. I didn't know what he would have said if a chime hadn't gone off.

"That's the door. Probably my admin, Arlene. I'll be back. You need coffee or anything?"

I shook my head.

"All right." He paused, pressed his lips together, then stalked through the office door, and pulled it closed behind him.

My eyebrows lifted. Maybe he always shut his office door. It could simply be habit. But it felt personal.

I swallowed the lump in my throat. I should have asked for water.

I thought about cracking the door, poking my head out, and seeing if that was a possibility. But no. If I had to guess, I was the big secret he didn't want getting out. His friends had called and texted a lot on Sunday—I guess Tristan missing church was still a big deal—and he hadn't mentioned me.

Not that I was eavesdropping or anything.

Okay, fine. Yes I was.

And I had no business being bothered by it. I'd been the one to walk. I'd been the one who disappeared.

I sighed and settled back down on the couch. I should've found another way. Something that didn't include Tristan. Because two days with him had made it very clear that fourteen years wasn't enough time for him to lose the ability to get me to do anything he wanted.

I wiggled the lid off the puzzle and set the empty box top face down next to the pieces. Step one? Find the edges.

Step two?

I guess I'd cross that bridge when I found it.

BY THE END of the day, I was positive that Tristan was doing his best to keep anyone from knowing I was around. He'd ordered lunch in. If I needed a drink, he fetched it. His admin needed to talk to him? He went out to her.

And when I'd needed to use the restroom, he'd gone out to create a distraction with Arlene so she wouldn't see me slip down the hall.

It was ridiculous.

"Good night, Mr. Lee." Arlene called from the front office.

"Good night." Tristan called back then moved to the door and cracked it open. He tilted his head.

Was the angle one that let him see her leave? Must be.

"We'll give her ten minutes, in case she forgets something." Tristan shut the door and returned to his desk.

"Does that happen a lot?"

"Not really." He shrugged and flipped open the folder he'd been referring to off and on for most of the afternoon. "Doesn't mean it won't."

"Right. And it would be horrible if someone knew I existed?"

He looked up, eyebrows drawn together. "You're hiding from the *Ortegas*."

"And your admin is an informant? And your friends?" I held my hands out palms up. "You're being seriously overcautious."

"Sure. And your sense of caution and self-preservation is why you're here."

"Wow." I blew out a breath. "I did a darn good job for fourteen years."

"You did. And then you didn't."

I couldn't even fight him on it. It was true. If I'd sensed the trap sooner, then I wouldn't have had to run. I would have found a way to turn down the work and relocate without it being a big deal. I'd done it before.

I closed my eyes and counted to ten slowly. I couldn't afford to fire off the retort that hovered on the tip of my tongue. I needed Tristan. And he did not need me. Which meant I was the one who had to suck it up.

"Maybe I should just stay in the condo. Your admin has to be wondering why you're being weird."

Tristan frowned.

"You know I'm right."

He grunted. "I wouldn't go that far. But she might have made a comment or two."

"Uh-huh." I wanted to point at him and sing "I told you so" but I held it in. "So maybe you can accept that I don't need a babysitter?"

Tristan was silent.

I fought a sigh. "Look. I promise I won't disappear."

"Your track record with promises isn't stellar." Tristan's gaze met mine.

My face burned as the memory of standing with him in front of a judge flashed to mind. I could almost feel the warmth of his hands holding mine as he promised to love, honor, and cherish me. I could hear myself echoing the words to him.

He nodded once.

I looked away.

"Come on. Let's head out. We need to make a stop."

Questions raced through my mind, but it was pretty obvious that he wouldn't answer them, so I kept quiet. I went out of his office and waited while he turned off lights and locked doors. We crossed the front room in silence and stepped out into the cool evening air.

Tristan locked the main door and tried the handle. He gestured for me to go ahead.

My stomach rumbled. Hopefully the stop would be dinner. But I couldn't imagine he was going to take me out to eat in a restaurant where people might see us. Which meant what?

The lights on his car flashed and it beeped as Tristan unlocked the doors. I went around to the passenger side and climbed in.

He used to make a big deal of holding doors for me. I'd lost that privilege now. Which was fine. Good, even. It wasn't like I expected that kind of treatment. I was perfectly capable of opening my own doors.

I pulled the door closed with a tad more force than strictly necessary, fastened my seat belt, and crossed my arms.

Tristan clicked his seat belt into place and glanced over. "Feel better?"

Oh sure. Sound smug. I wanted to growl. The problem was, I knew I was acting the fool. I didn't need him rubbing my face in it. "Not yet."

He laughed and started the car. "At least you're still honest about some things."

I hunched my shoulders and turned to look out my window. I was honest about a lot of things. I didn't need him judging me.

I'd done what I needed to do.

I'd done what was best for me.

If I'd learned anything from my parents, it was how to look out for myself, and I wasn't going to apologize for doing it.

5

TRISTAN

I glanced at Faith out of the side of my eye. The woman was an enigma. One minute, she was warm and funny like the girl I remembered. The next she was fiery and sassy...well, also like the girl I remembered.

Maybe she hadn't changed as much as it seemed.

Maybe I was the one who'd changed.

Not the important parts of me, of course. Oh, no. Not the part of me that loved her. And it was just as dumb and useless a feeling today as it had been fourteen years ago.

The reality of the situation, though? I didn't trust her not to run again. If we were going to work together to get her free—really free—from the mess she'd made? It was going to take time. And it was likely to be hard.

Seriously hard.

Which meant she needed the "babysitter" she so adamantly didn't want.

I backed out of my parking space and pointed the car toward Scott and Whitney's townhouse. As much as I wanted to keep this part of my life to myself, I couldn't delude myself that it was possible. Not anymore.

I'd been almost all the way to accepting it yesterday. My friends were...nosy. Oh, sure, they'd probably call it "concerned" or some other word that made them seem reasonable and me like I was acting suspicious. But seriously, a guy can't miss church now and then?

Or beg off poker?

And not answer the phone or texts all weekend without notice?

My lips twitched. Yeah, fine. I wouldn't let any of them slide like that, either. And probably, on some level, I appreciated it.

Just not right now.

"Is traffic always this bad?" Faith didn't turn to look at me when she spoke.

"It's not all that bad right now, honestly." We were moving. There were plenty of nights on my way home from work that it felt like I spent more time sitting and waiting than actually creeping forward. "Most of the backup is the stoplights."

"Ugh."

"I thought you were living in a city."

"I didn't leave the house much."

Right. I'd forgotten that part of her story. "If you're used to that, why is it so hard now?"

She managed a short laugh. "Come on. Things you choose are always easier than things forced on you."

Fair enough.

I gave the car a little extra gas and zipped through the light. I was going to absolutely defend the color as yellow if anyone asked. But no blue lights lit up in my rearview mirror, and that wasn't one of the intersections with the new red-light cameras attached. So yay for me.

We made it through the business district and into the residential streets—finally—and traffic thinned even more. I spotted street parking not far from Scott's townhouse, so I went ahead and pulled in, then turned off the car.

"What are we doing?" Faith turned and frowned at me. "This isn't your condo."

"Nope." I undid my seat belt and pushed open the door. "We're going to go meet some of my friends."

Faith's jaw dropped. She blinked.

I got out of the car, then leaned in and held her gaze. "Coming?"

"I have questions."

"Okay." I rested one arm along the roof of the car and tilted my head to the side. "Shoot."

Faith took a deep breath, paused, then blew it out. She scowled at me.

My eyebrows lifted.

After what felt like an eternity, she finally undid her seat belt and shoved open her door. I winced slightly. She didn't even look to see if she was going to hit something. Thankfully, her side of the car was against the curb.

I closed my car door and joined her on the sidewalk. She gave her door a firmer push than was really warranted, then crossed her arms.

"This way." I started down the sidewalk toward Scott and Whitney's end unit. I wanted, with everything in me, to check and see if she was following. But also? I kind of didn't care. She had questions, apparently, but wasn't going to ask them. Super fun.

Faith cleared her throat. "About these friends."

"Yeah?" I glanced back at her and slowed so we walked beside each other.

"Why am I meeting them?"

"First, because they're my friends."

She shook her head. "Bzzt. Not buying it. We've been cooped

up in your condo all weekend. And the office today. I don't think meeting your friends was something on the agenda until now. Try again."

I sighed. "Fine. That's second. Because you need a place to hang out during the day that's more interesting than my office."

"So they're potential babysitters."

"If that's how you want to look at it, then sure." I paused with my hand on the stair rail of Scott's front steps. "But they could be your friends, too."

The sound Faith made was decidedly inelegant. And also made it clear she didn't believe me.

Whatever. That was her choice. Just like running again would be her choice. I climbed the stairs to the front door and pushed the doorbell.

Faith had made it up two of the steps before the door opened.

Scott grinned broadly. "He's alive!" He dropped his voice to sound like a mad scientist.

"You're so funny."

"I think so." Scott stepped back. "Come on in. Are you begging dinner? Because that's cool, but also Beckett chose tonight so we had mac and cheese. There're leftovers."

I wrinkled my nose. "I'll pass. I don't want to take up a lot of your time."

Scott's eyebrows lifted when Faith finally joined me at the door.

"I wanted to introduce you to Faith Clarke." I stumbled over the last name. To my knowledge, Faith had never changed her name. Certainly when I'd searched for her, I'd always succeeded with Clarke. But I also had never even tried Lee.

"Nice to meet you." Scott shot a quizzical look my direction before gesturing toward the inside of the townhouse.

I stepped in and looked at Faith over my shoulder. She hesitated slightly before following.

"We can sit in the living room." Scott shut the door. As he crossed the foyer, he paused at the stairs and hollered up them, "Whit? Tristan's here."

"I'll be right down!" Whitney's muffled voice was barely understandable.

"Are we interrupting bedtime?" Maybe I hadn't thought this through as much as I should have. It was unlike me. But Faith tended to bring out all the things that most of my friends would consider unlike me. In my teens, I hadn't been sure if that was good or bad. Looked like the jury was still out.

"Nope. Just after-dinner playtime. Beckett wanted to build a train. Whitney had to get the bin down for him. He won't want her to stay and help—he's been getting more independent lately. He likes to build the tracks then call us to come see them." Scott took a seat in one of the living room chairs, leaving another chair and the couch available.

I wanted to take the other chair. Whitney and Faith could share the couch and that wouldn't be weird, right? Or should Whitney get the chair? I didn't particularly want to sit beside Faith. My nerve endings were all already on alert from the past three days in close proximity to her.

Faith's elbow dug into my side as she slipped around me and sat in the chair opposite Scott.

Okay. That solved that.

I sat on one end of the couch and avoided meeting Scott's gaze. He was looking at me like I'd lost a few marbles. And really, I couldn't blame him. He'd said to sit and I'd stood there like an idiot trying to figure out where.

I raked a hand through my hair.

"So. What brings you to town, Faith?" Scott frowned slightly. "I feel like we've met. Were you at college with us?"

She shot a quick glance my way, eyebrows raised. "For a semester."

I swallowed. I should have taken the time to explain to her ahead of this that I wasn't sure about spilling the whole story. But apparently, at least for now, she seemed to understand.

"That must be it." Scott smiled.

"Hi. Sorry. Beckett's really into his trains right now. We should swap the bin out with something else so he can get to it on his own." Whitney sat on the end of the couch nearest Scott and tucked her feet up under her. "I'm Scott's wife, Whitney. This is a nice surprise. Do you want something to drink? Or eat? I can make tea. Or some decaf."

I gestured to Faith. "This is my friend, Faith."

"Could I get some water?" Faith started to stand. "I can get it if you don't mind telling me where to find glasses."

"Don't be ridiculous." Whitney uncurled and stood. "I'll get it. Tristan?"

"Water would be great. Thanks." It'd be something to do with my hands, if nothing else, although right now my throat was parched. Stress would do that.

"Sure thing." Whitney headed into the kitchen, her voice raising as she continued talking. "Did you mention you were having company and I missed it? We probably wouldn't have harangued you all weekend if we'd known."

Faith cleared her throat. "He didn't know. It was a spur of the moment decision. I just showed up on his doorstep and he didn't turn me away. Which was nice of him."

"It was." Scott's piercing look turned my direction before turning back to Faith. "Will you be in town long? You could grab a spare room at Jenna's if you're crowded. Noah has this huge townhouse and she's living there on her own leading up to the wedding."

"We'll keep that in mind." I offered him a tight smile. I

understood what he was getting at, but he was one to talk. He and Whitney had lived together for several months—while dating—before they got married. Which, fine, nothing was going on between them. But it was the look of the thing.

Faith and I were married.

No one knew. But that was beside the point.

Or maybe it wasn't.

Whitney returned with two glasses of water. She handed one to Faith and I took the other as she passed by me to curl back up on the couch. "How long will you be in town? We'd love for you to join us on Friday when the girls hang out. The guys play poker. Coffee at the bookstore is way better."

"I..." Faith trailed off and looked at me.

"I'm helping Faith with some legal trouble. I'm not sure how long it's going to take, honestly, which is part of why we're here this evening." After a moment of hesitation, I reached across the gap between the couch and Faith's chair and patted her arm. I'd known better even before all the nerve endings in the left side of my body lit up from the brief contact. But she looked so nervous. I moistened my lips. "Two parts, actually, I guess. One, she could use a place to hang out during the day. It's better if she's not out touring DC or some-thing. And I don't want her to feel trapped in my condo. So I wondered if she could hang out here when I need to be in the office?"

Whitney's eyebrows lifted. She shot a quick, confused glance at Scott. "Sure. We're not all that exciting. Beckett has kinder-garten until one. Then it's a lot of trains or the park. Or both. Maybe some cartoons. You might be just as bored as if you were at Tristan's."

"I told him I'd be fine at the condo. He's adamant." Bitterness laced Faith's voice.

"You worried she's going to run off?" Scott's laughter was

barely contained. "C'mon man, she's a grown woman. Why are you trying to get her a babysitter?"

I fought the scowl I could feel forming on my face. I couldn't explain why I wanted Faith to be around someone all day without getting into the complete details of our relationship. And I wasn't ready to do that yet. "It was just a thought. I'm trying to be a good host."

Scott scoffed. "Going a little overboard."

"That said, you're welcome over here any time." Whitney's glance at Scott was pointed.

He reached out and linked his fingers with hers. "Yes. Of course. I didn't mean to make it sound like you weren't."

"Thanks. I'll keep it in mind." Faith sounded smug. Why wouldn't she? She'd won this one in a public setting and I couldn't do anything about it.

I sighed. "Okay. Then the only other thing I wondered is if you remembered the name of the FBI agent that was wandering around Robinson Enterprises a couple of years ago?"

Scott shook his head. "No. They were investigating someone in the computer security division. I was in government services pretty exclusively. Although maybe my old boss would know. I think his sister might have been involved somehow. I can send you his email if you want to reach out and ask."

"That'd be great. Thanks." I waited. It wasn't like Scott not to ask for details. The look on his face made it clear he was curious. "Just say it."

Scott laughed. "Come on. You know I want to know why you need an FBI contact. But if it's legal stuff I also know it's probably confidential. But dang, man. How do you keep all these secrets?"

"It's what makes me a good lawyer, I guess." I offered a tight smile and stood. "Do you think you could get me that email tonight?"

Scott took his phone out of his pocket and worked on it for a moment.

My phone chimed.

"There you go." Scott's eyebrows drew together. "You're leaving already?"

"I'm hungry. And as much as I appreciate the mac and cheese offer, I'm in the mood for something a little more grown up." I glanced at Faith. "If that's okay with you?"

Faith nodded and stood, the half-full glass of water in her hand. "I never mind mac and cheese but I could use a vegetable or two today."

I took the glass from Faith. "I'll put these in the sink on our way out. Thanks, guys."

"No problem. And seriously, Faith, if you get bored or want to see the chaos that is life as a stay-at-home mom, give me a call. Make sure Tristan gives you my number." Whitney grinned from her seat on the couch.

"Thanks." Faith nodded.

I carried the glasses into the kitchen, poured out the water, and set the glasses in the sink, then headed into the hall.

Faith was already standing by the front door.

I opened it and gestured for her to go through, then followed behind, and made sure the door latched.

"They seem nice."

I tried to decide if she was being sarcastic. "They are."

"That's what I said." Faith stopped at the bottom of the stairs and put her hands on her hips. "Why are you so antagonistic?"

"Me? Really?" I shook my head and started striding toward the car. "I'm not having this conversation on the street."

"Well when *are* you going to have this conversation? Because it feels like maybe you need to get something off your chest." Faith's voice rose with every word.

I scowled at her over my shoulder. "Keep your voice down."

"You're such a jerk." Her mutter was still loud enough for me to hear.

Probably on purpose.

I held back my retort. Nothing good was going to come from losing my cool. I needed to treat this like I would any other case with hostile witnesses and complex relationship dynamics.

Never mind that I didn't do divorces anymore because of both of those things. I still had the skills.

I wanted to say, maybe I was grateful for the divorce case I'd handled last summer as a cashed-in favor, but I didn't. That was taking it all too far. That case had been horrible and I was glad to be done with it, the client, and the client's friend, who I had at one point considered one of my best clients and almost a friend myself.

I unlocked the car and got in.

Faith was a few steps behind me. She pulled the car door closed with more force than necessary. "How about now?"

I closed my eyes. "After dinner, okay? I need food."

"Fine."

I started the car. She might say "fine," but I had a feeling it was anything but.

6

FAITH

Dinner was awkward and mostly silent.

Tristan had stopped at a taqueria on the way back to his condo. He'd assured me they were the best street tacos I'd ever had.

They were certainly close.

When we'd eaten and the dishes had been put into the dishwasher and the kitchen tidied, I was tempted to disappear back into my room and just leave it alone. I didn't want to fight with him. I didn't want to hear all the ways I'd messed up his life.

At the same time? If his problem with me was going to keep bubbling up as resentment and anger, we were probably both going to be better off getting it all out in the open. He'd heard my story.

Maybe now it was time I heard his.

I moved into the living room and settled in one of his ridiculously comfortable chairs. "Spill it."

He heaved out a breath and sat across from me. "You left."

My eyebrows lifted. "I left a note."

"Pfft." Tristan waved away my words. "Seriously, put yourself in my position and tell me a note would make it all better."

I winced. Okay, no. Honestly? The two of us were similar enough that I could see now—even though I'd kept myself from seeing then—that the note probably made things worse. "How many times do I need to apologize?"

"I don't...you're not understanding." Tristan closed his eyes and I could practically see him lining up the conversation in his mind. "I loved you. I know you thought I married you to help you out. And okay, sure, cool side benefit, but that's not why. You could've come to stay with me at college to get away without the whole marriage thing. You had to know that, didn't you? I thought we were going to figure it out and make it work. That you were at least willing to try to love me back."

I blinked.

Of all the things he could have said, that was not one that I was remotely prepared for. "I don't know how to respond to that."

He nodded and looked away. "Did you think I would have slept with you if it was all just for show? If I didn't plan for us to be together?"

My cheeks burned. It was good he wasn't looking at me, because I don't think I could have met his eyes. The years since then had done a good job of peeling away all the convenient lies I'd tried to believe and now all that was left was honesty. "No. But I tried desperately not to believe it."

"Why?" He turned back.

Now I couldn't look away. No matter how much I might want to. My throat was so tight it hurt when I spoke. "No one has ever loved me without strings. I figured sex was your string."

I'd never seen someone's face completely lose all its color. And it wasn't as if Tristan was tan to start with. Now he looked like he was about to pass out.

His Adam's apple bobbed when he swallowed. "I see."

He pushed to his feet and paced to the window.

"I don't think you do." I twisted my fingers in my lap. I'd known it wasn't going to go well, but I hadn't expected it to go *this* badly.

Of course, Tristan declaring his love for me wasn't something that had been on my radar, either.

"Oh?" He turned around and faced me, his head tilted to the side. "Enlighten me, why don't you?" Sarcasm dripped from his words.

I hunched my shoulders. "You're going to stand there and say I was far out in left field with that? Do you remember my father? The whole reason I wanted to get away from him?"

Pink tinged the tips of Tristan's ears. He nodded once.

"So. Given that dear old Dad didn't have any qualms about using sex as a string, why wouldn't I expect that's what was going on with us?" I crossed my arms over my chest. I didn't like to think about Dad. I did a good job of pretending he didn't exist. But he was the one person I'd always kept tabs on. The worst possible situation would be running into him again. When he'd died after having been shanked in jail a year and a half ago, I hadn't shed any tears.

"I wasn't the one—" He broke off and pressed his lips together. "You know what? It doesn't matter. Knowing how cheaply you saw me and my feelings for you explains a lot."

I opened my mouth to speak but Tristan was already striding down the hallway toward the bedrooms. My stomach twisted and I felt vaguely ill. This...had to be bad.

I'd barely started to wonder if I should chase him and make him finish this out when he returned.

He tossed a thick envelope down on the coffee table in front of me. "That's for you. Make sure I get it back. I'll still help you with this problem you've made for yourself, but as soon as we get the FBI to take it over? You're on your own. Got it?"

My fingers itched to snatch up the envelope and see what it

was. But the emptiness of Tristan's eyes as he looked at me kept me frozen.

He frowned slightly. "Is your silence a yes, you understand? Or do I need to be clearer?"

"I've got it. I'll find a hotel tonight."

"No. It's not safe yet. And I wouldn't want you to think I was using your safety as a manipulative string."

The barb hit home and I winced.

I swallowed. "I'll go to my room now, if that's all right?"

"Do what you want. It's all you ever do, anyway." Bitterness laced his words and he turned and strode from the room before I could respond.

My shoulders sagged and for a moment, I let myself fall back against the couch. Had I known he loved me? Really loved me? Was that why I'd gone out of my way to make sure to overcome his chivalrous nature and get him into bed?

He might have cut himself off, but I'd followed what he had planned to say. He wasn't the one who'd made the moves. And he was right about that. He'd offered marriage. I jumped on it. He'd given me a safe place and had been a gentleman about everything. But I'd seen how he looked at me.

And I'd justified getting him to follow through because I could tell he wanted it and we were married. His faith had always been a strong part of him—and we'd had conversations about his determination to save sex for marriage. So when he offered marriage? I'd absolutely believed he was offering us both a way to get what we wanted most.

I sighed and slid the fat envelope off the table, then stood.

I walked lightly toward the hallway and peeked around the corner. His door was shut. Okay. That was good.

I hurried past his room and into mine, then closed the door and pressed the button in the knob to lock it. After a moment, I dragged the chair from in front of the desk across the floor and wedged it under the handle.

It was unlikely Tristan would do anything. But at this point, I didn't feel like taking the chance.

I crossed to the bed and scooted so I sat against the headboard, my knees drawn up. I stared at the envelope. Finally, I pried the wings of the metal brad up and shook the packet of papers out onto the bedspread. I picked them up and scanned the first couple of lines before tossing them to the foot of the bed.

Divorce.

I swallowed and tears burned the back of my eyes. Which was ridiculous. This was the obvious move, and I shouldn't be surprised—or hurt—that he was prepared.

But I was.

I wasn't going to lie to myself. Seeing Tristan again on Friday had brought back all the feelings I'd squashed in high school and those six months that we lived together after our hasty marriage. He deserved so much better than anything I could offer him.

I'd kept him from finding that long enough.

I reached for the papers again and forced myself to read them. It seemed standard. It wasn't as though we had communal assets to divide. And I wasn't going to try to get him to pay spousal support or anything like that. He didn't owe me anything.

I probably owed him.

He was letting me off the hook for that, too.

I glanced over at the desk. There was a cup of pens sitting right there. I should sign the papers, put them back in the envelope, and slide them under his door. Then he could do whatever lawyer thing needed to be done next and we could both move on.

That was what I should do.

Instead, I folded them in half and pushed them back into the envelope and carefully pushed the brads down to hold the flap shut.

I couldn't deal with this right now.

I also couldn't explain why.

Divorce was obviously the right choice. It wasn't as if there was some grand reconciliation in store for us. Tristan had made that pretty clear. He'd said he had loved me. Past tense.

Because of course it was past tense. It would be ridiculous for him to have carried some mythical torch for me for fourteen years. Not after everything I'd done to him. Especially not after that.

I blew out a breath.

Here I was, doing it to him all over again. What had I been thinking, coming here? I should leave. Just...pack up and sneak out in the middle of the night and take my chances with the cartel. If they caught me? It wasn't as if I'd be getting anything less than I deserved.

The only problem with this plan—and it was a big one—was Tristan. I couldn't disappear on him again. Not now that I knew how badly it had hurt him the first time. So I'd explain first.

That was the adult decision.

I nodded once and took a deep breath to steel myself, then I slipped off the bed and crossed to the door. I moved the chair, grimacing at my silliness, and turned the knob.

Tristan's door was still shut. It didn't necessarily mean he was in there. He could have heard me pass by and gone out into the living room. Or out into the world, for that matter. He wasn't the one under house arrest.

I walked down the hall, not bothering to try to be silent but not stomping, and poked my head around the corner. The living room and kitchen areas were both empty.

Drat.

That meant he was in his bedroom.

My gaze flicked toward the main door. He might have left.

With a sigh, I went down the hallway and knocked briskly on his door.

I bit my lip as I waited. If he was in there, he was silent. Should I knock again?

No.

I was about to turn and head back to my room when I heard footsteps. After another few seconds, the door cracked open.

"Yeah?" His expression was unreadable. At least his eyes weren't completely flat still.

I fought the urge to clear my throat and fidget. "I thought I'd leave. Get out of your hair. I realized—belatedly, and I'm sorry—that all I've done is cause you problems. You don't need to clean up after me anymore. I shouldn't have come. I shouldn't have asked this of you."

Something flickered in his eyes. I couldn't put a name to it before it disappeared. "What about the cartel?"

I shrugged and hoped it seemed nonchalant. I was bone-deep terrified. But that was my problem. Not his. It should never have been his. "I can disappear. I know how."

"Uh-huh. That's why you did that instead of coming to find me." His eyebrows lifted. "I thought you wanted to get out from under all of this? Find a way to live a normal life."

"What's normal, anyway?" I managed a tight smile. "I feel like I read somewhere it's just a setting on the clothes dryer."

"Is this because of the papers?"

"The papers? Oh." The divorce papers. I shook my head. "No. Of course not. That would be ridiculous."

I needed to shut up. Immediately. I clamped my lips together.

At least he didn't call me a liar out loud, but I was pretty sure that was what he was doing in his mind.

"Honestly, I'm surprised you hadn't sent them to me already."

"I didn't know where you were, remember?" His eyebrows lifted.

I scowled. "I don't honestly believe that would have stopped you. Be honest—you kept tabs."

He shrugged. "Here and there."

I nodded. And yet he'd never reached out. Not even one time. He hadn't asked for me to come back. He hadn't looked for an explanation. He'd probably just made a note in a file and went on about his day. So yeah, he could go on and on to me about how he'd been in love and blah blah blah, but his actions painted a much different picture.

And that realization steeled my determination. "So. Like I said, I'll get out of your hair. I'm sorry—really sorry—for all the problems I've caused you. I hope..."

I let that trail off. I didn't know how to finish it. There were a lot of things I hoped, but not a single one of them was worth giving voice to.

I turned and went back to the guest room. I wasn't going to call it my room even in my head. It was too easy to like the idea of having space in Tristan's place. Or in his head. Or heart.

It didn't take long to toss everything back into my suitcase and close it. I gave the room one more quick scan. My fingers itched to strip the bed and offer to put on new sheets, but it was just one more way to prolong doing what I knew was the right move.

Leaving the first time had been hard.

Leaving tonight made that first exit feel easy.

I swallowed, but the lump in my throat didn't budge. I

grabbed the handle of my suitcase and dragged it across the room. I wasn't going to look back.

I was halfway down the hall when Tristan appeared. "You don't have to do this."

I didn't stop. "I think I do. I never should have come."

"Faith."

I shook my head and turned the corner at the end of the hall, heading for the front door. "Goodbye, Tristan."

Of course the fact that he kept his condo locked put a hiccup in my plan to sail breezily through the door. I finally handled the locks and stepped into the hall. When I turned to pull the door shut behind me, Tristan was there.

I bit my lip.

He reached out and gently touched my arm.

I jolted. It was as if he'd burned me.

Tristan's face fell. He shoved his hands in his pockets. "I'll keep working on the FBI angle. If you change your mind, you know where to find me."

I couldn't speak.

I just turned and made my way to the elevators.

The soft click of the door closing behind me echoed loudly in my ears. Something about it seemed harsh and final.

Which was as it should be. Tristan had always deserved better than me.

7

TRISTAN

Friday after work, I unlocked the door to my condo, stepped in, and once again—like I had all week—frowned at the silence. A week ago today, I'd come home to find Faith knocking. And then she'd disappeared again.

Maybe I should be willing to give her props for saying goodbye this time, but I couldn't quite get there.

With a sigh, I closed the door and flipped the locks before toeing off my shoes and kicking them over to the wall. I carried my backpack with me and turned to stare down the hallway that led to the bedrooms.

It was time.

I hadn't been able to bring myself to clean her room. No. Not her room. The guest room. My home office.

I needed to stop tripping over the box of files in my bedroom and go back to using my desk. I should change the sheets and make the bed in case—ha ha—someone wanted to come visit.

I should have done it before today, but I'd found excuses. On Tuesday, I convinced myself that she'd be back. Same on Wednesday. Thursday? I'd given up on her returning, but the fridge had been bare and I'd decided to shop in person instead of ordering online like I usually did. So I'd run out of time.

I couldn't come up with another excuse. Not even poker night—because the guys had decided they were coming here. So that only added a new reason for me to tidy.

"Better just get to it." I took a deep breath and strode down the hall. I gripped the doorknob and hesitated. "I can do this."

I twisted the knob and opened the door to the guest room. I could smell her.

I closed my eyes and breathed in the gentle scent of apples. It was her shampoo—she'd used the same scent all through high school. I'd teased her about it some when she switched, but she'd gone along with it.

I marched to the desk and put my backpack down in the middle. There. Reclaiming the space.

I wanted to call it enough, but it seemed cowardly. I checked the time—but there was still plenty before the guys showed up, so that excuse was out the window. Might as well get to it.

I turned and faced the bed and my heart stopped. The envelope holding the divorce papers sat in the middle of the bed.

Why did it surprise me? I'd given them to her. Of course she signed them and left them for me to deal with. I even sounded annoyed in my head, but I wasn't, really. I'd started the process. It made sense that it fell to me to finish it. Plus I was a lawyer.

And, bonus, given that she'd signed them easily, this shouldn't have to go to court and get sticky. It would be a simple, dare I say amicable, parting of ways. Done and dusted.

So why wasn't I happy?

I gave a derisive laugh. Because this wasn't what I wanted. I'd regretted tossing the papers at her almost as soon as they left my fingers. Oh, I stood by the decision—but it hurt. I'd loved Faith for a lot of years, and I wasn't quite sure how to stop.

But now I was going to have to figure it out.

I picked up the envelope and smacked it against my palm for a moment before taking it over to the desk and putting it on top of my backpack. Then I got to work stripping off the sheets, concentrating hard to ignore the urge to curl up in them and pretend, for as long as I could manage, that I'd traveled back in time and I was still in college and the reason she wasn't in bed beside me was because she'd gotten up to get us both coffee to drink while we cuddled.

I balled up the sheets and carried them to the washing machine, then pushed them in, added soap, and slammed the door closed, furious with myself for not only letting that memory loose, but luxuriating in it. That way lay madness.

I got the machine going, grabbed the spare set of sheets out of the linen closet, and made quick work of remaking the bed.

I still had twenty or so minutes before any of the guys would show up. I should have moved the files and set my desk back up. I should have looked over the divorce papers and made sure they were ready to file. Instead, I padded into the kitchen, grabbed a soda out of the fridge, and collapsed on the couch with my feet on the coffee table so I could scroll mindlessly through the various websites I followed.

I was relieved at the first knock. I left my soda on the coffee table and hurried to open it.

"Hey, man." Scott stepped in with a grin and kicked his shoes off and over by mine. "I'm surprised you offered to host with Faith here."

My eyebrows lifted. "Offered? You have an interesting definition of that word. Plus, she's gone."

"Yeah? She decided to join the girls? I'll let Whit know to keep an eye out. I'm surprised you didn't take her over. She's not walking home in the dark, is she?" Scott followed me back to the living room, peppering me with questions.

I resumed my seat and picked up my soda. "She's not joining the women. She's gone. Left. Disappeared. Again."

Scott paused and tilted his head to one side as he studied me. "This is not a good thing, I take it."

I shrugged, ignoring the tight ball in my chest. "She thought it was the right move."

"You asked her to stay, right?"

I took a sip from my soda.

"Dude." Scott shook his head and went to my fridge to get his own drink. "You really don't know anything about women, do you?"

"Guess not." I could hear the bitterness in my words, but it seemed to go straight over Scott's head.

"Hey, it's us." Austin's voice came down the hallway along with the sound of shoes getting kicked aside and bags rustling. "Wes brought eats."

"Eats are good." Scott frowned at me a moment before moving to help with the bags.

The rest of the guys had shown up as a group. That was reasonably typical. They tended to be on time, not early and not late, so they probably all got clumped together waiting for the elevator.

And wow, it was amazing the things I'd spend brain power on to avoid thinking about Faith. Or in this case, Scott's reasonably accurate summary of why Faith was gone.

I didn't know anything about women. And apparently what I thought I knew was wrong.

I should make a T-shirt.

"What'd you bring, Wes?" I pushed to my feet and joined the guys in the kitchen. They were all pretty comfortable in my place, but they also knew I liked things just so, so it was unlikely they'd root around if they needed something.

"Fried chicken." Wes reached into an enormous bag and

pulled out a box. "Got the dirty rice, mashed potatoes and gravy, and biscuits too."

"No fries?" Cody peeked in the bag. "How did you not get fries?"

"Fries go with burgers, not chicken." Wes grabbed the bag back and continued unloading it. "If you need fries, feel free to be the one who brings food next time."

"I cook for you guys a lot. It's not like I never contribute." Cody crossed his arms and scowled at the collection of boxes on the island. "Who doesn't get fries?"

"I probably have frozen fries if you need me to put some in the air fryer." I glanced at Cody. "Or we could order some for delivery."

Cody waved me off. "No. It's fine."

It didn't sound fine. "You all right?"

Cody pinched the bridge of his nose. "Yeah. Kind of. Not really."

"Which is it?" Austin frowned. "Is Megan okay?"

"Megan's fine. Our marriage is fine." Cody shook his head.

"It's work, right?" Noah grabbed a stack of plates out of my cabinet and brought them over to the island. He set the stack down and took the top one for himself. "Mr. Ballentine's announcement?"

Cody nodded.

"One of you needs to fill us in." Austin took the next plate and followed behind Noah, adding food to it.

"Seconded." I slid into line and grabbed two pieces of chicken out of the box. I scooped a big dollop of the dirty rice onto my plate, then opened my silverware drawer to get a stack of forks out for people to use. After ripping a paper towel off the roll, I went back to my seat.

I picked up one of the drumsticks and crunched into it.

Cody joined me on the couch. He sighed. "Ballentine is officially retiring at the end of the year. Jackson Trent has been doing a lot of honcho stuff for a while, so that's not as big a deal, but..."

"It's change." Noah took a seat in a chair opposite. "And it's hard to imagine that everything will stay the same. I actually knew a little before the official announcement because Jackson wanted me to know ahead of time that my new project wasn't going to be impacted."

"And you didn't tell me?" Cody scooped up a bite of rice.

"He swore me to secrecy."

"Who would I tell?" Cody frowned.

Noah shook his head. "Come on, man. A promise is a promise."

"Yeah, I guess." Cody sighed. "I just need to know if the fundraising schedule is going to change. Are we adding new events? Shifting to different events? Going virtual with everything?"

"Why would we go virtual?" Noah bit into a piece of chicken.

"You haven't been on the receiving end of one of Jackson's budget grillings yet. He...does not love the events that we do. But Mr. Ballentine has always believed it's important to see people face-to-face and give them a good time when you've got your hand out." Cody took another bite. "If we go virtual with stuff? I'm going to be out of a job. Or at least down to something half time. But probably completely out."

"Worried about keeping a roof over your head?" Wes grinned as he pulled a chair closer to the coffee table.

"I do have a wife now." Cody chuckled. "Obviously, no. But what would I do all day? I don't want to sit around and twiddle my thumbs just because I can."

"You can work at the bookstore with Megan." Austin pointed at Cody. "She'd love that."

Cody appeared to consider it.

I swallowed the bite I'd been chewing. "Maybe run that by Megan before you bank on it."

"Why wouldn't it work?" Cody turned to me, eyebrows raised. "I like books. I love Megan. Her store is amazing. And she just had one of her best employees leave because she's moving out of the area to somewhere cheaper."

"Oof. I hadn't heard that." Concern was visible on Austin's face.

"Just happened today." Cody shrugged. "Megan's still kind of in shock."

"Employees are hard." Wes glugged soda from his can. "I kind of knew that going in to opening a retail store. They talked about it some in the classes I took. But man, the reality of it is just...you can't describe it. I feel like I pay well. We have benefits. I bend over backward to schedule people when they want. And still it's like I'm some kind of evil overlord in their eyes."

Austin nodded. "Same. At least the folks at the tutoring center also believe in what we're doing. It's a little different than a retail worker. And still. I don't feel like I'm unreasonable either, but they appear to think otherwise. Mostly I've been letting Kayla handle it, because she has more patience than I do."

Wes laughed. "Sunshine is even more annoyed than me. But she's also doing some data crunching to see about adjusting our hours so we can handle it all on our own. I don't love running the store out front—I'd much rather do classes and plan trips—but she doesn't mind it, so it'd probably work."

I set my plate down on the coffee table. "You've been back from your island for what, a whole day, and she's already taking over the shop?"

"She's a go-getter. And it's all kicking ideas around right now. I'm not going to fire anyone who's currently working. But I know they'll start quitting eventually. It's good to have a plan in place.

Maybe the plan is 'hire a replacement.' Maybe it's not." Wes shrugged.

"I don't think I'd replace my admin if she quit." The words were out of my mouth before I'd really thought them through. Huh. Did I not like having her?

"Can big-shot lawyers answer their own phones? I thought that was against the code somewhere." Scott's eyes lit with laughter. "Or do you just want to make sure you don't miss a call from your girlfriend?"

The room went silent.

"Tristan has a girlfriend?" Cody scooted forward and looked between me and Scott. "This is news. How'd you find out?"

"He brought her by on Monday. Of course, he seems also to have scared her off. So maybe he doesn't have one anymore." Scott smirked at me and leaned back.

"This sounds like a story." Austin settled his plate on his lap. "I do like a dinner story."

One day I was going to get Scott back. Somehow. When he least expected it. I drained my soda and set the empty can on the table. "I do not have a girlfriend. I have a wife."

Everyone froze. It would have been comical in different circumstances. Forks hovered in mid-air, mouths gaped. And everyone's eyes were staring directly at me.

"A wife?" Wes held up a hand. "Hold on and roll that back. Sounds like you should start at the beginning."

What had I been thinking? I sighed. "I told you all about Faith."

"In college, sure." Scott frowned. "She hung around for like a semester one year. Right when we were getting to know each other. That'd be before you came to the group, Wes."

"Right. Well, we were married." I reached for the empty soda can and spun it in my hands. "Are married. Her home situation was bad. My folks had basically adopted her when we started middle school. Mostly we dragged her to church and had her over, that kind of thing. She was always glad to come along because it was out of the house. She was a lot less accident prone out of the house."

"Oh." Austin scowled. "I hate that. I've had students like that."

Of all the guys, Austin was the most likely to understand because of the demographics he'd taught and the kids he now served in the tutoring center. "Yeah. She never outright said her parents were abusive, but it was pretty obvious. I resented having her follow along for a little while, then we became friends. And then I developed a massive crush."

"I assume it was mutual, seeing that you married her." Cody leaned forward. "Where's she been?"

"Shhh." Austin reached over and flicked Cody's leg. "He's getting there."

"Nah. It was never mutual. And my parents were not on board with us being more than friends because she wasn't a believer. She accepted Christ toward the end of high school, but even then, they warned me to be careful since she was so new in her faith. But when I went to college, she still had a year of high school and her dad was drinking a lot more, and from what she said, the abuse was shifting in nature." I didn't want to have to spell it out. This honestly felt like I was giving away all of Faith's secrets without her permission. But it was part of the story, and I didn't think the guys would understand why I'd married her without the details.

Noah's hand contracted around his soda can enough that it started to collapse.

The sound broke the silence.

"That about sums it up." Scott took the soda can out of Noah's hand. "So she needed out."

I nodded. "She was eighteen. Just. So after Christmas break, she came back with me, we got married, and I kind of hid her at my place for a while. Until she left."

"She left?" Noah frowned. "She didn't go back home, did she?"

"No. Or, I don't think so. She didn't say, and the times I looked for her, I never found evidence that she had. But I didn't have the time, resources, or money when I was still in school to do as thorough a job as I would now." I cleared my throat. "Long story short, she's been missing from my life for the last fourteen years. She showed up out of the blue on Friday looking for help. Then walked out again Monday night because she didn't like how I thought we needed to approach the problem."

Scott's eyebrows drew together. "She's in trouble. Big trouble. That's why you were looking for the FBI contact info."

"FBI?" Wes's eyebrows drew together.

I glanced around. Everyone, save Scott, wore a similar expression of shock.

"Did you get it?" Scott reached for a napkin and scrubbed at his hands. "You're still going to help her, right?"

I let out an exasperated breath. "I talked to Christopher Ward and he put me in touch with his sister. I have a name and I left a message, but with Faith gone, I don't know how much help I can be. Or if she even wants me to try. I gave her divorce papers."

"What? Did you kick her puppy too?" Noah threw his hands in the air. "I thought you had more empathy than that."

I opened my mouth to defend myself, then snapped it shut. It had seemed like—no, it had *been*—the right thing to do at the time. And I wasn't going to apologize for it.

I crossed my arms.

"Chill, Noah." Cody looked between the two of us. "We don't know the whole situation."

"No, we don't." Wes put his plate down on the coffee table.

"Why is that, Tristan? The rest of us don't hold anything back from the group, but you're always over on the sidelines, aloof."

"I'm not aloof." I snorted. What a stupid word. "I'm a lawyer. I deal with people's confidential information. If one of us was a doctor, would you expect full disclosure from them on all their patients?"

"I'm not talking about your clients, man. You know that." Wes pointed at me. "After the crap you gave Sunshine this summer?"

"I apologized for that." Maybe I hadn't thoroughly meant the apology at the time, but I did now. Mostly. I did think we should all have a prenup when we got married, but none of the guys so far had taken me up on it. It was as if they figured...well, I couldn't figure out what they thought was going on. Maybe since they all had such fairy-tale-perfect marriages it wouldn't ever be an issue.

I didn't imagine I'd ever get that lucky though. My first marriage had been such a rollicking success, after all.

"Did she sign them?" Austin stood and moved to the kitchen to get another drink.

"I assume so. She didn't take them with her." I hadn't looked yet. Right now, they could sit there in that envelope like Schrodinger's Cat. But once I pulled them out and saw her signature? It was over. For good.

Austin tilted his head to the side. "You didn't look?"

"Didn't I just say that?"

Scott frowned at me for what felt like an eternity. "You're still in love with her."

"It doesn't matter. She left." Again. I didn't bother voicing that, but it was echoing in my head and heart anyway. When it came to Faith, I was easier to leave than her abusive family, and that stung.

A lot.

Scott and Austin exchanged a glance, then Cody cleared his throat. "We're playing poker right, not braiding hair, eating ice cream, and painting our toenails?"

I chuckled and it wasn't entirely forced. I glanced at Cody and gave a quick nod of thanks. "That's the plan. When the pigs are all done eating."

Wes made an incredibly realistic sounding series of snorts.

This time everyone laughed. And something that had been off kilter all week settled back into place. These guys might be a pain in the backside some of the time, but they were family. I should have told them all sooner. In college, even.

I stood, collected my trash, and carried it to the kitchen. Then I dug out the cards and poker chips and brought them back into the living room.

I shook the cards out of the box into my hand and started to shuffle. "Ready when you are, guys."

8

FAITH

I was probably paranoid.

Even so, I tucked my hands in my pockets and tried to act like I wasn't using the window of the store on the quaint, cobblestone street in Old Town, Alexandria, as a mirror. The handful of people out walking in the late afternoon looked normal. So why was the hair on the back of my neck standing up?

I'd almost convinced myself to keep walking when a flash of black caught my eye. I shifted, as if to get a better look at the books displayed, and squinted at the reflection in the window. Was it Manny?

It sure looked like Manny Ortega.

I fought a shudder.

Was he here on business for the family or were they onto me? The bigger question—one I'd been asking myself for the last week—was why I hadn't left the area.

A tap on the glass drew my attention to the woman inside the shop. Drat.

She grinned, held up the book, and gestured for me to come inside.

Caught, I slid down to the door and pulled it open. It would look weird if I didn't. And of the places it was unlikely Manny would ever enter, a bookstore rated high on the list.

"Good afternoon. Can I help you find something? You seemed to be enjoying the display of fairy tale retellings. This one is by a local author." The woman extended the brightly colored paperback.

I took it. I wasn't actually sure I was interested in a fairy tale retelling. Most of that was because I wasn't completely sure what that was. Fairy tales were fairy tales. How did someone "retell" it? I flipped the cover over and scanned the words. A gender swapped Little Mermaid? I snickered.

"Right? So clever. I'm Megan, by the way. Are you new in town or here on vacation?"

I looked up from the book and around the store. It was empty. Which was probably why Megan was beckoning people inside and then talking at them. Lucky me. "My name's Faith. Just passing through. Is this kind of thing popular?"

Megan's eyebrows lifted. "I guess it depends on what you like. This series is sweet romance."

My face must have revealed that I had no idea what that meant, because she chuckled.

"You're not a romance reader. That's okay, I have time. Come on in. Do you want to sit down?"

Megan took off through the shelves without waiting for me to answer. I should put the book down and go back on the street and get out of Dodge.

In more ways than one. Not just the store and the town. But the whole area. Tristan wasn't going to go comb the streets hoping to find me and convince me to return. That was obvious. And if it didn't make any sense to expect him to? So what?

And yet, despite everything saying that my next move should be to leave, I found myself trudging after Megan, book still in hand. I found her quickly. She'd curled into an overstuffed chair that was part of a cozy seating area.

I perched on the edge of the couch and glanced around. I wasn't super visible here. If Manny came in the store, he'd definitely see me, but if he just walked by? I should be safe.

"I do read, by the way." I settled the book on my lap. I wasn't illiterate. And I liked a book as much as the next person. "I'm just not obsessive about it."

Megan flashed a grin. "Sorry. I wasn't trying to be offensive. I live in the book world."

I nodded. "Go ahead and educate me. Sweet?"

"No sex on the page. It's kind of the opposite of spicy. Although there's this whole thing in the reader world about what the right words are and what they should mean and it can be a lot." She waved her hands. "You definitely don't care about all of that. Just know that the book there in your hands? You could let your teenage niece read it without worrying she'd find something she shouldn't."

"If I had a teenage niece, that'd be good to know." I looked down at the book again. "So it's like YA?"

Megan frowned a little. "Not really. It's not juvenile in style or content, if that's what you're asking. It's a really solid fantasy. And a clever twist on the fairy tale."

I'd buy it. I had enough cash on hand that I could splurge on something. And it'd be good to have more than the television in my cheapo motel to keep me occupied at night. I'd been trying to use the library computers to plan my escape—I didn't want to boot any of my electronics just in case—but it was a challenge to plan to disappear while using a machine literally anyone could walk by and gawk at.

"Thanks. I'll take it." I started to stand.

"You're not leaving already, are you?" Megan's expression morphed into a slight pout. "It's been a slow day."

I laughed in spite of myself. I could relate to the feeling. It wasn't that I was particularly used to hours and hours of exciting conversation, but I also wasn't in the habit of holing up in a motel room praying that no one would notice me. Well. Praying might be a stretch. But it was close enough that I wasn't going to have an argument with myself about it.

I sank back into the couch. "They say running a bookstore is a challenge these days."

Megan snorted. "That's putting it mildly. But I love books and I love helping people find the right books. And I love the friendships I've developed with local authors—and even some who aren't so local. I feel like I'm helping them. So I'm making it work. My husband thinks we should figure out a way to set up a café in the back corner."

I gazed over her head toward the area I assumed she was talking about. "Would you move this seating over there?"

"Probably. But all the permits and requirements for food service..." She trailed off. After a moment, she shook her head. "It's a lot."

"I guess I can see that. It's certainly different than books."

"So much different. Plus, I like the café owners down at the corner and I wouldn't want to undercut their bottom line just to try and make mine better. We have a little mutual promo that we're trying, but so far it feels like I'm sending a ton of people down there to get coffee and not seeing many people show up here to buy a book." Megan shrugged. "Anyway, there's no reason you would possibly care. Tell me what brought you into town."

I blinked. I'd hoped to have successfully sidestepped the question earlier. "Visiting an old friend."

"Oh, that's always so nice to catch up. Will you stay long?"

I shook my head. "No. I should be on my way out of town already, honestly."

"It can be hard to get away from home. Where's home?"

It was probably normal chatty small talk, but man it felt nosy. "It's kind of in flux at the moment. That's why I had the flexibility to make the trek out to see my friend."

"How exciting." Megan looked around the bookstore. "I love this place, but it makes traveling tough. I have some great employees, but they tend to have a lot of emergencies. Most of which I figure are probably just better offers than working."

"High school students?"

"And housewives and retirees. They're great, though. And mostly I don't mind shouldering the bulk of the work. But sometimes I dream of being able to get away for more than a week at a time." Megan sighed.

The bell over the door jingled and I looked over, my heart frozen.

But it wasn't Manny. I let out my breath.

"Hey, babe." Megan popped to her feet and hurried over to greet the man with a hug and kiss that were on the steamier side of publicly acceptable. "Come meet Faith. She's leaving town soon, but she popped in because of the fairy tale display."

"Faith?" The man looked over at me, his expression considering. He followed Megan to the seating area.

I wanted to rush from the store. Why? I couldn't put my finger on it, but the urge to flee was real. Generally, I didn't ignore a gut feeling like that, and my mind raced trying to figure out how I could gracefully excuse myself without it looking like I was running away.

"Faith, this is my husband, Cody. Cody, Faith." Megan reclaimed her seat.

"Nice to meet you." I offered a tight smile. "I should go and let you two have some time together."

"Don't be silly. He just comes and hangs out on nights I have to work, but it's not like I'm not working."

"Right. And that's the other thing, you're working. I don't want to take up your time. But I appreciate this." I lifted the paperback and gave it an awkward wave. I edged past Cody. "Nice to meet you both."

Megan started to speak, then instead she got up and hurried past me to the cash register. "You really don't have to leave."

"I appreciate that, but it really is past time for me to be on the road." I put the book down on the counter and dug into my bag for my wallet. Of course it was upside down and I hadn't zipped it, so all the random slips of paper that I stuffed in it went spilling out. "Sorry."

I scooped at the papers.

Megan bent down and collected the pieces that had floated behind the counter. She frowned slightly, her head tipping to the side. She put a business card down on the book. "You know Tristan? Cody and I have been friends with him forever. He's so great."

My mouth went dry. I glanced down at the card. Why had I grabbed that? I knew why, but sometimes decisions were dumb. This appeared to be one of them. "A little."

"Is he who you came to visit? Or, I guess you could be a client. But I shouldn't ask that, right? Because he's a lawyer and everything, so it's probably confidential." Megan rang up the book.

I stuffed all the loose papers—including Tristan's card—into my bag and pulled out a twenty-dollar bill. Maybe if I ignored the question, she'd let it go.

That hadn't been the case so far, but that didn't mean she wouldn't eventually get the hint, did it? I didn't want to outright lie—but I also didn't want to get into the inevitable follow-on questions of how did I know him and why was I leaving and so on and so forth. If Megan and Cody were his friends, they probably knew all the sordid details, and I just...couldn't go there.

"Here's your change." Megan held out the money.

I took it and dropped it into my wallet, taking care to zip the thing this time. "Thanks."

"I hope you enjoy the book." She looked like she wanted to say more.

"I'm sure I will." I took the book and hugged it to my chest as I headed for the door. I wasn't going to look over at Cody. His gaze was unnerving. And if they were good friends with Tristan, I needed to get out of the area before they called him and let him know they'd seen me.

Would he come looking?

No. That was dumb. Of course he wouldn't. He hadn't asked me to stay. He hadn't chased me down at the elevator. He hadn't taken any of the opportunities to change my mind either time I'd left.

I pushed through the door and, keeping my head down, started back toward where I'd left my car. It was time to get out of Virginia. Past time.

I covered the distance to my car in just under ten minutes. That was much faster than when I'd been meandering and window shopping earlier. Of course, since exercise wasn't something I did a ton of, my shins were killing me from the fast walking. Or it could be my shoes. They were old and beat up. Maybe once I figured out where I was going to land, I'd—

"Oof." I bounced off the solid mass of muscle-covered-denim. "I'm sorr—"

Strong fingers clamped around my arm. "Did you really think you'd get away?"

I jerked my arm, but Manny's grip was steel. "Kinda hoped so, yeah. Any chance you're going to let go and we can talk about this like civilized people?"

Manny shook his head.

"Figured." I sighed and darted a glance around. Of course

the residential street where I'd parked was devoid of the crowds that had been on the main shopping street. Which was why there'd been parking. I was maybe twenty feet from my car. But I couldn't remember if Manny could run or not. Some of the Ortega boys were fast. Others weren't.

"Faith!"

I recognized Tristan's voice. Dang it.

Manny's fingers tightened, but he looked toward the sound.

I put everything I could into swinging my left fist into his gut, then stomping forward. Manny's cowboy boots meant that didn't do much damage, but the movement was enough for me to get good leverage with my other knee as it came up between his legs.

He dropped my arm and I took off, digging into my bag for my keys as I sprinted. I clicked the fob, praying—ha—that this time would be one of the times it worked, and yanked at the handle.

It opened.

I dove in, slammed the door, and mashed the lock.

Manny's open palm smacked on the window by my head and I jolted.

"Don't run. It'll be easier on you if you don't run."

"Yeah, sure." I muttered as my shaking hands took three tries to get the key into the ignition. I really, *really* wished I could have found a used car with a push-button start. Next time.

A bubble of semi-hysterical laughter tore free. Next time?

I got the engine started, shifted into Drive, and started to ease from the space. I didn't *want* to drive over Manny's foot, but if he didn't move, I wasn't going to be responsible for the damage.

"Hey!" He pounded on the window. "Stop! Now!"

I cleared the back bumper of the car in front of me and stepped on the gas. There was a thunk and I caught a glimpse of

Manny hopping and rubbing his leg before he took a few steps after my car.

I blew through a stop sign, waving at the cars I cut off as they blared their horns.

It took longer than I wanted to get to the Beltway entrance. Once there, I merged into traffic. I could circle DC until I figured out my next step.

What I wanted to do was pull over and let the adrenaline work its way out of my system. But there'd be time for that later. Hopefully.

I slammed my brakes as a car from the right lane swerved in front of me.

Maybe driving on the Beltway wasn't going to decrease my adrenaline any.

I blew out a breath. I needed to think. I had to leave the area. The problem was, I had no idea where to go. If Manny had found me here—and how that had come about was something I needed to unravel—was anyplace safe?

I was going to need a new car now, too. Manny knew this one. I chewed my lip. That was probably the first step. Ugh. I could use a cell phone right about now. Of course, that was the same as lighting a big sign over my head for the cartel.

I checked my mirrors, changed into the right lane, and then moved into the exit lane. I'd find a convenience store and see if someone there could direct me to the right place to find car dealerships. I didn't have time to dig through the online listings, which meant I was going to end up paying more than I really ought to. And I was going to have to tap an account.

None of this was ideal.

Why hadn't I left last week when I could've gotten away easily?

I bounced my head against the headrest as I came to a stop

at the traffic light at the end of the off ramp. I spotted a 7-Eleven to the left and flicked my signal.

A car pulled up behind me before the light changed. They flashed their headlights. I frowned and checked, but it was still red.

Flash. *Beep. Beep.* Flash.

"Look buddy, if you're in a hurry and want to run the red, feel free to go around," I muttered and tried to ignore whatever problem the dude behind me had.

Finally, the light changed and I hurried to turn.

Did the guy go around me? Of course not.

Scowling, I slid into the turn lane at the next light so I could get to the 7-Eleven. Of course the impatient guy was behind me. I closed my eyes and started counting.

The tap on my window startled me. I whipped my head around, eyes wide.

"Tristan?" I hit the button to lower the window. "What are you...did you *follow* me?"

"Of course I followed you. Go to the 7-Eleven and park." He pointed, as if I was too stupid to see the enormous sign in their ubiquitous color scheme. Then he stomped off before I could retort.

"Like I wasn't going there already." I huffed under my breath. I squeezed the steering wheel, considering my options. I could sit through the turn arrow, then swing into the straight lane and...and what? I needed information. And knowing Tristan, he'd just follow me and be angry about it. Because apparently now that he'd decided to chase me down, he was serious about it.

The light changed before I made up my mind. Tristan laid on his horn a little longer than necessary.

I made the turn and pulled into the parking lot in front of the convenience store. I slammed the shifter into Park and cut the engine, then wrenched open the door and climbed out. I leaned against my car, arms crossed, and waited.

Tristan pulled his much nicer car into the spot beside me and got out. He looked at me over the hood of his car, head tilted to the side. "Hey."

"Really? You're going with a breezy 'hey' like you didn't just accost me in a near road rage incident?"

To my utter amazement, he laughed.

"I'm not the one with road rage. The Mazda that cut you off might have it, though."

My lips twitched. Darn it, I wasn't going to smile. Or act like this was all normal and not a big deal. "What are you doing, Tristan?"

"Helping you. Like you asked." He crossed his arms on the top of his car and leaned. "Or do you have it all under control?"

I wanted to protest that yes, I certainly did. But he'd been there and seen Manny with his gorilla hand on my arm. "You don't want to help me, remember? You want a divorce."

He flinched.

Where had those words come from? They weren't the issue here. They couldn't be. Not with the Ortegas on my tail. "Forget I said that."

"Kind of hard to do."

My eyebrows lifted. "I'm not the one who had papers just sitting around in his apartment."

"Uh-huh. You're also not the one who got walked out on. Twice."

It was my turn to flinch. I held up my hands in surrender. "Okay. Peace. All right?"

He nodded slowly. "I didn't realize you knew how to sing." He mimed an elbow to the solar plexus, stomped his foot down, and threw his head back like he was smashing someone's nose in the self-defense moves that used the SING mnemonic.

My lips twitched. "I forgot the N. But I've always loved *Miss Congeniality*, you know that."

"I do."

I wanted to groan. Why did he have to say those words? And say them that way? Looking at me steadily with those eyes that I'd always gotten lost in. "Tristan..."

"Let me help you, Faith. Please? Stay and let me help you."

Something in his voice was so vulnerable that my throat tightened. I wanted to object and declare that I'd be just fine all on my own. I wasn't positive that was actually reality though. Beyond that? I didn't want to leave Tristan.

Stupid.

He wanted a divorce. That was the right way to go. The delusional little voice in the back of my mind that said there was a way to make things work between us was, well, delusional.

I sighed. Even with all that, I still needed help. "Do you think you can? Really?"

"I do."

Was he doing it on purpose? Those two words were little barbs in my heart every time he said them. Totally unfair! I wasn't the one who'd put the divorce papers together. I'd just run off and disappeared. So yeah, totally not innocent here. I got that. "Manny knows who you are now."

"Manny?" Tristan looked perplexed. "Oh. The guy on the street? I don't think so. He knows someone called out, but I have no reason to believe he can figure out who I am."

I shook my head. "Don't underestimate these people, Tristan. If he got a photo of you or your license plate, it's a matter of time before they show up at your condo. Your office. Your friends' houses. You get the idea."

"I'll let everyone know to be cautious. None of that changes the fact that I want to help you get out from under this and be free to have a life."

I looked away as my eyes filled. Having a life—a real one—sounded amazing. It was also a pipe dream. I knew that, but I couldn't stop myself from yearning for it. If I was going that far, I might as well go ahead and pretend there was a way for Tristan and me to end up as a happy family.

I blinked back the tears and, when I was certain they wouldn't betray me, looked back at Tristan, fully intending to say no.

"I'd like that."

"I can't believe you're wearing a suit."

I turned at Faith's words and tilted my head to one side. "I'm not wearing jeans to meet the FBI."

Faith glanced down at herself then back at me. "Am I underdressed? I don't have a lot of options."

"You look lovely."

"But you—"

"I am an attorney." I gave her my best shark-tooth smile. "I need to look the part. I don't want Special Agent Orbison thinking he's going to be able to pull a fast one because I haven't danced with the FBI before."

"I'm surprised."

I shrugged. I'd had a few opportunities when I worked at the firm. Before I struck out on my own. I hadn't wanted to then. Didn't really want to now. But I'd do it for Faith. I checked the time. "We should go. Late isn't a good look with the feds. Although we'll be waiting, I'm sure, once we get to Orbison's office."

"Why?"

"Power move." I opened the door and let Faith walk past me.

It'd been two days since I'd chased her on the Beltway and convinced her to come back home with me. So far, there'd been no sightings of anyone from the Ortega cartel. I prayed constantly that would remain the case. But I was also glad that the FBI had finally returned my call.

"I hope you're wrong." Faith crossed her arms around herself. Her eyes were wide and she'd pulled her hair back into a ponytail. It made her look young and fragile.

"Why?" I checked the locks, then gestured toward the elevator.

"I don't want to be a pawn in someone's power game." She snorted out a laugh. "Too late. I get that. But I don't want to add any new players."

I pushed the call button. I could understand what she was saying. But yeah, it was probably too late to keep that from happening. "I'll do my best. Christopher—Scott's friend from his old job—insists this guy is legit. Hopefully, that'll turn out to be true."

The elevator arrived, empty, and we stepped in. The ride down was silent and uneventful. When we stepped out into the parking garage, I took a quick look around. Nothing looked out of place or unusual. I couldn't promise that I'd recognize a threat if it was subtle, but my paranoia had me continuing to try.

We hurried to my car. Faith was obviously as on edge as I was. I clicked the fob to unlock the doors and she pulled her side open before I could reach it. She waved me off. I frowned slightly, but went around to the driver's side and climbed in. When both doors were shut, Faith punched the lock button.

"Okay. Let me get the GPS set up and we'll be on our way."

Faith nodded.

I pulled up the location on my map app and got the directions started before hooking my phone into the stand on the dashboard. I started the car, then reached over and took Faith's hand.

"Don't tell me it's going to be okay." Faith tried to tug her hand away. "You don't know that."

"I wasn't going to. I was going to ask if you wanted to pray." The times I'd tiptoed around the topic of church and faith and how her spiritual life was going, she'd deflected. Masterfully. But this situation wasn't going to get fixed with legalese and feds alone. We were going to need the kind of help only Jesus could bring.

"Oh. If you want to, go for it. I don't really...I haven't been..."

I waited to see if she'd finish either statement. When she didn't, I just squeezed her hand and offered a short prayer, asking for guidance, clarity, and protection. Then I started the car and headed out of the garage.

We'd made it through town to the highway before either of us spoke again.

Faith cleared her throat. "You still do all the Jesus stuff?"

"Yeah. I take it you don't?" I didn't love categorizing my faith as "Jesus stuff," but that didn't seem like the hill to die on right now.

"Not really. It's hard to go to church and tell people you help with forgery and money laundering." She offered a tight smile. "It's not like I didn't know I was crossing lines. I never pretended to be, I don't know, Robin Hood or anything. But I honestly did try to make sure my clients weren't hurting anyone."

I held my tongue. I didn't see what she'd gotten into as a victimless crime. I understood the rationalizations she'd made, but I disagreed with them wholeheartedly. At a minimum, she'd helped people avoid paying their taxes, which in the long run hurt everyone. I didn't love taxes. I certainly thought that there were areas where they'd gotten out of control, but the government had to be funded somehow, and I liked this option better than the others available. Plus there was the whole render to Caesar thing.

Faith blew out a breath. "I'm too far gone now, anyway. Even if I can get the cartel off my back, I know I blew my chance with Jesus."

"That's not a thing." I glanced over at her before checking my mirrors and shifting lanes. Maybe it was my paranoia, but I didn't like the way one of the cars behind us was acting.

"What do you mean?"

"You can't blow your chance with Jesus. He loves you. He loves all of us. If you confess your sin and repent and ask Him to help you change, He's going to do that."

"I already did that, though. In high school. I meant it at the time, I really did. But life got hard, and it was like He didn't seem to care—He sure wasn't showing up like I needed Him to. So I handled it. Even though I knew I wasn't doing what God would have wanted, I had to survive. Like I said, I blew my chance."

I saw her shoulders jerk up and fall.

My heart hurt for her. "Do you think I never sin?"

"Not anything big."

"Jesus doesn't see big or little. It's just sin or no sin. Humans are the ones who try to rate sin on a scale. God can't tolerate *any* sin because He's holy. So believers have to keep confessing and repenting and allowing God to change us. It's not a one-and-done thing." I glanced in the rearview mirror. The same car was hovering two cars back. We were nearing our exit. I didn't think they could cause mischief between here and the FBI. And then once we were there, they wouldn't be able to follow us. They'd know our destination. But that was it. So it would be okay.

I hoped.

Faith didn't respond. Maybe that was just as well. I'd come perilously close to a sermon, which was never my intention. Mom and Dad had always been believers in loving people to

Jesus. I tended to agree with that approach over all the other options.

I waited until the last possible moment to slide over three lanes to the exit. The car I was worried about attempted to follow, but couldn't get through the traffic. I allowed myself a brief smile as we slowed at the end of the ramp and waited for the light to turn. That was even better. They could look at the exit we'd taken and make some guesses about where we were headed, but it didn't automatically mean the FBI.

The rest of the trip was relatively short. I didn't see any suspicious cars. No one cut us off or T-boned us in the middle of an intersection. All the things I'd been half-worried about the whole way here.

The building itself was fairly nondescript. If you didn't know better, you might think you were pulling up to a standard office building. I couldn't have said what I expected, but it wasn't this. There were even visitor spaces near the front doors.

I pulled into one of those spots and turned off the car before looking over at Faith. She'd gone pale. Maybe *paler* was the right way to phrase it. She twisted her fingers together in her lap.

"Hey."

She jolted and looked at me, eyes wide.

"This is good. You taking a good, first step toward being able to live the life you want. The life God wants you to live." I hesitated before reaching over and covering her hand with my own. I ignored how cold her skin was and squeezed. "I'm with you every step of the way, okay? Promise."

Faith made a fractional nod.

She didn't look convinced, but I wasn't sure how I could prove it other than continuing to do what I said I'd do.

I squeezed her hand one more time, then pushed open my door. "Come on. We don't want to be late."

"Right." With almost robotic movements, Faith climbed out

of the car and closed the door. She crossed her arms around her middle.

"Come on." I smiled, praying that she'd see the encouragement in it, then I started toward the doors.

The glass was tinted, so I could only see the reflection of us as we neared the entrance. I paused to let Faith catch up, then pulled open the door. The first glimpse of the lobby showed the security I'd been expecting. There were bag scanners and X-ray arches to walk through all before you could even get to the reception desk to state your business. Even after that, there were turnstiles that needed a badge to operate.

"ID please." The guard by the nearest bag scanner held out her hand.

I reached into my pocket for my wallet and slipped my driver's license out, then handed it over. The guard looked at my ID, her eyes darting up to my face several times as she did so. Then she took a tablet off the scanner table, used her fingerprint to access it, and scrolled on the screen. "Last four digits of your social security number?"

My eyebrows lifted and I rattled them off.

She nodded and handed me my ID back. "Put anything metal, including cell phones, into a tray for the scanner, then walk through. Wait behind the tape line on the other side."

I did as she said, taking a second to double-check my pockets for any stray metal that would set things off. I wasn't excited about the prospect of a pat-down. When I was convinced I wasn't going to make the thing beep, I stepped through the archway.

Not a peep. Excellent. The basket holding my pocket items and my briefcase chugged through the X-ray and into reach. I grabbed them and reloaded my pockets as Faith went through the same ID verification with the guard. After a minute, she stepped through and joined me.

Faith hadn't brought anything with her besides an ID.

I'd tried to talk her into bringing her records along, but she'd insisted that since they were all on her laptop, she didn't want to risk turning it on until she had a better idea of how things were going to shake out.

I hadn't pushed.

I'd convinced her to come back home with me. I'd convinced her to let me help her. That seemed like enough. At least for right now.

I crossed the lobby to the desk. "Tristan Lee and Faith Clarke for Special Agent Orbison."

"One moment." The guard-slash-receptionist-slash-whatever barely glanced up before she started typing. She clicked and typed some more, then went through the process of activating two badges, each with a huge, blue "V" on it. She hooked them to lanyards then placed them on the counter in front of me. "You'll each need to wear this at all times. You have to swipe for the elevator and to request a floor. These will only work for the ninth floor, where you'll find Special Agent Orbison. Once you get to nine, check in with the reception desk, and they'll let him know you're here."

"Thank you." I took the lanyards and offered one to Faith before looping the other over my head.

Faith followed suit.

"The elevators are through the turnstiles." The woman gestured vaguely to her left.

I guess that was helpful? I strode to the turnstile and tugged on the badge. It had a reel under the clip that allowed it to extend for swiping. With a beep, the two partitions slid open so I could pass through. They snapped closed quickly behind me.

No one was sneaking in on someone else's swipe here.

Faith pressed her badge to the sensor and hurried to join me.

We crossed to the elevators, and I pressed the call button.

Nothing lit up. Faith pointed, then swiped her badge on a sensor near the button panel, then pressed again. This time it lit.

I shot her a smile.

The smile I got in return looked sickly.

I wasn't sure what to do. I would have loved to put my arm around her shoulders and squeeze, but I didn't want the people watching on the inevitable cameras to think there was more between us than there was. Same issue with taking her hand.

I settled for a whisper. "It's going to be all right."

"You don't know that." Her swallow was audible. "What if this was a terrible idea?"

I sighed. "Even if it is—which I don't believe—it's still the best of the options."

"Is it?"

The fear and uncertainty in her eyes nearly undid me. I didn't know what I would have said if the elevator hadn't chosen that moment to arrive. We stood aside as a small group of men in suits strode out. Each one glanced over at us as they passed, and I could almost feel their gaze lock on the visitor badges.

We stepped into the elevator. This time, I remembered to swipe the card first and then press nine. When the doors closed and the car began to rise, I looked at Faith and injected as much confidence as I could into my voice. "This is the right first step."

It didn't take long to reach our floor. The car didn't stop along the way—was that because we were visitors? I wouldn't put it past the FBI to have some way to program the elevators to work different ways for different badges. The front desk had said we were only cleared for nine.

We stepped out into a sterile reception area. Leather chairs were pressed up against any empty wall space. Thick beige carpet covered the floor. A young man sat behind a tall, wood desk.

He looked up from his computer. "Can I help you?"

I walked closer. Faith hung nervously back by the elevator doors. "Tristan Lee and Faith Clarke for Special Agent Orbison."

The man nodded and looked at his monitor. His fingers flew over the keyboard. "Take a seat. Someone will be out to get you soon. If you'd like coffee or water, you can help yourself."

I followed the man's brief glance toward the corner where a small, bar-height table held a Keurig, a few mugs, and a rack of pods. A water cooler stood beside the table. "Thanks."

I made my way back to Faith. "Would you like a drink? Coffee?"

She shook her head. "I don't think caffeine is a good idea right now."

"Water?"

She shook her head again.

"Okay. Let's take a seat." I looked around, then nodded to a set of two chairs next to each other.

Faith sat and folded her hands in her lap.

I sat. I was tempted to get out my phone and check email. I probably didn't have anything urgent, but it was something to do, since having a conversation with Faith was a nonstarter right now. She was too nervous. Besides, what would we talk about? Did we even have anything in common anymore?

I sighed. How long would Special Agent Orbison keep us sitting here? After the security and check-in process, we'd ended up only being about seven minutes ahead of our appointment time. Obviously, we'd have to wait for at least that long, but would he keep us cooling our heels in the reception area for another fifteen or twenty minutes? Thirty?

It probably depended on how important—or unimportant— he thought this appointment was. Given that it had taken two weeks for him to return my call? I was banking on the latter.

I fought the urge to check the time and let my gaze roam around the reception area. I spotted two cameras, but there were probably more that I didn't see. No clock. No cheerful waiting room music. No TVs, like in doctor offices. Just silence broken by the clicking of the receptionist's keyboard and his murmured conversations on the phone.

It felt like it had been an hour when a door finally opened. An older, somewhat portly man, glanced around then spotted us. "Tristan Lee?"

I stood. "That's me."

"Special Agent Orbison. Come on back." He backed up against the door and gestured for me to go through.

I nodded at Faith to go first. I followed her through the door, nearly plowing into her when she stopped abruptly in the hallway.

"Go on to the right. I'm all the way at the end." Special Agent Orbison's voice was booming.

It didn't take long to reach his office. He gestured to the receptionist out front as he ushered us in. "Sorry for the wait."

"It's no problem." A quick glance at this wall showed that we were only five minutes past our appointment start time. Huh.

"Can I get you some coffee? Or we probably have sodas somewhere." Special Agent Orbison offered a sheepish smile. "I gave up soda last year and made them move it to another fridge and not tell me which one."

Faith chuckled.

He glanced at her and his smile turned kind. "I could go looking. They know it. I know it. But they'd also rat me out to my wife the first chance they got, and it's not worth the headache that would cause."

He moved around his desk and sat. "So. Tell me what brings you here to see me?"

10

FAITH

I glanced at Tristan. He'd said he'd be taking the reins. At least until we knew how things were going to shape up.

Tristan cleared his throat. "We have information about the Ortega cartel."

Other than a slight lift of his eyebrows, Special Agent Orbison didn't react. "Oh?"

"My client," Tristan made a slight gesture in my direction "was tricked into doing some business for them. Once she realized what she'd done, she refused to do additional work and has had to go into hiding."

Special Agent Orbison gave a soft snort as his attention shifted to me. "I bet."

My face heated. I wanted to squirm under his steady scrutiny, but I made myself be still.

"I believe the information she has would be instrumental in helping disrupt their operation in the United States on a fairly large scale. But I also believe it would be easily traced back to her. So we need some assurances."

Silence stretched across the room. It was miserable. I wanted to say something. Crack a joke. Anything to ease the tension. But it was the wrong move. I would have known that even without Tristan's pointed side-eye.

Finally, Special Agent Orbison nodded. "The Ortegas are a considerable concern for us. We've been trying to infiltrate their operation for several years, but our agents are inevitably identified."

"I don't think—"

I cut Tristan off. "I'll do whatever you want."

"Faith." Tristan turned, his knees bumping mine. "There's no way they'll believe it. Not now. They know we came here."

"Do they?" I forced my voice to stay steady though it wanted to shake. "You said yourself you lost the tail on the highway. There are a lot of places we could have ended up."

Special Agent Orbison straightened. "You were followed this morning?"

"They've had someone watching me—us—Faith—for a little over a week."

"What?" I swung my head to stare at Tristan. "No. That's not possible. Manny found me on Tuesday, but before that they had no idea I was here."

"Manny Ortega is in town?" Special Agent Orbison lifted a finger before he turned to his computer. The keyboard clicked noisily as he typed rapidly. "Where did you run into him?"

"Old Town Alexandria. He's probably on cameras in the main shopping area—I know he followed her to my friend's bookstore."

My jaw dropped. I scowled at Tristan. "How do you know that?"

"We'll talk about it later." Tristan's voice was a whisper.

"Yeah, we will." I hissed the words under my breath.

"Did you have any altercations with Manny?" The special agent's gaze traveled between Tristan and me.

I sighed. "He tried to grab me a few streets over when I was running for my car. Tristan bought me enough time to get away."

"Hmm. So he'll recognize you?"

Tristan winced. "Afraid so."

"It's fine. They probably have a whole file on you if she came to you and they found that out." Special Agent Orbison drummed his fingers on his desk. "If they didn't follow you into the parking lot, I have to agree that they may not know where you came today. There are plenty of choices between here and the highway that would make just as much sense. It's a calculated risk, but not overly more dangerous than any other."

"I don't think Faith trying to get in with the Ortegas is a good idea. She ran and tried to disappear. Now, what? She gives up and says 'just kidding'?" Tristan leaned forward. "How does that do anything other than put her right into their hands where they can get rid of her?"

"If they wanted to get rid of me, they would have." I crossed my arms. "I'm still useful to them. They want my skills."

"I'm afraid I have to agree with Faith on this one. Sorry." The look he shot Tristan suggested that he was, in fact, apologetic. "I understand your hesitation. It's the same one I've had every time we've authorized another attempt at a mole."

"With her information, wouldn't you no longer need someone undercover?" Tristan leaned down and grabbed his briefcase. He clicked the clasps open. "She really knows quite a lot about their operations."

"I don't doubt that. The problem isn't information. We have lots of information on a generic level. What we don't have is proof."

"You have an eyewitness." Tristan gestured to Faith. "That's not enough?"

Special Agent Orbison turned his steady gaze on me. "Who did you interface with?"

"Manny, mostly." I grimaced. "He was introduced through a different client who I didn't realize had connections to the Ortegas."

The special agent nodded. "That's pretty typical. We could probably use your information to get Manny off the street, but I doubt it would make much of a dent in their operations in the long run. And honestly? They're so used to Manny getting nabbed, they get him back out within a week."

I frowned. "They have people everywhere."

"They do. I'm reasonably confident they don't have anyone in my organization, but nothing is ever a hundred percent."

"Especially if your plants keep getting identified." Tristan shifted, leaning back in his chair. "Maybe coming to you was a mistake after all."

I started. Those were not words I'd expected to hear from Tristan. Ever. He was Mr. Straight-and-Narrow. Now he was having second thoughts? He couldn't have done that yesterday? Or the day before?

"We're here now." I put my hand on Tristan's arm.

Tristan turned to look at me. "We are. But we can leave. Figure it out on our own."

"You can." The lack of inflection in the Special Agent's voice was a dead giveaway of what he thought of our chances.

I shifted my attention back to Special Agent Orbison. "But?"

"But it then becomes how long, how far, and how fast you can run." He shrugged and leaned back in his desk chair, looking for all the world like a man discussing something innocuous. "Is that what you want for the rest of your life?"

I heard the underlying implication that it wouldn't be a long rest of my life. I sighed. Here I was, right back at the decision point Tristan had put me in. Or I guess it was me who put me here when I hadn't turned down the job that seemed too good to be true.

"You can't guarantee that isn't what she ends up with anyway." Tristan scowled. "You're just asking her to potentially make that life even shorter."

"What were you hoping I'd offer here?" Special Agent Orbison reached for the pen resting on his desk and began to flip it between his fingers. "Some kind of magical get out of jail free card?"

I flinched.

"No." Tristan squeezed his eyes shut for a moment. "Although, ha, that would be great. I guess I was hoping you'd take the information and find a way to keep her safe until you were able to get the Ortegas handled. But without even knowing the information she has, you're saying it won't help. So I don't think there's anything more for us to do here."

"Tristan." I reached out and grabbed his sleeve again as he started to stand.

"Faith. There's got to be a better way. Honestly? We can go live on an island. They won't be able to get to you and if they get close, sharks can dispose of bodies pretty well, I'm told."

I shook my head and stayed seated. "No. That's not the way. You were right all along. It's time to fix this. If the information I have isn't enough, then I can go back and get more."

"How? You ran and hid. They're going to see straight through you if you go back skipping and whistling a happy tune."

"No one is recommending skipping. Or whistling." Special Agent Orbison lifted his eyebrows and nodded toward Tristan's seat. "They'd have to think they caught her."

"Are you kidding me?" Tristan planted his hands on his hips. "What if they decide she's too big a liability and kill her? Do you have any way to know they won't do that?"

"Tristan." I reached out and grabbed his hand, then gave it a hard tug. "Sit down. Of course he can't promise safety. No one can. Not even you."

Grudgingly, Tristan perched on the edge of his seat. "You understand we came here for help, right? Not for her to volunteer as some kind of tribute?"

Special Agent Orbison's lips twitched, but he nodded. "I realize that. I also realize there's not a lot we can do in any sort of permanent way without more information. From the inside. Information that Faith seems uniquely suited to acquire."

I didn't like that it made sense. Tristan seemed to think that I was excited about the prospect of recklessly throwing myself back into association with the Ortegas. There wasn't anything further from the truth. But also, now that the idea that I could be free—really free—had taken root? I wanted that. Even if it meant doing something risky. "I'm in."

"Faith." Tristan frowned at me. He searched my face and something in my expression must have conveyed that I was serious, because he sighed. "How do I help?"

Special Agent Orbison cocked his head to the side and studied Tristan. "You want to help?"

"I want to keep Faith safe." Tristan shrugged. "That's all I've ever wanted."

I took a quick glance at Tristan as his words sank into my heart. I didn't deserve him. I never had. I certainly didn't now. The difference between me now and fourteen years ago? Today I wished there was some way that I could.

"Hmm." Special Agent Orbison drummed his fingers on his desk a moment, then abruptly stood. "I'll be right back. Talk amongst yourselves."

I waited until he'd left the room before I turned in my seat. "You don't need to do this. Just go home. Live your life."

Tristan shook his head. "Until you're safe, I'm with you."

"Why?" I should have stopped the word before it escaped.

"You know that answer." Tristan held my gaze for a moment before he looked away.

I wanted to object that no, I didn't. But maybe I did. At least I knew what Tristan had told me a week ago. Had it only been a week? He thought he loved me. Maybe he did. I shouldn't qualify it when he hadn't, but I wasn't used to being on the receiving end of love, so how was I supposed to judge?

I cleared my throat. "You still don't have to do this. You keep saving me from my messes. That's not your job."

"But it is. You're my wife. I should never have let you leave in the first place. I should have chased you, convinced you to come back."

I shook my head. "You didn't know where I was."

"Not at first. But when I looked—really looked—I found you. I kept tabs. Off and on." His face reddened. "I convinced myself that leaving you alone was the right decision. But I think that was just my hurt speaking."

"I wish you'd reached out."

Tristan shrugged.

It was as good a response as any, really. "I shouldn't have said that. It's not as if I reached out to you."

He offered a tight smile. "I've always been a lot easier to find."

"I'm sorry."

He waved it off. "I wasn't looking for apologies."

"What were—" I broke off when the door opened.

Special Agent Orbison entered, followed by a man who, frankly, looked homeless. "Sorry about that. This is Special Agent Blake. He's been under for a while, trying to get absorbed into the Ortega cartel in some capacity. While he hasn't been blown, they're also not biting."

Blake nodded once and leaned against the wall.

I swallowed. "So why is he here?"

"I have an idea. One that will allow Tristan to be involved as well without—hopefully—looking fishy. The Ortegas have plenty of legal representation, but I've also never seen them turn it aside. Particularly when the attorney in question has a squeaky-clean reputation. Or mostly squeaky-clean. You did a divorce case this summer that blurred some lines."

Tristan flinched. "That was a favor that I couldn't get out of."

Orbison nodded. "And that's exactly how the Ortegas try to lure people in."

"He was connected to them?" Tristan straightened. "I didn't see any of that when I was doing a deep background."

"It's tangential. You wouldn't find it if you didn't know already. I don't think they'll be coming to you trying to muscle you into doing more work for them, if that's what you're worried about. But it gives us a little bit of leeway in setting it up for you to represent Blake in a shadier deal. And it lends credence to why Faith here sought you out." Orbison tented his fingers. "Why don't I run through what I'm thinking?"

Two hours later, as Tristan and I walked back out to his car, I still couldn't quite wrap my mind around everything that had been said. It was...a lot.

Tristan paused beside the passenger door and opened it for me.

"Thanks." I started to sit and glanced up at him as he stood there. My heart did a slow roll in my chest. "Do you think this will work?"

Tristan hesitated. "I honestly don't know. But I hope so."

With that, he waited until I was completely in the car and then closed the door. It wasn't the reassurance I needed. But it also wasn't false hope. I had to appreciate that, didn't I?

We drove back toward the highway and I pointed to a fast-food restaurant. "Should we stop and get something?"

"I could eat." Tristan flashed me a grin before shifting lanes so he could make the turn. "And I guess it plays into the idea that we've been out shopping or something."

"Right. That, too." Ugh. I didn't love having to second guess every move. It was one of the big reasons I'd run. The first time and every time since. Life was easier when I could pretend there was nothing wrong and no one was looking for me.

When was the last time that had been true?

Those months I'd been with Tristan was the closest I could come up with. Even though my parents probably wondered, they weren't the kind of family that did things like look for someone who walked away. Not once I was a legal adult. They might have been hoping I'd stick around so they could charge me rent and utilities and keep mooching a portion of my paycheck. And Dad had had his...friends. I wrinkled my nose. Those friends who were glad to hear I was of age.

I fought a shudder.

"You all right?" Tristan glanced over before turning into the drive-thru line.

"Yeah. Just thinking."

"What are you in the mood for?"

I didn't want to tell him that my appetite had just gone on vacation, so I eyed the menu. "Do you think I could just get a kids meal?"

His eyebrows lifted. "You sure?"

I nodded. "With a Coke?"

"Okay." He looked like he wanted to say more, but he didn't. When it was our turn at the ordering sign, he asked for my kids meal and then got himself a double cheeseburger with large fries. At least someone was hungry.

When we had the food, and the cups were nestled into the cupholders, Tristan made his way back out to the road that would lead us to the highway and then home.

Home.

I shouldn't call it that. No matter how much I might want to.

I dug into the bag and got out Tristan's fries. "Here. You should eat these first while they're hot."

He laughed. The sound lifted my spirits. "Always looking out for me."

It wasn't true. We both knew it. He was risking his reputation as a lawyer for me now. Special Agent Orbison didn't think there'd be any permanent damage, not once things were finished and the FBI could make a statement thanking Tristan for his assistance. But until then?

I chewed my lower lip. "You know you don't have to do this, right?"

"I do."

Those words again. My heart ached even as I tried to decide what he meant. "You know or you do have to?"

"Both." He glanced over with a smile before shifting onto the ramp for the highway.

I sighed. I didn't have any way to repay him. Except...I swallowed and turned to look out the window at the cars and buildings as they whizzed by.

I'd sign the papers. That would be the repayment he needed. It would be the best thing I could do for him. No matter how much I wanted to keep him and see if there was a way to make things between us work for real, it was time to set him free.

11

TRISTAN

The hardest part about the FBI's plan—other than the waiting—was not being able to talk to the guys. Special Agent Orbison had been adamant that no one could know the plan. I understood his theory, but at the same time? It wasn't as if the guys were going to say anything. And at the end of the day, I could use the prayer support.

Which was why I found myself pulling up in front of Wes's dive shop just before close of business a little over a week after Faith and I had met with the FBI. Best case scenario, Orbison would never find out, and I'd get the support from my friends that I needed. And also, I wouldn't be hiding things from them once again.

The buzzer on the front door of the shop went off as I pulled it open.

"Welcome to—oh, hi Tristan." Sunshine, Wes's new wife, grinned from behind the sales counter. "How's it going?"

"Can't complain. You?" I glanced around the shop. I didn't see any customers, but that didn't mean they weren't doing a brisk business. I didn't really understand Wes's business model, but he seemed happy with it, and ultimately that was what mattered.

"Pretty good. Got some folks in earlier today who signed up for three certification courses and our January dive trip. Plus, I'm pretty sure they're going to end up wanting to buy all their own gear instead of renting."

"How do you figure that?"

She laughed. "Mostly from the woman's vibe. She had on designer athleisure, coordinating designer bag, flawless—if casual—look from head-to-toe. And the guy didn't look like he'd ever tried telling her no. So if she decides that being able to color coordinate her BCD, regulator, and wetsuit is the next critical thing she has to do in her life? He's going to plunk down his shiny gold credit card and make it happen."

I nodded. "Nice for you."

"And them. Because even if they don't care, we give good value for what you spend here and we'll make sure they're trained well enough to be safe. I've gone diving with some people who had certification cards who should never have graduated. We don't let that happen."

"True." I tipped my head to the side and studied her. "I feel like I probably owe you an apology."

"No, you don't." She held up her hands. "The more I experience your friend group, the better I understand. I probably would have worried too. I like that you were willing to speak up to protect your friend when you thought it needed doing."

"Thanks." I stuffed my hands in my pockets. "I'm still sorry. I could have been nicer about it."

Sunshine laughed. "That's true of all of us, a lot of the time. Let's call it bygones, all right?"

"All right. Thanks. The guys meeting in the back?" I nodded toward the hallway that led to changing rooms, a conference-slash-classroom, and Wes's office.

"Yeah. Although I think you're the first one here. Wes is back there, though. Probably in the office. Look around and you'll find him. Could you tell him I'm going to order you all pizza?"

"Sure. Thanks." I walked through the artfully displayed gear, towels, sweatshirts, and other assorted dive-related things and down the hallway. I poked my head in the conference room, but it was empty, so I kept walking. I knocked on the office door.

"C'mon in."

I cracked the door and peeked in. "Hey."

Wes swiveled in his chair and ran a hand through his hair. "Oh wow. It's that late?"

"Apparently." I glanced at his computer monitor. "Cooking the books?"

"You're such a riot." Wes made a show of slapping his knee. "Just trying to make sure things are balancing like they're supposed to. Which they aren't."

"Uh-oh."

"Nah." Wes shook his head. "I'm sure I'll figure it out. I probably forgot to enter an invoice from an order. It happens."

I watched as he saved and shut down the machine and stood. "You don't have to wrap up."

"It's all good. I'll figure it out tomorrow. Or I'll have Sunshine take a look. She's a whiz with numbers. Who knew?" He grinned and bumped my shoulder with his. "Married life is pretty good, isn't it?"

"Bro."

"What? You drop a bomb that you have a wife and you don't expect a little ragging?" Wes shrugged. "Anyway, she came back, right? So that's good."

It was a little—or a lot—more complicated than that. But I was going to save my breath because trying to explain that to Wes now seemed like an exercise in futility. Plus, I'd have to go through it all when everyone else got here anyway. So yeah. Let it go.

I followed him out of the office and back into the hall.

"Hmm." Wes stopped in front of the conference room and squinted at me. "You didn't agree. Which suggests it's not good."

"I'm here on a Monday to talk to you guys. Draw your own conclusions." I sighed and pushed open the conference room door. "Sunshine said she was ordering pizza."

"Nice. I'm going to go check in with her real quick. Make yourself at home. There are sodas in the fridge under the credenza."

I looked around the room and spotted the low shelving unit on the far wall that was probably what Wes had called the credenza. I crossed to it and pulled open one of the cabinet doors. Except it wasn't a cabinet, it was a mini fridge. "Clever."

I squatted to get a better look at the contents and settled on a Sprite. I didn't need caffeine in the evening. It was probably a sign of age. I wasn't going to dwell on it.

I closed the door and straightened, then carried the drink over to the table and sat. I'd barely popped the top and taken the first sip before Scott came through the door laughing as he looked over his shoulder. Austin followed in behind him.

"Hey, guys." I lifted a hand.

"Heya. Where's the soda?" Austin nodded toward my can.

I pointed.

"Cool." Austin crossed to pull open the door and looked at Scott. "You want?"

"Sure. I'll live on the edge. Does he have an orange soda in there?"

Austin moved cans around, then held an orange one in the air. "You're in luck. You know what? That sounds good."

I winced. "How can you drink that?"

Scott scoffed. "Oh please. It's all just bubbly sugar water anyway."

"Yeah, but orange?" I gave a mock shudder.

Austin chuckled and popped open his can, then took a long drink. "Ahhh. Just like radioactive fruit should taste."

I laughed in spite of myself. "I don't have a mechanism for comparison there, so I'll take your word for it."

"Everyone's a comedian." Austin shook his head and took another drink. "Why are we here on a Monday?"

Scott jammed his elbow into Austin's side. "Wait for Wes."

"Ow." Austin glared at Scott. "Just trying to get a feel for how long it's going to take."

"You don't have to be here." I couldn't help that annoyance laced my words. Here I was trying to do what the guys were always nagging me about and keep open and honest communication, and Austin was already trying to leave.

"That's not what I said. Or meant." Austin sighed. "Kayla gets antsy when she doesn't know exactly when I should be home. I'm putting the blame solely on pregnancy hormones and praying it changes when the baby's here."

"At Christmas." Scott shot Austin a look. "That's like three months still."

"You don't have to remind me of this." Austin reached for his soda.

"You should turn on your location sharing. Then she can track you like a stalker on her phone and you can be less annoying to your friends. Everyone wins." I spread my hands. "You're welcome."

Austin clicked on his phone, tapped, and then held it up so I could see the screen with location sharing enabled. "She can see where I am whenever she wants. Doesn't seem to make a dent in her anxiety."

I winced. So much for that. "And her doctor says it's normal?"

"Eh. Her doctor says sometimes pregnancy hormones cause paranoia and if it gets unbearable to let her know and she'll discuss options." Austin shrugged. "So far, keeping her in the loop is enough to make it all work, so for now we're letting it ride."

It didn't sound like it was working to me, but what did I know?

Wes came back, this time with Noah and Cody in tow. "Pizza's almost here. I'll wait for it and then be back. Just another couple minutes, promise."

The same conversation about soda and general greetings batted around the table for Noah and Cody. I leaned back in the chair—it was a lot more comfortable than my desk chair. Maybe I ought to give in and buy myself something nicer for work. It wasn't as if I couldn't afford it. Just because I'd gotten the office furniture for a steal didn't mean I had to stick with it.

"You okay?" Noah dropped into the seat beside me and cracked open a can of Sprite.

"Not really." I pressed my lips together. I'd planned on saying that sure, I was fine. It was one thing to keep the guys in the loop. It was a completely different thing to admit that I wasn't dealing with this whole situation very well.

Noah nodded. "Reasonable. Probably a lot to deal with, with the whole secret wife showing up out of the blue thing."

I closed my eyes. "Is that going to hound me forever?"

"Probably, yeah."

I turned to glare at Noah.

He held up his hands. "Come on, man. If we'd done it, you'd be the first in line with the barbs."

"I must be really annoying."

"You get used to it. Then you're kinda fun to be around." Noah grinned.

I snorted. Why did I hang out with these people again?

"Pizza!" Wes came in, closed the door behind him, and dropped two large pizza boxes in the center of the table. "One sec and I'll get plates. If you don't like the toppings, pick them off and don't complain."

"Aw, that's half the fun." Cody flipped open one of the boxes and closed his eyes as he breathed in deeply. "Mmm."

Wes crouched in front of the credenza, opened another of the doors, and pulled out a stack of paper plates. He turned and slid them down the table. They bumped into the nearest pizza box. "All right, someone pray and let's dig in."

Scott said a quick blessing for the food before he reached for the plates and started passing them out.

I waited until everyone had one before leaning forward to snag a slice out of the closest box. It looked like it was supreme. Good enough.

Once the noise from getting food settled, I swallowed the bite I was chewing, took a drink, and cleared my throat. "Thanks for coming, guys."

"Pizza on Monday. I'm good." Cody grinned.

"What's up?" Wes reached for a second slice of pizza and added it his plate.

I wasn't really sure where to begin. "I texted you all when Faith came back and agreed to let me help her with her situation. So for part of that, we met with the FBI agent that one of Scott's former coworkers at Robinson knows."

Wes glanced over at Scott. "Is that Christopher's sister?"

Scott nodded. "Yeah."

"Nice." Wes nodded. "I heard a little about that whole situation. Seems like he's a good guy?"

That was the impression I'd gotten from Christopher and his

sister. I wasn't completely sure it was accurate after our meeting with him, but I was trying to give the benefit of the doubt. I let the comment go without response. "Turns out, Faith agreeing to testify wouldn't really do anything useful. Orbison—that's the FBI guy—had a whole song and dance about why. I don't completely buy it, but it's not my area, so maybe I'm off base. Anyway, what he wants—and what Faith agreed to—is for her to essentially go undercover and get more dirt on the cartel. Something more actionable."

"What's actionable mean?" Noah frowned. "That sounds super unspecific."

"Tell me about it." I blew out a breath and looked down at my pizza. After a moment, I took a bite and chewed. No one spoke. It was probably a good thing that they were interested and listening. "Hopefully she'll know it when she sees it."

"Aren't they going to be suspicious if she shows up and says hi?" Cody leaned back in his chair. "I'm not a criminal mastermind, but that just doesn't seem like it's the kind of thing they'll just be okay with."

I snickered. "I had similar thoughts. We're supposed to let her get 'caught' by them. Meanwhile, I'm going to take on a client who looks dirty on the surface so maybe they'll trust me enough that I can keep an eye on her."

"What?" Austin shook his head. "That's the stupidest idea I think I've ever heard. What about your reputation? No one's going to hire you if it comes out that you were an attorney for a cartel."

"I had those reservations. The FBI has assured me that it won't come back to bite me."

"I can only imagine how much those assurances are worth." Scott scowled. "Why would you agree to this?"

"Because Faith said she was in. And this was the only way I could think of to help. I don't want her to have to do it alone." I studied my pizza again before taking another bite. It tasted like dust and I wasn't all that hungry anymore. Every time I thought or talked about this dumb plan, my stomach twisted into knots. But what else was I supposed to do?

No one spoke.

I took another bite. I didn't have anything else to add. They might be expecting me to have more to say, but I was going to need for them to give me a hint before I could.

"Wow." Cody propped his elbows on the table. "That's a lot."

I nodded.

"How can we help?" Cody glanced around the table. "I'm assuming everyone wants to help if we can?"

The guys all nodded.

A lump formed in my throat and I swallowed. "I wish I had a clue."

Cody laughed. "Man, we've wished that about you for a long time."

I chuckled along with the rest of the guys. "Seriously, though. I just wanted you to be in the loop, since you're always telling me I don't share enough."

"You have to admit, leaving out a whole wife was kind of a big deal." Noah pointed at me with the pizza crust he was holding. "So we aren't wrong."

"No. You're right. I'm so used to keeping things quiet. Client confidentiality and all that." Of course, my marriage to Faith predated any kind of lawyerly privilege, but maybe they'd let it slide.

Noah shot me a look that conveyed, clearly, that he saw my hedging. At least he didn't say anything about it. I'd take the small favor.

"We can pray." Scott looked up from his perusal of the pizza in the middle of the table without taking another slice. "That's not a last resort, you know?"

I winced. "You're right, too. And prayer is absolutely something I need. I'm not as faithful with that as I'd like to be."

"Who is?" Wes reached for his drink. "Honestly, it's easy to fall into the trap of saying you'll pray and really meaning it, but then life happens, and it's the first thing to go."

Austin cleared his throat. "This might be cheesy."

I laughed. "With an intro like that, I can almost guarantee it."

"Quiet, you." Austin gave me his sternest teacher glare. "But Kayla and I have set some alarms on our phones to remind us. We translated the month and day of our birthdays into times to remind us to pray for each other. Her due date reminds us to pray for the baby. That kind of thing."

"So you pray at twelve twenty-five every day for the baby?" Cody's grin was huge. "I love that. Although I still feel for the kid if he's born on Christmas."

"He? Wait, do we know it's a boy? How'd I miss that?" Scott's gaze bounced between Austin and Cody.

"We don't." Austin held up a hand. "Kayla refuses to be told. I thought about sneaking the info out of the doctor, but I know I'd slip up. I just try to use random pronouns, because 'it' doesn't seem right, and as far as we know there's just one in there, so 'they' is confusing."

"Teachers and their grammar nerdiness." Scott's grin made it clear he was joking. "Back on topic though? I love that. I'm also adding the twelve twenty-five in."

Noah looked at me, one eyebrow lifted. "Your birthday is July fourth, right?"

I nodded. I'd hated it growing up, but slowly learned to appreciate having a built-in celebration every year. Now that I was older, mostly my birthday slid by with only my parents mentioning it. But that was also fine. At this point, I bought what I wanted when I wanted it, so it wasn't as if I was in need of gifts.

"All right, seven oh four it is. I'm going p.m. myself, because I don't want to have to form coherent thoughts at seven oh four on Saturday mornings." Noah looked up from his phone and glanced around the table. "You can all choose what works for you."

"I can add information to my alarms." Wes sounded slightly amazed. I guess he wasn't big on using phone alarms for things, because I already knew that. He frowned at his phone. "Should I just put 'Tristan' in there, or do you have specific things you want us to pray about?"

I sighed. "Ultimately, Faith and I want to be in the middle of God's will with this whole situation. But personally? I have some feelings on what I hope that means."

"Then we should pray for that." Cody set his phone down. "We're told to bring our requests to God. It's good that you're seeking His will, but it's not wrong to say 'hey, this is what I'm hoping for.' You know?"

He was right, but it felt...greedy? "All right, well, obviously safety, because this whole thing could go sideways in big ways. And then our marriage."

It was so weird to say that out loud in front of people. Even though these were my friends—basically my brothers—I had to overcome a lot of years of pretending.

"You gave her divorce papers." Scott's eyebrows lifted.

"Because it seemed like what she wanted." I rubbed my forehead. It still seemed like what she wanted most of the time. Maybe because there was so much else going on that our relationship, such as it was, was the furthest thing from her mind. But still. "Not because I want it. Anyway, she didn't sign them."

"She didn't?" Scott cocked his head to the side. "Why didn't you know that when you first came clean?"

"I couldn't bring myself to look, okay?" I scowled across the table at him. "If Whitney walked out on you for the second time, would you be rushing to see if she also went ahead and took care of all the paperwork before she left?"

"Point taken. Sorry." Scott blew out a breath. "But if she didn't sign them, doesn't that mean she wants to stay married?"

I shrugged. I honestly had no idea. It could mean she had been in such a hurry to disappear again that she forgot. Or she didn't want to agree to the terms in the papers I'd drawn up and wanted to get her own made up. I was a billionaire now, so maybe she was going to try to take half.

I'd probably let her.

I wasn't sure what that said about me.

I'd let her have it all if she'd stay.

And I knew, deep down, that solidified just how pathetic I was. Pathetic and in love. Just like the fourteen years had never happened.

12

FAITH

I squashed the urge to glance over my shoulder and ignored the sense of déjà vu as I strolled down the main shopping street in Old Town. I was trying to do as Special Agent Orbison had recommended and make myself available to Manny—or someone else from the cartel—to find. But I didn't love it.

I also didn't love kicking around Tristan's apartment with nothing to do. I'd been working some kind of job or other since I was fourteen and able to apply for a work permit. Sitting around idle just wasn't for me. So today I was going to find a job. If I got grabbed off the street, maybe I'd be able to convince the cartel to let me keep living my life and doing work for them in the evenings. I could probably sell it as needing to look normal so Tristan didn't get suspicious.

I bit my lip.

I *thought* I could sell it at least. Time would tell.

I looked in the windows as I passed the shops. I didn't particularly want to do food service, but it might be my best and only option. I wrinkled my nose. I'd go there if I needed to, but I wanted to play out a hunch, first.

I walked past the ice cream shop—definitely higher on the list than waiting tables—and another two shops until I reached the bookstore. The bookstore that Tristan's friends ran. Or owned. Or something. I needed to get the full scoop there. But since they'd recognized me—eventually—and called Tristan when I ran off, I figured the chances were high that they were good friends. Which made them good people, because other than his association with *me?* Tristan always surrounded himself with good people.

It had been one of the first things that drew me to him.

I pushed that thought away. I couldn't concentrate on that right now. I'd looked for the divorce papers when Tristan had brought me back to his place after chasing me on the Beltway, but they were gone. I wasn't going to ask him about them. But they weren't signed. I knew that. I was pretty sure he knew that. So...what did it mean?

Ugh.

I didn't want to go down that rabbit hole. Not right now.

Instead, I fixed a smile on my face and pulled open the bookstore door, my spirits lifting a little with the sound of the jingling bells overhead.

"Hi, welcome—oh it's you!" Megan's polite smile morphed into an actual grin. "I'm so glad you came back. Did you get through the fairy tale already?"

"I did, actually. And I really liked it." Which I hadn't expected to, but there didn't seem to be a reason to say that out loud.

Megan's grin broadened. "Come sit down and tell me what kind of book you're looking for today."

"Actually." I took a deep breath. "While I do want another book, I'm also wondering if you might be hiring."

"So you're sticking around? You seemed pretty keen to leave

last time you were here." Megan nodded toward the seating area. "Let's sit. You can tell me about it."

I groaned quietly. Maybe I should've run this past Tristan. I got the feeling he'd told his friends everything. First, because that was just the kind of man he was. And also, because he'd been a lot more relaxed since Monday, and I figured it had to do with his evening meetup with "the guys." That was what he'd called them when he let me know he'd be late, because he was having "a meetup with the guys."

He probably would have told me all about it, but I wasn't going to pry into his personal life. Was I supposed to?

I chose an armchair rather than the couch this time. I folded my hands in my lap and tried not to squeeze them together too tightly.

"So." Megan smiled as she sat across from me. "You're staying?"

I nodded. "Can we be honest?"

"I always prefer that."

"Good. Me, too. I feel like you probably know the whole situation already. You're married to one of Tristan's friends—I got that much information out of him—and I figure he keeps his friends in the loop. So, while I can answer questions, I don't want to just babble on and on about stuff you already know."

Megan snickered. "That...is honest. And fair. Maybe I wanted to know your take on things, though?"

I shrugged. "I can't imagine Tristan's version was skewed. But the short version is we're married, I run when there's trouble, and that's what I did fourteen years ago and more recently. I came back because I thought Tristan could help me. He is. But I tried to leave when I realized how unfair it was to expect him to do anything for me after all this time. Now he's dug his heels in, and I'm scared enough and tired enough that I'm willing to try it his way."

Megan pursed her lips before nodding slowly. "Okay."

What did that mean? I swallowed and started to stand. "You know what, never mind. I'll go fill out an application at the ice cream store."

"Wait wait wait. Sit down." Megan held my gaze until I lowered back down into the chair. "You keep things close, don't you?"

My eyebrows lifted. Did she expect me to spill all the sticky details and the ins and outs to her just because she knew Tristan? She might be his friend, but she was still a stranger to me. "I guess. Is that a problem?"

"Not necessarily." Megan drummed her fingers on her leg. "I could actually use some help. One of my high schoolers just quit because she made varsity basketball and doesn't have time in the afternoons anymore. Totally legit and I support extracurriculars, but it did leave me in the lurch. My understanding is that you might disappear again, though, as part of the solution you're trying?"

I pressed my lips together. Tristan had told them the details. Which was fine. Maybe even good. "I'm hoping not to. I think I can make a case that it'll be better if they let me try to keep up the appearance of normal."

Unless, of course, they killed me before I had a chance to talk. But I really didn't believe they'd send Manny if that was what they wanted. They had people who were much better suited for making people disappear than Manny.

"How...no, maybe I don't want to know."

"It's probably better if you don't." Also, it wasn't like I had a grand plan. Just kind of the vague hope they'd see reason. Which, when dealing with these people, was a big enough gamble that I didn't think even Vegas would take the odds. My stomach twisted. Maybe I should just go. Leave town. Take my chances. And if I lived to tell the tale, see about getting useful information to the FBI.

"Okay. You're hired. When can you start?"

I blinked. "Just like that?"

Megan shrugged. "I need help. Tristan matters to me and to my husband. And it seems like you could use a friend. I'm finding I'm pretty good at that. So yeah. Just like that."

I wasn't sure I appreciated how on target she was. I could use a friend. Or two. But that had been such a constant state in my life, I wasn't used to people seeing it. Tristan had. His parents had. But other than that? No. "Well. Thanks. I can start whenever. Now. You tell me."

Megan laughed. "Now works. It's a slow day. Which is sadly not unusual. But it makes it good for training."

"All right." I stood and looked around. "Where do we start?"

"With lunch."

"Lunch?"

"That's right. I usually bring something. I did, in fact, bring something today. But hiring a new employee calls for a celebration and I'm really not in the mood for a sandwich of compressed chicken anyway. Though I will share the Twinkie if you want."

When was the last time I had a Twinkie? "I might take you up on that, for nostalgic purposes if nothing else."

"Excellent. So, as the low woman on the totem pole, you get to go pick up lunch at the Café down the block."

"The Café?" There were so many restaurants around, I wasn't sure I'd get the right place.

"That's its name. The Café." Megan shrugged. "When I saw it, I tried to convince my grandmother to rename the bookstore 'The Bookstore,' but she wasn't having it. She's a diehard Stephen King fan, so Portable Magic is her homage. At this point, having seen what's involved in changing a business name? I'm leaving it all alone. Even if it confuses people."

"Maybe just tack on 'A Bookstore' after it? At least in your ads and fliers and stuff? Doesn't necessarily have to be a legal name change." Because it seemed to me that knowing what a store sold was critical to increasing the bottom line.

"That's...not a bad idea. I'm appreciating my decision to hire you already." Megan laughed as she stood and strode to the front desk. She slipped to the side where the cash register stood and pulled out a notepad from wherever she'd had it tucked away. She wrote on it, then ripped off the top sheet and slid it toward me. "That's my order. Let me get you some cash."

"I've got it." Tristan had been adamant about giving me money. He called it "walking-around money," even though it was more like "withdrew-the-max-from-the-ATM money" in my mind. I appreciated that he didn't want to leave me destitute, but I didn't like not paying my way. Even if he could afford it. "I'll be back in a few."

I started toward the door, then stopped. I pointed to the right. "Down the block that way?"

"Yep. You can't miss it. There'll probably be a line. And an amazing smell. If you see a pastry you can't live without, get two."

"What if it's something you don't like?"

Megan patted her stomach, which was completely normal sized. Maybe not skinny, but also not fat. "I like it all."

I chuckled and pushed the door open. Clutching the paper holding her order, I stepped out onto the sidewalk.

I'd made it past two stores and had spotted the café when I sensed someone behind me. I slowed and glanced over my shoulder, then stopped and turned. "Hi, Manny."

He froze then blinked. "You gonna run?"

"No." I lifted the paper. "But I need to get this lunch order and take it back. Maybe we could arrange a time to meet up and talk?"

He frowned at me.

"Look. I'm tired of running, okay? I want to talk about how we can all be happy." My heart thundered in my chest. Could he see my pulse racing? My hands wanted to shake and my knees were weak. This was where it could all go wrong.

"I gotta make a call." Keeping eye contact, Manny dug a phone out of his pocket, tapped the screen, and lifted it to his ear.

Jesus, are You there? Tristan says You are. I don't know what I think anymore, but I could use a hand here. Maybe if not for me, for Tristan? I don't think that's actually how You work, and maybe even talking like this will make You mad—sorry. I just—

Manny took the phone away from his ear and stared at me. He nodded once. "Boss says seven tonight at the seafood place on the water. Bring your boyfriend."

"Look, Tristan doesn't—"

"Bring him. Seven o'clock." Manny gave me a hard stare before he turned on his heel and marched back down the street.

I blew out a breath.

That could've been worse. A lot worse. *Was that You? If so, thanks.*

I hurried the rest of the way to the café and got in line.

Megan had been right about the scents. The sugar and yeast and something fruity in the air made my mouth water. For the first time today, my stomach unknotted enough that I thought I might actually be able to eat a proper meal.

I sure wasn't going to be eating tonight.

I made my way to the counter and placed our order, then slid around the pickup area. There was an empty stool pushed out of the way against the wall, so I hopped up on it to wait, and dug out my phone.

After a moment's hesitation, I opened a text to Tristan.

> Met up with Manny a few minutes ago. Dinner tonight with the boss at seven. Seafood place on the water? They want you to come.

I hit send and bit my lip.
Tristan replied quickly.

> I know the place. Seven is fine. Are you okay?

My lips twitched and I couldn't stop my heart from turning to mush. What was I going to do when this was all over and Tristan gave me those papers again? The right thing was to sign them and leave him to have a good life. The kind of life he deserved. One without me in it.

I tapped back.

> Yeah. Thanks.

I stuffed my phone back into my pocket without waiting to see if he said more.

I felt my phone vibrate a couple of times while I waited for them to call my name for the lunch order, but I resisted checking. I couldn't trust myself not to beg Tristan to give me another chance—to give *us* another chance. It was the worst possible thing I could do.

"Faith?"

I glanced up as my name rang out, then slid off the stool and headed to the counter. "That's me. Thanks."

The kid—honestly, he looked twelve, but since it was the

middle of the school day he had to be at least eighteen, didn't he?—smiled and handed me the paper bag of food. "Have a good one."

"Thanks. You, too." I took the bag and headed toward the exit, weaving between tables and patrons. I was looking for Manny, but didn't see him. Maybe with our appointment set for seven, I didn't need to be looking over my shoulder constantly?

Oh, who was I kidding? I was going to end up paranoid for the rest of my life.

I enjoyed the short trip through the sunny yet cool fall day back to the bookstore. I paused outside and looked up at the sign above their plate glass window. They could absolutely add "Books and Coffee" or something along those lines underneath. It'd make a good addition, honestly. And coffee always drew people. Maybe Megan's husband was onto something with his idea.

I went in, the bell on the door jingling cheerily and, I assumed, causing Megan to poke her head out of a door in the back.

"Oh, great. Long line, I guess? Come this way."

She disappeared into the room before I could answer, so I crossed the store to the far wall. Looking through the doorway, I saw a desk with a laptop, and a four-person round table squeezed into the corner. A dorm-sized fridge hummed in the corner near the desk.

"Welcome to the staff room." Megan spread her arms grandly and laughed. "It's not much, but most of the time I'm here alone, so it works. Have a seat and let's eat."

I chuckled at her rhyme and moved around the table to the far side so I could see out the door into the bookstore. It wasn't that I necessarily wanted the wall at my back, but also? I really didn't want an open door at my back.

I sat and opened the bag so I could pull out the enormous Cobb salad Megan had ordered.

"Have any trouble with the modifications?" Megan took the container as she sat across from me.

"No. Once I started listing them, they asked if it was for you and just took the paper."

Megan laughed. "I guess I eat there too much. Or I order the salad too much. Their sandwiches are great, but I'm trying to cut carbs."

I frowned. This was the second time she'd made a dig at her weight. "You look great. Also you have a Twinkie in your lunch. Sandwich bread is better for you than that."

Megan's cheeks flamed red and she sighed. "I should cut sugar completely. I know that. But sometimes I just neeeed it."

"Dopamine is a thing." I unwrapped my sandwich and took a bite. I studied Megan as I chewed. "Why the weight worries?"

Her eyebrows lifted and she looked down at her salad, then started stabbing her fork into it. "The doctor said it'd help with getting pregnant if I lost ten to fifteen pounds."

"Seriously? You'll disappear."

Megan laughed. "Hardly. But thank you. That's what Cody says."

"You've been trying a long time?" This was starting to feel like wading into too much information. "You know what? We barely know each other. Don't answer that."

"It's okay. I don't mind if you don't. And no, not really. We got married this summer and we haven't been not trying, you know? I just kind of figured it'd happen. People talk about honeymoon babies all the time and..." Megan shrugged. "I guess I was hoping for that."

Wow. Okay. I couldn't process the idea of actually wanting to get pregnant that fast in a marriage, but it wasn't like I had a super healthy example of marriage anywhere in my life to draw on. Or not many. Tristan's parents were amazing.

Ohhhh. What must they think about this? They probably hated me.

"What are you thinking? I can take it." Megan watched me.

"Nothing about that, really. Just a tangent." I waved it away and took another bite. "I know my opinion doesn't count here, but honestly, I don't think you need to lose weight or worry yet. Focus on being healthy."

"It's like you're listening in when Cody and I talk." Megan shook her head and sighed. "I'll try. It's hard not to obsess. Especially with Kayla due in December. And I know Noah and Jenna are going to try to start their family as soon as they're married on New Year's Eve. I don't want to be the last one with no kids."

Since I couldn't think of anything to say, I just nodded.

"Saying that out loud makes me sound horrible. Especially when I know Whitney can't have kids, so she and Scott won't be trying. And Sunshine is in her forties, so while possibly she and Wes could have a kid, it doesn't seem super likely. So I'm not even the odd one out for real." She frowned down at her salad. "I should've gotten a sandwich."

I laughed and nudged the untouched half of mine toward her. "I'll share if you have a plate or something to scoop some of your salad onto."

"Really?" Megan brightened. "You're already my favorite employee."

"As long as I'm not your only employee."

She shot me a grin and shook her head.

"Speaking of that, though, I have a thing tonight that I can't miss." I could imagine how well it'd go over to miss dinner with whoever Manny had called. The answer was "not well." At all.

"Oh that's no problem. I was already planning to close today.

And I'll probably have you take over mornings once you're trained. If that works?"

"It should." At least I thought so right now. If something happened tonight that changed it, I'd let her know.

"Perfect." Megan scooped half of her salad out into the lid of the container it came in and pushed it across the table along with a fork. "After we eat, I'll show you the ropes."

13

TRISTAN

I unlocked my front door and toed off my shoes as I shut it behind me. "Faith?"

I cocked my head to the side and listened, but the place was quiet. The kind of quiet I was used to coming home to. Or at least I had been used to it. Now, I'd already become accustomed to the little sounds of life that another person existing in my space created.

I loved it.

Was that because it was Faith? Probably. At least, I knew it helped, even though I tried to deny it. She'd made her stance clear. Even if she hadn't signed the papers before she disappeared the last time, she didn't love me. I should be doing something to internalize that and work on getting over her. When she left, when things were officially over between us, I needed to be ready to throw myself into the dating game right away.

If I didn't, I'd just spend the rest of my life mooning over the one who got away.

I padded down the hall and turned toward my bedroom. I wanted to change out of the suit I'd worn today. I didn't always break out the full lawyer look, but I'd had a court-ordered mediation session for one of my clients, and it didn't do to show up looking unprofessional. In the end, that session had gone well and the client had been persuaded, finally, to agree to a compromise. A good one, in my opinion. He was unhappy, but I'd been straight with him from the beginning that he didn't have a strong case, and that what he ended up with was the best he could hope for.

I shrugged out of the suitcoat and hung it on its hangar. Then I paused. Dinner at the seafood place could run casual or dressy. The restaurant didn't care, but it was upscale and pricey and people took prom dates there. A suit wouldn't be out of place. Would it be intimidating to the Ortegas? Or would I look like I was trying too hard?

Maybe I'd wait for Faith to get home and see what she thought made sense.

I hung up the suitcoat and went back out into the living room, stopping by the kitchen for a glass of water. I plopped onto the couch and unlocked my phone, frowning when I saw she'd read my last three texts but not responded.

I sighed and switched to social media and scrolled aimlessly through the shiny happy version of people's lives, pausing to watch clips from standup routines and dogs being crazy. A dog.

I switched to the web browser and navigated to the animal shelter. I'd been planning on getting a dog at the start of the month. Then Faith had shown up and that got moved to the back burner. But now? Were things stable enough that I could explore that option again? Or would that just be someone else who was heartbroken when Faith left?

The sound of a key in the door shifted my attention from the amusing, dating-site-like bios of the dogs at the shelter. I clicked off my phone and stood, tucking my hands in my pockets.

"Tristan? I'm ho—" Faith broke off as I stepped into the hallway. "Hey."

"Hey. You're okay?" I was trying not to let her see how worried I'd been when she didn't respond to my texts. But it probably leaked out.

"I am. I should have texted you back, I'm sorry. I got a job." She grinned as she stepped out of her shoes and reached behind her to push the door closed. "I'm working for your friend Megan at her bookstore."

"Yeah? Nice." I caught myself before I made a quip about cooking the books. Probably best not to go down that route just yet. Maybe this whole situation would be funny at some point in the future, but we weren't there yet. "Congrats."

"Thanks." Faith closed the distance between us.

I held my breath. In a normal marriage, this would be where we'd embrace and see where things went.

She slipped past me. "What's the dress code for this restaurant?"

I closed my eyes against the surge of disappointment. It was stupid on about twelve levels to be disappointed. But the longer she lived here, the longer she was back in my life, the harder it was for me to keep the memories of the months when we lived truly as husband and wife out of my thoughts. And heart.

I turned. "I wanted to talk to you and see what you thought. Patrons run the gamut. I've seen people in shorts and flip flops in the summer and kids going to prom. Most people are probably on their way home from work or after church, so maybe a little dressier than jeans. But jeans would be fine."

"That is completely no help."

"Sorry." I glanced down at my slacks. "Do you think if I wear my suit it'll intimidate them? Or will I just look like I'm trying too hard?"

"You do look good in a suit."

She said it under her breath, so I tried not to take it too much to heart, but I couldn't deny that it warmed me.

"So wear the suit? Jacket or no jacket?" I brushed a hand down my tie. I wouldn't mind ditching the tie and wearing the jacket, but most people seemed to feel that a shirt and tie was more formal than a jacket and no tie. Even though my parents had drummed Miss Manners into me as a teenager and she said the opposite.

"Might as well wear the jacket. I have a skirt suit, I'm pretty sure. Then we can both be fancy and businesslike. Let them know we're serious." Faith frowned. "Though I'm not sure how much that'll matter. It bothers me that they want you there. And that they think you're my boyfriend."

"Ouch."

Faith shook her head. "Not because you wouldn't be a great boyfriend, but if they've been digging on me to track me down, shouldn't they know we're married? I don't know what it means, but I feel like it has to mean something."

"It could just mean that they tracked you down some other way and not through me." I pulled out my phone and glanced at the time. "We should leave in about an hour. It doesn't take long to get there from here, but we wouldn't want to be late."

"No. We wouldn't." She sighed. "I'm going to go rest for thirty minutes before I get ready, if that's okay?"

"Yeah, of course." I'd been about to suggest we could watch something on TV together, but maybe this was better. I shouldn't get used to having her around. She wasn't permanent.

What I ought to do was get a dog.

I watched Faith go down the hall to her bedroom. She closed the door behind herself without looking back. I sighed and resumed my spot on the couch, flipping back to the animal shelter website.

I'd narrowed my choices to two by the time I heard the door down the hall open and shut again. I listened as her soft footsteps traveled to the bathroom, and that door clicked shut, followed by the snap of the lock. Then running water.

With a sigh, I turned my attention back to the web page and filled out the contact form. It didn't hurt to get information, right? Maybe this wasn't the perfect situation to bring a dog into, but when was life ever perfect? It felt like having something better to focus on than the nebulous state of my marriage was a good thing.

When I'd submitted the form, I stood, and crossed to stare down at the river from my big window. There weren't any boats out. Not surprising, seeing as we were in the final days of September, and evenings were cooling off. There was still plenty of activity during the day though. And the dinner cruises ran all year long.

I rested my forehead on the cool glass.

"Ready?"

I turned. The shoes dangling from straps in her hand explained why I hadn't heard her come in. The combination of bare feet, bright red toenails, and that dress did something crazy to my insides—like they froze and turned to molten lava all at the same time.

"What's wrong? Is this not okay?" Faith brushed self-consciously at the dress.

"It's great. You look great. Amazing." I winced inwardly as the inanity tumbled out of my mouth. I sounded like a besotted teenager. I cleared my throat. "Let's go."

She tipped her head to the side and studied me. My heartbeats ticked off the time. Finally, she nodded and bent to slip her feet into the shoes.

Mmm. Well then. The shoes added something even more to the outfit. And that was a road best not traveled.

I started toward the door, careful not to brush against her as I passed. I didn't think my haywire system could handle that.

Since I had no idea how she'd react to an offer of my elbow or hand, I didn't.

But I did hold the door for her. Some manners shouldn't be forgotten.

Her lightly floral scent filled my senses as she walked by much closer than I'd done in the living room.

I swallowed.

Silence marked every stage of our journey to the restaurant. I would have classified it as awkward, but from the way Faith knitted her fingers together, maybe on her end, at least, it was just nerves.

I found a parking spot in the restaurant's lot. I decided to take it as a sign that God was looking out for us. In fact...I shut off the car and turned slightly to look at Faith. "Can we pray?"

She blinked at me. "Uh. I guess. Sure."

Before I could stop myself, I reached over and took her hands in mine, then I bowed my head. It took a moment for me to clear my thoughts enough to speak. "Heavenly Father, protect us. Help us to know what to say and when, and when to be silent. Work in this situation to free Faith, once and for all, from the mess she's in. Amen."

Faith sighed. "You really think God's going to intervene when this is a mess I made myself?"

"I do." Maybe I wasn't a hundred percent positive, but it was better not to say that aloud. She needed reassurance. And really, I did believe that God was well able to fix the situation. It was more a matter of how much He'd do. Were there consequences Faith was going to have to bear beyond those she already did? Time would tell.

Faith just nodded.

Belatedly, I realized I was still holding her hands and released them, then I pushed open my door and climbed out of the car. She didn't move, so I made my way around to her side and opened the door for her, then squatted down so I was at eye level. "Hey. We're going to be all right."

"I want to believe that. I just don't know if I can."

I reached in and took her hand then stood and gave a little tug.

Faith fumbled to unlatch her seat belt, then swung her legs around and stood.

I squeezed her fingers before closing the car door and reaching into my pocket with my free hand to click the lock button. The car chirped and the lights flashed.

We turned toward the restaurant. Faith didn't pull her hand away, so I kept the contact. It was reassuring to me—I could only imagine that it was bolstering her, too.

It was a short walk from the car to the restaurant door. Manny waited for us in the lobby.

"Good. You're not late." He shot me a seething glare then shifted his gaze back to Faith. "This way."

Faith trembled slightly. I gave her fingers another reassuring squeeze as we followed in Manny's wake through the lightly crowded main dining room into the back area that was usually reserved for parties and was separated from the rest of the space by thick draperies. When we'd passed between them, Manny unhooked the ropes that held the drapes open.

The sound from the main dining room disappeared.

"Welcome, welcome." An older man—probably nearly seventy—stood. "Please. Sit."

I reached for a chair, beating out Manny, and pulled it out for Faith. When she was seated, I took the spot beside her.

"Such a gentleman." The man gave a slight nod. "Manners like that are hard to come by these days. Or so it seems. But my grandchildren tell me I'm out of touch. I am Marcos Ortega."

I couldn't stop the lift of my eyebrows.

He smiled. "You are surprised that I take care of this myself, yes?"

"A little. Yes." I spoke before Faith did.

She glanced at me, worry in her gaze.

Marcos simply nodded again, then he shifted his attention to Faith. "You've caused quite a bit of drama in my organization."

Faith's swallow was audible. "That was never my intention."

"I'm sure." Marcos's eyes shone with humor that was quickly damped. "The question is, what do we do about it?"

Manny grunted.

Marcos glanced briefly over at him and shook his head. "Manny, of course, feels that violence is the best option. Not what I've always found to be the case, but we all have our preferences."

Faith glanced over at me.

Did she expect me to know what to say to that? Because I had no clue. I could probably go off on a long-winded lecture about violence never being the answer, but it didn't seem like the time. Maybe this was time for the lawyerly wait-and-see.

Silence stretched through the room.

Marcos chuckled. "I see you also know the value of silence. Very well. My proposal is this: come work for us."

"But—" Manny snapped his mouth shut at the look Marcos sent.

"If we know where your loyalties lie, we won't feel the need to chase you. You have to know hiding can't last forever." Marcos spread his hands on the table. "We found you here, after all."

"For how long?" I leaned forward slightly.

Marcos tipped his head to the side. "I'm not sure I'm following."

"How long would she have to work for you?"

Under the table, Faith reached over and took my hand. Her

fingers might as well have been made of ice. I gave them a light squeeze.

"Indefinitely." His tone implied the "of course" that he didn't bother to say.

"That's unacceptable. Thank you for your time." I scooted my chair back slightly.

"Interesting." Marcos gestured for me to sit. "I don't think you're unintelligent. You know who I am. What our family represents. But you'd negotiate?"

I eased back into my chair. "For Faith? I would. Yes."

His eyebrows knit together. "You've known her a week. Maybe two? This seems unwise."

My thoughts raced. Maybe Faith and I should have talked about this ahead of time, but it was too late now. If she wanted our marriage kept secret...well, it was too bad. "That's inaccurate."

Marcos scowled at Manny and he rattled off something in gruff Spanish.

Manny replied.

The two of them spoke back and forth for what felt like several minutes, but was probably nowhere near that long. It didn't seem like the right time to check. Finally, Manny made a disgusted sound and stomped out of the private dining area, the curtains swinging behind him.

"My apologies." Marcos tented his fingers on the table. "Explain to me your relationship."

Faith's fingers tightened around mine.

"We've been married for fourteen years." The truth slipped out before I'd decided how much—if any—to hedge.

"But—" He looked at Faith. "You are separated?"

"We were?" Faith's voice went up, indecision obvious on her face. She cleared her throat. "It's complicated."

"The best relationships are. Tell me. From the start." Marcos leaned back in his chair, his gaze steady on Faith.

I would have loved to have stepped in and done the talking, but it was clear—to me at least—that this was something she would have to do. I squeezed her hands, hoping it was encouraging. And then I started to pray.

14

FAITH

"You didn't have to take the day off." I brought my coffee over to the living room and hesitated a moment before joining Tristan on the couch. There was still a cushion between us, but sitting in a chair across from him felt too far away.

He glanced up from his phone and shrugged. "I don't have a lot on the books today. It's easy enough to take the day while we wait for Mr. Ortega to verify our story."

I wrapped both hands around my mug, letting the warmth seep into them. "I don't understand why he feels like he needs to do that. Is he really considering dropping it?"

Tristan shrugged. "It sounded like that was a possibility. But I agree it seems far-fetched. I texted Special Agent Orbison to see if he had any insight."

I nodded and sipped the coffee.

"Would you like to go do something?"

I looked over at Tristan, eyebrows raised. "Like what?"

"I don't know. It's DC. There's all kinds of stuff we could go do downtown. Or there's Mount Vernon, which isn't too far. We could even rent bikes and ride down there if you wanted. It's a nice trail along the river." He shrugged. "Sky's the limit. Literally. I don't think anyone's using the plane. We could fly somewhere."

I blinked. "The...plane?"

Tristan nodded. "The plane. The guys and I own a plane together."

"Wow. That's a big investment to share." He could afford his own, but maybe it made sense that he would share with his friends. And still, I couldn't stop the question: "Why do you still live here?"

"What's wrong with here?" He frowned at me. "I like the view. It's paid for. And it's more space than I need. I'd be fine with a one bedroom, honestly. But my parents like having a place to stay when they're in town."

I couldn't help but smile. That was Tristan in a nutshell. It worked, so he stuck with it. And he made room for his parents.

"So. Would you like to go somewhere? I should make sure we can get a pilot if that's the case."

I laughed. It was so surreal. Imagine being able to call up a pilot and then zip off to wherever simply because the whim struck.

"We could make a weekend of it. If you wanted. And you have a passport." Tristan tipped his head to the side, little sparks of mischief ignited in his eyes. "Did you ever get to Paris?"

I snickered. "Oh, sure. I've jetted off to France all the time. It fits in so well with my stay-under-the-radar lifestyle to date. Nobody just flies to Paris for the weekend. But I do have a passport."

"Sure they do." He grinned as he tapped at his phone. He waited, then tapped again.

I watched as he texted with someone. It was fascinating to see his billionaire side emerge, even briefly. I'd known about the money—sort of—but his lifestyle made it easy to forget.

He looked up from his phone. "You mind if Noah and Jenna

tag along? I guess Jenna's working with a designer in Paris for her wedding dress and while they've been doing most of it virtually, she was going to go for her final fitting soon anyway."

"Um. Sure. I guess. The dress is ready?" I didn't have any idea how fancy Parisian designers worked, but I didn't imagine that someone could simply show up on their doorstep and say they were ready for a fitting.

"Jenna's checking on that now. But she believes so." Tristan shrugged. "You really don't mind? They'll leave us alone if we want."

"I really don't mind. They don't even have to leave us alone. But I want to do touristy stuff." If we were going to live in this surreal world where jetting off to Paris was a thing, then I was going to embrace it.

"Obviously." Tristan stood. "Go pack. I'll take care of the details. We should plan to leave in a couple of hours."

"Sure." I started out of the room, then turned. "This is really weird, you know that, right?"

He chuckled. "I do. Mostly, I pretend the money's not there."

I nodded. That explained a lot. Like why he was still working. Why he lived in this condo, which sure, was nice, but it wasn't exactly billionaire lodging. Then again, I hadn't looked up housing prices in the DC area, so maybe it was. A view of the river probably didn't come cheap.

I went down the hall to the room I was using, and closed the door before stretching out on the bed. I had no idea how to pack for a weekend in Paris with a billionaire.

So maybe I should just pack for a weekend in Paris with Tristan.

I rubbed a hand over my aching heart. We'd talked about going to Paris for a honeymoon. It had been all talk—we'd both known that. He was a student. I was a high school graduate— barely—who desperately needed out of her home situation.

And Tristan had been my best friend. My only friend, really. He'd given me the solution I needed and I'd latched on with two hands. I'd cared for him then. Still did. But back then, I hadn't realized that his feelings ran deeper than he let on.

Maybe it was fair, since he obviously had no idea that my feelings had been changing over the last month.

And I needed to keep it that way.

Regular man Tristan deserved so much better than me. *Billionaire* Tristan? Yeah, talk about out of my league. We weren't even playing the same game anymore.

With a sigh, I sat up. Time to look through my sparse collection of clothes and see what would work for a weekend in Paris.

After an hour, I gave up. I was going to have to go shopping. I had a couple pairs of jeans that would work. Some shirts that were okay for doing things like walking around and visiting the Louvre. But if we were going to eat anywhere other than a sidewalk café—and even then I might be underdressed, depending —I didn't have the right clothes. I had what I'd worn to the FBI, but that was more business than fancy. Dinner in Paris? That needed fancy.

Didn't it?

I closed my suitcase and lifted it down off the bed, then wheeled it behind me as I made my way back to the living room. "Tristan?"

"I'm in here."

I turned.

Tristan leaned on the frame of his bedroom door. "You're ready?"

I winced. "Kind of. I need to go shopping. I really just have jeans."

"Jeans are good."

I scowled. "Where are we staying?"

"That's a surprise." He crossed his arms.

I tried to ignore just how good he looked, leaning casually in the doorway like some kind of *GQ* model. "But it's fancy, right? I bet everything you've arranged is fancy."

It took him a moment, but finally he inclined his head slightly. "Maybe."

"So yeah, jeans aren't going to cut it." I rubbed my head. I had some money—and now that the Ortegas knew where I was, it probably didn't matter if I spent it. "So. Where's the nearest Walmart?"

Tristan laughed. "You're going to find fancy for Paris in Walmart?"

That was a point. My shoulders slumped. "Probably not."

"Why don't we go shopping in Paris?"

"Tristan." I shook my head. "I can't afford that."

"I can."

"But—"

He held up a hand, then pushed off the doorway and closed the distance between us.

My breath caught. I took a deep breath and instantly regretted it as his scent filled me. The air between us seemed charged and warm.

He lowered his head so our eyes were level and his voice was quiet. "Let me do this for you. Let me give you Paris."

I looked away, unable—maybe even unwilling—to process the emotions that had tears welling in my eyes.

"Faith."

I closed my eyes.

Tristan's hands curled gently around my arms. He leaned in and his arms slid around me. He didn't squeeze. In fact, his touch was almost feather-light. And it couldn't have been more potent.

I burrowed my face into his chest and my arms wrapped around his waist without conscious thought. Somewhere in the back of my mind, there was a little click and for the briefest moment, everything made sense.

I sniffled.

"Hey." Tristan eased back and tipped my chin up with one finger. Concern filled his eyes. "Don't cry."

I swiped at the tears. "I can't help it. I don't deserve this. I don't deserve you."

"But I deserve you."

The way he said it, left no room for misinterpretation. He didn't feel I was some kind of penance. He saw me as a prize.

I swallowed the lump in my throat. All of my will to fight disappeared. "Okay."

"Okay?" His eyebrows knit in confusion.

"You can give me Paris." There was more I wanted to say. I wanted to tell him I was sorry. For everything. I should have stayed. Or come back sooner. Or even kept in touch. I regretted it all. But the words were stuck somewhere in my throat and I couldn't shake them loose.

Tristan smiled, holding my gaze, and pressed his lips to my forehead. "Then I will."

Apparently, when Tristan leaned into his whole billionaire thing, the wheels moved seamlessly and fast. Before I knew what was happening, we'd driven to the airport, climbed aboard a slick-looking jet, and were buckled in sipping Coke and munching on chips while we waited for Noah and Jenna to arrive.

"Hey guys, sorry we're late." Noah stepped in from the stairs and handed his suitcase to the pilot.

"It's my fault." Jenna had to duck to get through the hatch. It didn't even look like she could stand completely straight without nearly touching the ceiling. "I couldn't decide how much to bring. Noah had to talk me down."

Noah chuckled. "Mostly I just told her to bring it if she thought she'd want it."

"Which is why my bag is at the bottom of the stairs and we're actually using the cargo hold instead of stowing everything in here like usual." Jenna's cheeks pinked. "I'm not usually like this."

"It's true." Tristan gestured to the seating. "Noah and Jenna, this is Faith. Faith, Noah and Jenna."

"It's nice to meet you." Surprisingly, it was. Tristan had always had good taste in friends. I didn't imagine that had changed.

"Thanks for letting us horn in on your trip." Jenna grinned. "It's my fault. I was nosy when Noah got the text."

"It's not a problem." I settled back into the seat. "I'm still trying to wrap my head around this whole thing."

"Right?" Jenna laughed as she plopped down beside me and nudged my shoulder. "Imagine my surprise when I get back in touch with Noah after moving to the area and find that he's rolling in it. And yet he still needs a backup date."

"Why settle for the rest when I have an in with the best?" Noah winked at Jenna and took a seat beside Tristan. "And hey, turns out I'm not the only one keeping secrets. I think Tristan out-secrets all of us."

Tristan's face flamed red. "No one asked."

"Right. Because it's obvious that we should have asked someone we've known since college if he happens to be married." Noah rolled his eyes. "Duh."

I laughed. "He has a point."

"I guess." Tristan shrugged. "Are we ready?"

Everyone nodded.

Tristan unbuckled his seat belt and stood, making the short trip up to the cockpit area. He poked his head through the divider and I listened to the quiet rumble of voices, not taking in the actual words. He was probably telling them we were ready to go whenever.

He made his way back to his seat. "Just waiting on clearance from the tower. Shouldn't be long."

The reality of the situation crashed over me. "We're really flying to Paris for the weekend?"

Tristan reached over and took my hand. I didn't think about it, just threaded my fingers through his and held on. "We really are."

15

TRISTAN

Even a private jet couldn't make the trip across the ocean fast. The benefits still far outweighed commercial travel though. No one minded if you needed to stand up and pace a little to stretch your legs. The food was better. And ultimately, after watching two movies on the big screen, we played poker together to pass the final hours.

"So is this what your Friday nights with the guys are like?" Jenna studied Noah. "You know the girls could all play poker, too, right?"

"Seeing as how you just cleaned everyone out, yes, I realize that girls can play poker. But now I'm even more sure that I don't want you to join us. With the guys, I have a remote chance of winning occasionally."

I laughed. "A small, remote chance."

Noah flicked his fingers at me. "Whatever. Cody and Wes are the card sharps of the group."

"True. Although I think that term means they cheat, and I don't think I'd go that far." My ears clogged. I worked my jaw to clear them. "Feels like we might be starting our descent."

As I finished the thought, the pilot came on over the speaker and said just that.

"Look at you. Psychic." Jenna chuckled as she reached for her seat belt.

"Just sensitive ears." I shrugged and leaned forward to get a better view out the window. "It's still plenty light. We should be able to see the Eiffel Tower, I would think."

Faith's face brightened and she swiveled to press her nose against the window like a kid at a candy store display.

Jenna looked at me and sent a subtle thumbs-up.

I was glad for her approval, at least. The guys hadn't loved the fact that I was willing to potentially sully my reputation to help Faith get out of her mess. They understood why. They even understood that I didn't want a divorce. Would bringing Faith to Paris help her see that I still loved her? Or would she think I was trying to buy her? Because I definitely didn't want that.

I sighed. Maybe this was all a dumb idea.

Faith glanced away from the window. "Are you okay?"

"Yeah. Tired. I don't know what it is about air travel." It was true. Maybe not the whole truth, but enough of it. For now, at least.

She nodded. "We can go for a walk after we're checked in. That'll help."

"Ooh." Jenna beamed and bounced slightly in her seat. "That's a great idea. Can we come? Maybe we'll find a nice outdoor seating area for dinner."

Noah laughed. "If they say no, you and I can head off in a different direction. It sounds like the perfect way to spend our first evening in Paris."

"I don't mind if you join us." Faith glanced at me. "Do you?"

"Nope."

"Yay!" Jenna clapped her hands. "Even better. Maybe if we're out long enough, we'll see the Tower lit up."

"We can make that happen." Noah reached for Jenna's hand. "It feels like a requirement for any trip to Paris."

I nodded. It did. Also? I couldn't help but be glad that Noah saw the fun of this trip. Of course, before he and Jenna got engaged, they'd taken a quick trip to Chicago for a date, so he wasn't new to the over-the-top gesture. Cody had taken Megan to New York City.

Both of them had asked what the point of all the money was if they couldn't use it now and then for something special. Maybe I hadn't understood as well at the time, but I did now. One look at the unfiltered joy on Faith's face made me want to promise her every weekend in Paris.

The landing was smooth and disembarkation quick and painless. There were benefits to private travel that extended beyond less cramped seating and good food. Noah had arranged for a limo to pick us up. The chauffeur loaded our bags in the trunk, and before long, we were whizzing into the city.

I tried not to look out the window. The man drove well, but he didn't always seem to understand the size of the vehicle—squeezing it into breaks in the traffic that didn't seem possible. Still, we arrived in one piece outside the exclusive boutique hotel just a block away from the Champs-Élysées.

Inside, I took care of checking us in while Jenna and Faith obviously tried not to gape. I couldn't fault them. The lobby oozed opulence. Honestly, it was over the top. I was worried I was going to bump into a table and knock some priceless vase onto the floor. I could probably cover the replacement cost, but how embarrassing was it going to be?

"Your butler will bring your bags to the room. If you need anything at all, he's at your complete disposal." The man behind the counter slid a paper folder across the marble to me. "Enjoy your stay."

"Thank you." I took the folder. I assumed they were keys, but something about the whole setup suggested I didn't want to look right then. Like I'd be exposing my ignorance and lack of class. I headed over to the rest of the gang. "We're on the top floor."

"This is amazing. Where'd you find it?" Noah's voice was low as he fell into step beside me. The girls had made a bee-line for the elevator.

"Google." I shrugged. How else did you find hotels? "I was going for fancy, but this might have exceeded my expectations. We have our own butler. Like just assigned to our suite."

Noah's eyebrows lifted. "Bougie."

"Yeah." I couldn't decide if it was good or not.

Jenna pushed the elevator call button and the doors slid open immediately with a dignified ding.

We all boarded and I swiped a keycard and then pressed the button for the *Grand Palais Suite*. They didn't label the buttons by floor. Each one had a little plaque with the names of suites on the given floors. Ours was all alone beside the button. Ooh la la.

When the doors opened, an older man in a somber black suit greeted us. "Welcome."

"Thank you." I waited for the ladies to exit, then followed behind Noah. I looked around and tried to keep my jaw from dropping.

"Your luggage is just here. I can unpack for you, if you'll inform me of the sleeping arrangements."

"We'll let the ladies choose their room. Noah and I will share the one they don't choose."

"Very good."

Maybe it was because of his refined French accent, but it sounded like he meant the opposite. I couldn't say why. Possibly I was paranoid.

I trailed behind the group as they went into the main living area. There were burgundy velvet tufted sofas and coordinating leather chairs. Tables that looked antique were covered with little dust catchers and stacks of books. The whole thing was like walking into a palace.

"This is gorgeous." Faith ran a hand over the back of a velvet sofa. "Tristan. It's too much."

I shook my head. "Go choose a room."

Faith frowned slightly.

"Come on." Jenna hooked her arm through Faith's and dragged her off.

I tucked my hands in my pockets and turned to Noah. "Is it too much?"

"No. This is fantastic. And honestly, I can't imagine that either room is going to be less than the other." Noah strolled to the large window that ran along one wall of the living area and looked out. "Man, you can see the river."

I came over and looked out. The cars down below zipped and zoomed like every driver had a personal vendetta against the others. Maybe the limo driver hadn't been so bad after all. I looked farther out and caught the glint of light on the water. It wasn't really a river view, but it was still impressive.

Faith's laughter preceded her into the room. "We want the corner room. You can see the Eiffel Tower!"

"I'll take care of the bags. Will you be eating here this evening?" The butler hovered in the doorway.

"We're going to walk and find a place. Maybe you have a recommendation?" Jenna beamed at him. "Something casual?"

He seemed to thaw. Jenna had that effect on people. "Of course. There are many options if you turn right as you leave the front door. I recommend you go the few blocks to Rue Marbeuf then continue toward the river. There are many lovely cafés there."

"That sounds perfect. Thank you." Jenna turned to look at the rest of us. "Everyone ready?"

"I'm set." Faith hooked her purse strap over one shoulder.

Noah nodded.

I gestured toward the doorway that would take us out to the elevator. Faith hung back and waited for me. She took my hand and squeezed it. "This is amazing, Tristan. Thank you."

My heart felt like it might explode. I tugged her close. "Thank you for letting me."

16

FAITH

I stepped out of the bathroom and hesitated. The afternoon and evening in Paris had been beyond my imagining. We'd walked the route the butler had suggested, stopping to admire architecture—apparently that was Jenna's thing—or anything, really, that caught our eye. Closer to the hotel than what he'd indicated, there was a street branching off that had a whole row of different Asian restaurants. We'd almost stopped there, but in the end, the lure of a French café was too much for us to resist.

It seemed necessary, somehow, for a first night in Paris.

And we'd found one with little tables out front behind a wrought iron railing and under a striped awning. The servers wore black with small white aprons. Honestly, it was like something out of a movie. And the food?

Sublime.

After dinner, we'd walked down to the Seine and walked along the bank until the sun had set and the temperature started to drop.

Now, back at the hotel, the reality of sharing a room with

Jenna hit me full force. It would be fine. Except that I wasn't used to sharing a room with anyone, let alone a bed. I hadn't since the few months when Tristan and I lived together after we eloped.

"Hey. Cute jammies." Jenna grinned from where she sat on the little two-person sofa between the windows of our room.

I glanced down at the cartoon alien and Hawaiian girl doing the hula. "Thanks."

"We're a lot like that, you know?"

My eyebrows lifted. "You're aliens?"

Jenna laughed. "No. We're family. We don't let anyone get left behind. Or forgotten."

I sighed.

"You don't believe me." Jenna pointed a finger at me.

"I do. I'm just not sure it applies across the board to everyone you run into." I crossed my arms, suddenly chilly.

"Hmm." Jenna patted the seat next to her. "You're not exactly a stray from off the street. You're Tristan's *wife*."

I winced and dragged myself across the room. I would have loved to find an excuse—any excuse—not to. I perched on the sofa as far from her as I could get.

"I don't bite." Jenna laughed. "But I also get being over-whelmed by this group. And you haven't really even met all of us yet."

I nodded. Tristan had mentioned church and getting together with everyone. I'd found an excuse to get out of going every time he did. "Don't blame Tristan for that."

"Oh, I don't. I know he's persistent. Noah said—and I guess you have to figure that all the guys talk to their ladies, so we pretty much know it all—"

Jenna paused. I nodded.

She smiled and continued. "So I heard about the divorce papers."

I winced and looked away.

"You know he doesn't actually want a divorce, right?"

I closed my eyes. "I don't know that, no. He has the papers. He's obviously thought about it. And honestly? It's probably better for him."

"You didn't sign them."

I wanted to groan, but held it in. "No. Maybe I should have."

Jenna shook her head. "You know better than that."

"I know what he said, but—"

"Is there a reason you can't accept what he said at face value?"

I blinked. "You're blunt."

"Guilty." She smiled, not looking guilty in the slightest.

I chuckled in spite of myself, then sighed. "I don't think I'm good for him."

"I do."

"You barely know me." I frowned. Jenna had no idea if I was good for Tristan. For all Jenna knew, I was a serial killer hiding out from the feds.

"I know Tristan, though. He's happier now that you're here. He's...softer somehow." Jenna lifted a shoulder. "Watching him tonight? He's in love with you."

I swallowed. It was one hundred percent what I wanted to hear, but how did I trust it? "He just wants to save me."

"Wow. You're a tough nut." Jenna drummed her fingers on her knee. "I'm not going to push, even though I'm pretty positive you're wrong. You don't know me super well, so I'm going to point out that this is a big concession for me. But we have to share a bed and I don't want you to smother me in my sleep."

I laughed. "In the interest of brutal honesty, I want it to be true. I just...have a hard time believing it."

Jenna studied me for a moment.

I wanted to squirm.

Finally, she reached over and rubbed my leg. "Maybe work on that. I'll be praying for you."

"Can I ask you a question?" The words blurted out before I thought about them.

"Sure." Jenna settled back.

"The praying thing. If, hypothetically speaking, someone used to be pretty good about praying and reading the Bible and then stopped. Is God really okay with them coming back? No matter what?"

"Absolutely."

"You say that fast." I bit my lip.

"Because it's an easy answer." Jenna leaned forward. "God wants everyone to come to Him. Read Luke fifteen."

That sounded familiar. "Is that the Prodigal Son?"

Jenna grinned. "Got it in one."

I just nodded. I'd read it. Mostly I felt sorry for the older son. How was it fair for the ones who'd been faithful for God to welcome back the ones like me who fell away and then wanted to come back? Why would He want me back?

Jenna stood. "You should read it again, anyway. It's a good one. I'm going to get ready for bed. Choose whichever side you want."

She was halfway to the bathroom when she turned back. "Do you want to come to my dress appointment tomorrow?"

"Oh. I think Tristan and I are going to play tourist." That was the plan, wasn't it?

"Right. Much more fun." Jenna turned and headed into the bathroom, then closed the door firmly behind her.

I eyed the bed and, after a moment of thought, crawled in on the side farthest from the bathroom. I plugged in my phone, then before I could talk myself out of it, opened a web browser and put in Luke fifteen. It didn't start out with the family story. First there was a lost sheep. Then lost coins. Finally, the lost son.

Lost.

The word implied that the thing in question was wanted. No one said they lost something unless they were sad about it and wanted it back. That was definitely the theme in the chapter, too. We were lost and God wanted us back. Because He loved us? Me?

I couldn't really see in the overall scheme of things why I'd matter to Him.

I'd come from a home that defined broken. Tristan and his family had rescued me from that. They'd dragged me to church any time the doors were open. At first, I'd gone along because it was better than being at home. Then I'd kept going because something had called to me. When I'd finally broken down and given my heart to Jesus, I'd been counting on everything getting better.

But it hadn't.

Not really, at least.

I changed, a little, but my home life was still a disaster. Maybe it even got worse, because Dad was definitely not a fan of me being gung-ho about Jesus. And that was when Tristan had thrown out another lifeline. I'd grabbed it with both hands, believing maybe it was God finally fixing everything for me.

For a while it was. And then it wasn't.

So I'd run.

And I could look back and see just how well that had gone for me. I sighed and turned off my phone before setting it on the nightstand. I clicked off the lamp on my side of the bed and snuggled down under the covers, scooching as close to the edge of the bed as possible without falling off.

I didn't know if Jenna was taking her time in the bathroom for me, or if she really had a long evening ritual, but I was ready to sleep. Even on a private jet, flying across the Atlantic wasn't something I was used to doing.

I was drifting in that not-quite-asleep-but-also-not-awake state when I sensed the room darken fully and heard the rustling of sheets. The mattress dipped slightly.

"Good night." Jenna's voice was a whisper.

It would have taken too much effort to respond, so I just let myself sink further into sleep.

"Wake up, sleepyhead."

I cracked open one eye and scowled.

Jenna laughed. "Get up! You're in *Paris*. You don't want to sleep the day away, do you?"

Paris? I blinked and rubbed my eyes. My brain kicked in and I pushed to a sitting position. Paris. With Tristan. And Jenna and Noah, but that was beside the point.

"There you are." Jenna grinned. "There's coffee and pastries in the main room for breakfast. The guys are getting ready."

I studied her for a moment. Since she was still wearing her pajamas—at least, that was what I assumed they were, since I couldn't quite picture her heading to a couture bridal appointment in cotton pants covered with frogs—I figured I probably wasn't too far behind everyone else.

"I'll throw on some clothes and then go eat. What time do you have to be wherever you're headed?" I slid my legs out from under the covers and stood, then took a moment to stretch my arms over my head, trying to will alertness into my muscles.

"Couple of hours. I might try to get Noah to stop by the Eiffel Tower first. Or something. We're in Paris!" Jenna bounced a little with her last words.

I chuckled. "So you said."

"Oh, come on. You have to be a little excited."

I shrugged. "I am. More than a little. But also I need coffee."

I opened one of the dresser drawers and grabbed clothes, then hurried into the bathroom to dress. Maybe I ought to be fine changing in front of other women, but it had never been in my comfort zone. Even in high school, I'd been the weirdo taking her gym clothes into a toilet stall to change. None of the mockery from the other girls had mattered. Of course, there'd been better reasons, then, to make sure no one saw me without a shirt. Dad didn't care about cuts or bruises when they'd be covered with clothes.

I pushed those thoughts away and finished getting ready.

The bedroom was empty when I emerged and I heard laughter from the main room. I took a deep breath, and headed out.

"Good morning." Tristan's gaze snapped to me, and everything in me felt steadier. "Let me pour you some coffee."

"Thanks." I crossed the room, consciously keeping from crossing my arms against the sudden awkwardness.

Jenna tipped her head to the side and pointed to a chair. "Sit. You have to have one of these croissants. I'm sure it's a cliché, but they taste nothing like what we get at home."

I eyed the tray of golden baked goods and decided on a more rectangular looking one than the typical croissant shape. The first bite confirmed my deepest hope: it was filled with chocolate.

I closed my eyes and savored the sweet and crispy treat.

"Your coffee, madame."

The scent of the drink had my eyes popping back open. Noah was directly in front of me, the mug held tantalizingly close.

I wrapped my hands around it. "Mm. Thanks." I took a sip and felt my eyebrows lift. "This is good coffee."

"Bougie French coffee." Jenna's eyebrows waggled.

I chuckled and took another sip. "This may ruin me for breakfast for the rest of my life."

"You're easy to please." Noah slid his arm around Jenna's shoulders. "A croissant and good coffee and you're set? I thought Jenna was low maintenance. Apparently not."

"Hey." Jenna jabbed her elbow into Noah's side. "I'll have you know I am incredibly low maintenance."

"Mmhmm. That's why we're in Paris for a wedding dress fitting."

"Oh shush." Jenna's cheeks flared red. "I get one shot at a wedding. A wedding with a billionaire groom, by the way. I feel like I can go a little out with it."

Noah leaned over and kissed Jenna's cheek. "You absolutely can. You know I'm teasing."

"I do."

Jenna beamed. "I like how that sounds."

Tristan met my gaze and rolled his eyes. "Lovebirds, am I right?"

I laughed. "It's cute."

"Hmpf."

I shook my head. I didn't buy Tristan's grumpiness at all. I could see he was happy for his friends. And honestly, I was, too.

I made quick work of my breakfast, though it felt like sacrilege to rush that amazing food. On the other hand? I was in Paris. There was probably another bakery where I could indulge in yet another kind of treat that would be equally amazing. If there were bad pastries in France, I didn't want to know it.

"Ready to roll?" Tristan stood and collected the dishes before loading them back on the room service cart.

"Yeah. Eiffel Tower first?" I couldn't wait to go up to the top and take in Paris from the sky.

"Sounds good." Tristan looked at Noah. "You two want to join in for this? Is there time before your appointment?"

"Should be." Noah checked the time then glanced at Jenna. "Does that work?"

"Absolutely." Jenna stood and brushed crumbs off her shirt.

"Let me text the driver." Tristan paused and tapped at his phone. He waited a moment, then nodded. "He's on the way and will be here soon. Let's go wait in the lobby."

It took us a couple of minutes to do the last-minute check for all the things we wanted to take along. Then we took the elevator down to the lobby and I had to keep my jaw from dropping again at the opulence. Yet again, I was faced with the reality that Tristan—my neighbor and friend from when I was a kid, the man who had saved me from a horrible home—was loaded.

A limo pulled up in front of the hotel and a uniformed driver stepped out from behind the wheel, then headed into the hotel lobby. "Lee party?"

Tristan lifted his fingers.

The driver nodded and gestured for us to follow. He opened the back door as we approached the car. I laughed to myself as I climbed in.

"Share the joke?" Tristan scooted next to me.

"Just this." I waved my hands at the car and then the hotel. "It's surreal. And a big step up from ramen and mac and cheese."

"I still like both of those things, though." Tristan took my hand and squeezed. "It's not like this all the time."

"I know. But it could be." I shrugged. "I wouldn't want that, mind you."

He squeezed my hand again.

Noah and Jenna finished settling in their seats, and the driver shut the door.

"Does he know where we're going?" Jenna twisted in her seat to look into the driver's side.

"I told him when I texted." Tristan settled back against the seat. He didn't let go of my hand.

I took a deep breath and just let all the sensations flow through me. I couldn't describe how his touch could set every nerve ending on fire while, at the same time, be exactly like coming home after a long time gone.

17

TRISTAN

The ringing phone jolted me out of my drifting thoughts. "Tristan Lee."

"Mr. Lee. This is Marcos Ortega. How was Paris?"

"Wonderful." I probably shouldn't be surprised that he knew where we'd gone. For all I knew, he'd had someone flown over to keep an eye on us, on the off chance we decided to run. The idea might have crossed my mind once or twice, but it wasn't realistic. He had to know that, too. Did that also mean he knew about the FBI? If so, he hadn't said anything. "How was your weekend?"

He chuckled. "You're very cool."

I didn't quite know how to respond to that. I glanced at the time. It was almost the end of the day. Arlene would be packing up and heading out any minute. I wouldn't be far behind her.

"Well. I spent the weekend profitably. You're not a hard man to discover. Is that on purpose?"

My eyebrows lifted. "I don't try to hide who I am, if that's what you're asking. But I also don't tend to put it out on the front page of the paper. At the base of it all, I'm an ordinary man."

"No. Ordinary is not the word that describes you." Mr. Ortega sighed. "And it makes my problem slightly more challenging. If my people had investigated your wife more thoroughly in the beginning, I would never have allowed them to do business with her. The reality is, a billionaire—even one who lives his life mostly under the radar—has entirely too much governmental oversight in his life to be associated with my organization."

"That makes sense." Why wasn't it something that had occurred to me when I was thinking of solutions in the first place? Actually, that was easy to answer—I didn't tend to focus on my money. It was just there, doing its thing.

"We won't bother you, or your wife, further. We do ask that you and your wife agree to keep what you know of our organization to yourselves. In fact, I've sent you a contract, via messenger, along with a small retainer. That should cover you in terms of privilege, which in turn covers us."

The man was cunning. I didn't love the idea of having the Ortegas as a client—even just on paper as this would surely be —but it was better than any of the other alternatives. "I'll wait for it to arrive before heading home this evening. That way, I can look it over and get back to you tomorrow. You know I can't— won't—actually represent you, right?"

Mr. Ortega made a sound that might have been a laugh. "Of course. This is purely a paper agreement. Think of it more like an NDA. You can reach me at the number on the contract. Give my regards to your wife."

The phone went dead before I could respond. I shook my head and set the phone down on my desk, then stood. I crossed to my door, opened it, and moved to the main room.

"You're not leaving, Mr. Lee?" Arlene was already shutting down for the night.

"I just had a client call saying they'd messengered something over. I'll wait for it so you can head out." I tucked my hands in my pockets. "Hopefully it won't be long."

"You're sure? I don't mind staying if I can be helpful."

I waved that off. "Go ahead. I'm going to grab it and take it home with me to look over. I'll probably wrap everything in my office up and just wait out here."

"All right. I'll see you tomorrow?"

I nodded. "That's the plan. I should be in around nine. Maybe nine thirty. I don't have anything on my calendar."

"No. But you have court next week, so you'll want to be sure you're ready. I have a checklist set up for that on the shared drive."

"You're a lifesaver." I grinned at her. "Go home. Have a nice night."

"Thanks. You too." She scooted out from behind her desk and strode quickly out of the office.

I turned back down the hall and went into my own office so I could do as I'd said I was going to and shut down. I'd been so preoccupied with Faith and this situation with the Ortega cartel that I'd forgotten about court next week. The case itself didn't worry me. It was pretty straightforward, particularly since my client just wanted to formalize the verbal agreement they'd been operating under.

But sometimes people got sticky when there was a change from informal to formal. So the checklist was a necessity to make sure I had all my ducks in a row.

My usual habit would be to take work home and spend the evening reviewing it unless the guys talked me into plans. With Faith here, that didn't appeal nearly as much as it used to. Especially after a weekend together in Paris.

We'd spent all of Saturday playing tourist, ending it all with dinner in the Michelin starred restaurant in the Eiffel Tower. Sunday, we'd strolled along the Seine with Noah and Jenna before heading back to the airport for the flight home.

She'd let me hold her hand.

There had been moments—several of them—when I'd considered kissing her. I wanted to more than I could put into words, and Paris seemed the perfect place.

So why hadn't I?

I blew out a breath.

I didn't have a concrete answer that went beyond it not feeling...right.

I turned off the lights and pulled my office door shut behind me, pausing to check that it had locked, before heading back out to reception. I took a seat in one of the guest chairs and pulled out my phone, then tapped to open the word game I enjoyed when I had a minute of downtime.

I'd made it through three levels when the door opened and a burly guy in a messenger service uniform lumbered in.

I stood, tucking my phone in my pocket as I rose. "Can I help you?"

"Delivery for Tristan Lee."

I held out my hand. "I'll take it."

"You're Mr. Lee?"

There was no reason for my hesitancy to admit it. But it was there, nonetheless. "I'll see that he gets it."

The messenger scowled and looked like he wanted to object.

"Or you can come back tomorrow. But the receptionist will probably tell you the same thing. I'm only still here because Mr. Lee was expecting the delivery." What was I doing? I opened my mouth with the intention of clearing it all up but was cut off.

"Fine." The guy grunted and thrust a cardboard envelope at me, then a clipboard. "Sign here."

"Been a while since I've seen a clipboard. I figured everyone was electronic these days."

The guy shrugged.

I scrawled an unreadable signature on the receipt line,

barely finishing before he yanked the clipboard away and squinted at the squiggle.

With a grunt, he turned and stomped out of the office.

I waited another couple of minutes before locking up and exiting myself. I really didn't want to run into the guy in the parking lot. Or ever again. Did the Ortegas have their own goon delivery service? Apparently. All brawn, no brain, but the envelope had reached its destination, so maybe that was all that mattered.

I kept alert as I made my way to the car, but I didn't see a messenger service truck or the guy anywhere. That should have put me more at ease than it did.

The drive home was typical, but I was wired by the time I reached my parking space in the condo's garage. Even as I hurried to the elevators, I imagined footsteps that echoed mine just slightly off rhythm. But there was no reason for anyone to follow me.

Mr. Ortega knew where I lived. He knew where I worked. And he'd released us from any threat of retribution.

Basically.

I guessed I wouldn't know for sure until I read through whatever document was in the envelope I carried. And his retainer. Ugh. Should I return that? I didn't want his money. There was no situation where money from the Ortegas was legit.

On the other hand, returning the money might be seen as rejecting his deal. And that wasn't what I was going for either.

I offered a tight smile to the small family that climbed into the elevator at the lobby. Their daughter jumped from one foot to the other as she waited for permission to push the button for their floor. Then she pushed the already lit button for my floor for good measure.

I leaned against the back wall as the car ascended. It paused on the family's floor and they got off, the little girl dancing and hopping as her parents laughed. It stirred a sense of longing in my chest that I didn't know what to do with.

Finally, I reached the top floor and made my way down the hall to my place. I unlocked the door—it was good Faith had been keeping it locked while she was home—closed it behind myself, and locked it again, then took off my shoes.

"Tristan?" Faith's voice called out and after a moment, her face appeared poking around the corner from the kitchen. She smiled. "I was starting to worry."

"Sorry." I held up the envelope. "I had to wait for a messenger delivery from the Ortegas."

Faith stepped fully into the hall. She wrapped her arms around her waist and I could almost feel the nerves pumping off of her. "Oh?"

After a moment's hesitation, I moved to her and pulled her into my arms. She was stiff and unyielding. "It's a good thing. I think. I guess I should read it before I make any guarantees."

Faith laughed. It was a short, shrill sound that belied any sense of humor.

"Hey." I eased back. "It's going to be okay. No matter what. Ortega called and the gist that he said is that I'm too high profile."

Faith frowned. "You're hardly high profile."

I shrugged. "Not according to the IRS."

"Oh." Faith's eyes brightened. "I guess they do like to keep track of the guys with all the cash, don't they?"

"They do. Which means that I get a little too much governmental oversight—those might be his exact words—than he's comfortable with. And you're married to me, which means you're in the same boat."

"But..."

I waited for her to speak. When she didn't, I prompted her, "But?"

Faith cleared her throat. "The papers. You wanted a divorce. I...I owe you that much."

My heart sank into my stomach and my mind started to race. I was thankful, yet again, that the guys liked to play poker because my reaction didn't immediately show on my face. After our weekend in Paris, I'd been hoping the topic of the papers never came up again. Not the most mature response, sure, but it felt like sometimes acting like things hadn't happened was okay.

Apparently, she didn't feel the same.

I hedged. "Let's go sit down and read what it says."

I didn't wait for her to agree—or disagree—I just stepped past her and went into the living room. I plopped onto the couch and ripped open the top flap of the mailer, then drew out the packet of documents inside.

I glanced at the money order paperclipped to the front page and my eyes widened. That was not a small retainer.

"Is that money?" Faith perched on the edge of the couch beside me.

I nodded and unclipped the paper then handed it to her.

"This is a quarter of a million dollars!" Faith dropped the paper on the coffee table as if it burned her. "You can't accept that. They're just getting you even more under their thumb."

Since I'd had a similar initial response, I didn't refute her statement. Instead, I held up a finger and continued reading the first page of the document.

Honestly, Mr. Ortega had a pretty decent attorney on staff. Maybe I shouldn't be surprised, but I was. This went beyond a standard nondisclosure agreement. And it was probably even enforceable—if only because the specific crimes Faith had been part of were outlined in detail in the pages. Neither she nor I would want this document being read in court.

He was banking on that.

It was going to pay off.

Thankfully, the terms were basically what he'd outlined in our phone call. The retainer provided attorney client privilege between me and the Ortegas. But it clearly spelled out the terms of Faith's freedom.

"Well?" Faith stood and paced to the window then back. "Can you read aloud or something?"

I snorted. "You don't want to hear a whole bunch of legalese, do you?"

"Not really. But also yes, if it means you're going to talk to me."

"Sorry." I cleared my throat. "It's a decent document. It protects them, obviously, but you, also. As long as we're married and neither of us talks about your prior work for them, they are considering your service to the Ortega family complete and relinquish all claims to your time or resources. We both need to sign and date the last page. When the money is deposited—I have to send them a screenshot verifying the deposit—and they've received the signed document, they'll be out of your life."

"I can't sign that." Faith shook her head. "It's a nice idea, but I'm not going to do that to you."

"Faith."

"No." She held up her hands. "I took advantage of your generosity when you were in college. I didn't understand what you were giving up—I only thought of how it would help me. I can't—I won't—do that to you again."

I scowled. It took everything I had not to tell her to stop being stupid. That probably wasn't the way to go here. Nor was grabbing her by the shoulders and giving her a good shake. "I don't understand. This is everything you want. Without the uncertainty of the FBI's plan, I might add."

"You deserve to be free. To marry someone you love and have a family." She turned and walked to the picture window and stood with her back to me.

I bit my lip and tossed a mostly inarticulate prayer heaven-ward. While I didn't get a clear message of the exact words to use to get her to see reason, I did feel peace creeping through me. I'd take it. "Why don't we spend the evening praying about it? We can talk about it again in the morning."

"What's there to think about? I should just go."

"No." I stood and crossed to stand beside her. I wanted to reach out and take her hand, but unlike during our time in Paris, I didn't get the feeling she'd welcome it now. She didn't turn to face me, so I stood beside her looking out at the river. "You should stay."

"Tristan." My name was a frustrated sigh.

My lips twitched up and I tried to mimic her tone. "Faith."

"You're not being realistic. Did you even absorb what Ortega said? You really want to be married to me forever? Just so, what, you can be some kind of martyr? Don't you want a real wife? A family?"

"I don't actually think being married to you forever and having a real wife and family are mutually exclusive." I swal-lowed and tried to ignore the throbbing in my chest her words had caused. Did she really not see that we could have it all? Together? "I guess I thought, after this weekend, you were begin-ning to believe it, too."

I looked over and saw her close her eyes. Her face scrunched up like she was in pain. But I had no idea how to interpret her expression, and given my apparent inability to understand her at all, I wasn't going to try.

I cleared my throat. "I'm going to sign the papers from Mr. Ortega. Let me know what you decide."

"Don't you want dinner?" She still didn't turn.

"I think I'm going to go for a walk. I'll probably stop and get something at some point. If you want me to bring you some-thing, I can, but I don't know when I'll be back."

"You don't have to leave. I can go."

"No." I shook my head even though she still wouldn't turn away from the window. "I'd like the walk. Help yourself to anything in the fridge. Or order something in. Or text me, I guess, if you change your mind about me bringing something by."

I sat on the couch and flipped to the back of the document then signed and dated on the lines indicated for me. I dropped the pen on the papers and stood. I opened my mouth to say something about how it was all right here for her, but stopped. She wasn't a child. I sighed. "Think about it, okay? I'll be back in a bit. I have my phone."

18

FAITH

I listened as Tristan's steps carried him down the hall to the door. It took everything I had not to turn and ask him to stay. But he needed to really think about this. Was he honestly okay with the idea of me as his wife? Forever?

It was one thing when we were kids and he was getting me out of a terrible situation. But now? He had so much to offer and I was just...me. If I was honest, I brought a lot of negatives to the table. Always had.

Look at how this whole mess had started in the first place. His parents—Mrs. Lee in particular—had taken pity on me and dragged me to church with them. I was reasonably positive she'd been responsible for Tristan giving me the time of day. I could imagine her patient voice in my head, lightly scolding him to make me feel welcome.

The door opened, closed, and the locks clicked with a distinctive *snick*.

I blew out a breath and let my gaze drift to the door. Should I have stopped him from leaving? Did I have any right to ask him to do this? To want him to?

I crossed the room and picked up the papers off the coffee

table, then settled on the couch. I hadn't read them in depth yet. Maybe I wasn't a lawyer, but I was reasonably certain I could see past the "whereas" and "thereuntos" to see what the Ortegas were getting at. And maybe, just maybe, since I'd spent so much time on the other side of the line between black and white, I might see something in here that went beyond a straightforward release.

Halfway through the first page, I started to get a dull throb behind my eyes. The thing read like the lawyer got paid by the word. Twenty minutes later, I set the papers back on the coffee table, leaned my head against the back of the couch, and closed my eyes.

I didn't see anything off in there. After wading through all the language, I wasn't sure I would have even if it was obvious. So much for that idea.

Tristan...would have seen it. And he hadn't. Or maybe he had, and he just didn't care. Either way, he'd signed it, and the space beside his name for my signature mocked me.

In my pocket, my phone vibrated with an incoming call. I dug it out as hope speared through me. The only one who could possibly be calling was Tristan.

Or a number I didn't recognize.

I frowned and tapped the "screen call" button. It was one of the reasons I'd gone with this model phone and it saved me from all kinds of telemarketers. And clients I didn't want to deal with right then.

My eyebrows lifted as the transcript began to scroll across the screen and I hurried to accept the call. "Hello?"

"Oh, Faith, honey, this is the right number. I was so worried I'd written it down wrong and was going to have to tell Tristan he was right and have him text it to me after all." Mrs. Lee's voice was exactly as I remembered it.

"Hi, Mrs. Lee."

"I would think, at this point in our lives, you could call me Angie. Especially since Tristan just let his dad and me in on a rather large secret he's been keeping. The turkey."

I winced. "I hope you're not too angry—"

"Shush. Tristan's been in love with you since about six months after we started taking you to church with us. Honestly, I've been frustrated these last ten years or so that he let you disappear. Of course, I didn't realize exactly how that had happened. He just said college had you drifting apart."

It was sort of true. But it was also the kindest possible spin he could have put on it. Which was just like him. "I thought you were overseas."

"We're on our way home. If we can finagle the flights, we should be in the DC area on Wednesday. I can't wait to see you."

"You're coming here?" My chest tightened. Sure, she didn't sound angry on the phone, but how could I possibly show my face after all of this?

"Of course we are! As soon as Tristan explained that you were in town and that you were married, well, we have to come. It's no big deal to change our plans and come early. Steve is busy on his phone with the airlines, or he'd be backing me up."

"Where will you stay?" I blurted out the words before I could think better of it.

"With you two, of course. Tristan has that lovely spare bedroom, and we promise not to stay too long and cramp your style. I realize you're still basically newlyweds with all the time you spent apart."

I opened my mouth to explain that I was staying in the spare room, then stopped. Tristan hadn't mentioned it to them. Obviously. But why wouldn't he have? I swallowed and prayed my voice didn't sound as tight as it felt. "Wonderful."

"Isn't it? Now, fair warning. I plan to talk you into a real wedding. Or at least a nice reception. But it'd be so great for you and Tristan to renew your vows with a minister. There's nothing wrong with eloping. I'd never say that. But I do love the idea of making those promises in a church. What do you think?"

"Um." I blinked. I couldn't think. I was still stuck on the idea that, unless Tristan wanted to spill all the details of the whole sordid story to his parents, I wasn't going to have my own room while they were in town.

Angie laughed. "I took you by surprise. Well, think on it, and we'll chat when we're there. I just can't wait to hear all about—" Her husband's voice rumbled in the background "—what, honey? Oh, okay. Sorry. Steve says to hang up so we can get a move on. That man. See you soon! Love you, bye!"

The call ended and I sat staring at my phone. What had just happened?

I was so out of it, I didn't process the sound of the key in the lock until the front door closed.

After another moment, Tristan came down the hallway in his socks holding a paper bag. "I went ahead and got you a burger and fries even though you didn't text. If you don't want it, I can stick it in the fridge."

"A burger sounds good." I stood robotically and moved to the kitchen island. "How was your walk?"

"Good." Tristan followed me. He set the bag on the island and went over to the fridge. "Soda?"

"Ginger ale?" I couldn't remember if he had any, but I could use something to settle my stomach.

With a nod, he pulled open the fridge and got out two cans. He put one in front of me, then pulled out his stool and sat. He opened the bag and lifted out two foam to-go boxes and slid one over before popping open the top on the other. "They're the same. No tomatoes, right?"

I nodded, my heart melting. How could he remember all those little things about me? The answer was, I guess, easy. He paid attention. He always had. And apparently, I mattered to him.

I opened my takeout box and breathed in the savory aroma. I took a fry and bit in. It was crispier than I expected, given the to-go situation. "Sweet potatoes?"

"Yeah. That way you can pretend you had a vegetable."

I chuckled. "Your mom called."

Tristan's hands stilled. "Oh?"

"Don't act all innocent."

He shrugged. "She called while I was walking. They're heading back to the States."

"So she said. To Virginia, in fact." I turned and watched him closely. His expression didn't betray anything. "To your guest room, actually."

He nodded and picked up his burger. "That's where they usually stay."

"You're good with that?"

Tristan turned to look at me. "Why wouldn't I be?"

I broke eye contact and looked down at my food. Did he really not understand the problem or was he playing at something? "You told them we were married."

"I did. I should have a long time ago. Believe me, I got an earful about that."

I frowned. His mom—Angie—had been so kind and excited. "Sorry."

"It's not your fault."

"It really is." I picked up my burger, but my appetite had gone. I set it back down and turned in my chair to face him. "You wouldn't have married me if I hadn't been such a mess. You wouldn't have hidden it if I wasn't such a mess. And you wouldn't have had to deal with fourteen years of secrets if I—"

"Stop. You're wrong all across the board. And I don't understand why you won't hear me. I married you because I was in love with you. Yes, you needed out of a bad situation, but I probably could have come up with other ways to help you. Like telling my folks. You know they would have let you come live with them."

"I..." I tipped my head to the side. "You're right. Why didn't you?"

He just lifted his eyebrows and stared at me.

I swallowed. It was starting to sink in. For real. "Why didn't you say anything?"

"I thought I had time."

I winced.

"That wasn't a dig." He reached out, hesitated for a moment, then took my hands. "I should never have let you go. I have so many regrets, but marrying you isn't one of them."

I blinked as my eyes filled, and looked away. "I don't understand you."

He laughed and squeezed my hands. "I could say the same thing. Faith."

He paused so long I turned back to face him.

He caught and held my gaze. "I love you. That was true fourteen years ago. It's true today. I realize I haven't always done a great job telling you that, but I hoped you'd see it in my actions."

"I did. I do." I pressed my lips together. "You really want to do this?"

"I do."

I couldn't stop the flash of memory of the two of us in jeans and T-shirts, ridiculously young, facing a judge in a small room at the courthouse. Tristan had said those words with the same fervor then as he did now.

"Okay."

"Yeah?" His face split into a grin and he stood and tugged me to my feet. He pulled me into his arms and held me close in his strong, safe grip.

I relaxed into his embrace and nestled my head into the hollow of his shoulder. "Your mom wants us to get married again so she can watch."

"No."

I tipped my head up so I could see his face. He was watching me, his expression serious. "Really? It seems like a simple enough thing to do for her."

He shook his head. "Not happening. I have no interest in the circus that my mother would plan for something like that."

"She said simple."

"Oh, please. Do you remember my mom at all?" Tristan kissed my forehead and released me.

I shouldn't have missed the warmth of his embrace as badly as I did, nor should I be disappointed that his lips had barely brushed against my head rather than seeking my own. If we were doing this married thing, wasn't kissing going to be part of it?

I cleared my throat. "I guess I should sign that document."

"Eat first. I'll send it back tomorrow. You start up at the bookstore in the morning, right?"

I shot a glance at the papers on the coffee table then resumed my seat at the kitchen island. "Yeah. Or, at least I think so. Megan was going to text me, and I haven't seen anything yet."

"Hm. That's unlike her. Why don't you reach out after dinner? I know she appreciates having employees who take initiative."

Who didn't? "Is it going to be weird that I'm working for one of your friends?"

"Why would it be?" Tristan took a huge bite of burger.

I still couldn't quite bring myself to eat. My stomach had stopped churning, but there'd been enough up-and-down drama this evening that I was unlikely to want food until tomorrow. I shrugged. "I don't know. I'm not on equal footing with anyone. You're all billionaires and I'm just me."

"The girls aren't billionaires except by association. You're my wife. You're on exactly equal footing. If you don't want to work for Megan, don't. You can stay home. You can find another job. You could start your own company. What do you want to do?" Tristan reached into the bag and pulled out a napkin, then wiped his fingers and mouth, balled the napkin up, and dropped it in his empty container.

"I don't know. The bookstore honestly sounds like fun."

"Then do that. As long as you're enjoying it. If it changes, do something else."

I scoffed. He made it sound so easy. Just do something else. It wasn't as though I had a résumé that would set the work world on fire. I had a high school diploma and years of not-quite-legal work that I was never going to talk about. The only jobs I could put on any sort of paper were the fast food and delivery jobs I'd had as a teenager.

That wasn't a ringing endorsement in my thirties.

"You could go back to school, if you wanted." Tristan studied me. "You used to want to do marketing. There's still time."

Marketing. A big PR firm. How long had it been since I'd given any thought to that as a career? If I could have jumped into it without education, I probably would have given it a try instead of falling back into the shadows where I'd grown up.

"I'll think about it."

"Pray about it." Tristan took my hand and brought it to his lips. "I'll pray, too. We can pray together."

I nodded and looked away.

"What's wrong?"

I took a minute to gather my thoughts. "In Paris, Jenna said something about how God always welcomes us back. I want to believe her. I read the stuff in Luke. But what about Paul getting mad at people for sinning so they can get grace? Or I found another article about something in Hebrews about there not being any more sacrifice for sins. That one didn't make a lot of sense, but it sure wasn't the father of a prodigal dancing for joy."

"You've been digging." He smiled. "That's good. I don't necessarily have all the answers, but I do know 1 John 1:9 says if we confess our sins, God is faithful to forgive us and cleanse us of unrighteousness. There's no limit given on that. Nowhere says it's a one-time thing. You were serious when you accepted Christ in high school, right?"

I nodded. I could remember the joy of that moment and the days following. The sense of wonder and awe that had faded gradually as the world around me stayed the same. In my mind, I'd painted a picture of everything improving somehow because I had Jesus. I'd talked to the pastor then, and he'd explained that we were what God changed, not always our circumstances. It had made sense.

But it was also disappointing.

"And now you're coming back."

I nodded again, even though he hadn't asked it as a question. "I just...worry, I guess."

"Then we'll pray about that together, too."

19

TRISTAN

"Thanks for meeting me here." I offered my hand to Special Agent Orbison as he pulled out a chair across from me at the small coffee shop in Fairfax.

"It's always good to get out of the office." He glanced around. "This isn't exactly private."

"No. But I thought that might make it seem less like I was trying to hide something."

"Are you?" His eyebrows lifted.

I laughed and reached for the latte with fancy foam art on top. "No. But I didn't want it to look like I was, either."

He sat and lifted his to-go cup to take a drink.

I cleared my throat. "Anyway, I wanted to show you this. It seems like neither Faith nor I are going to end up being any use to you after all."

I slid the manila envelope containing the Ortegas' document across the table, then picked up my coffee and drank. I hadn't actually wanted a beverage. I just needed something to do with my hands to keep the nerves from showing. I probably shouldn't be nervous, but it wasn't as if I spent a ton of time dealing with the FBI.

Special Agent Orbison undid the clasp on the envelope and pulled out the document. His eyebrows inched up as he read. By the time he flipped to the last page, I had a hard time reading his expression.

He set the papers down, then flipped them over so the blank back was up. "Well."

I waited. There had to be more, didn't there?

"This is unexpected." Special Agent Orbison tapped a single finger on the document. "You've signed it, I see."

I nodded. "That's actually my copy. I sent the signed originals back to Mr. Ortega yesterday."

"I see." Special Agent Orbison took a drink from his cup. "That certainly changes things."

"Does it? I mean, I realize we aren't going to be able to help with your undercover investigation, but you had to know that the possibility of anything seriously useful coming from what Faith or I did was slim." I'd puzzled through that over the last twenty-four hours as Faith had dribbled out more about the types of things she'd been doing while she was off the radar.

I'd tried to tell her it didn't matter to me, but she was determined to confess to someone. And while I thought that was taking it a little far, I also didn't mind listening to her if it helped. Plus, she'd spent the time snuggled up at my side on the couch while she poured it all out, and I was definitely not going to rebuff that contact.

"She was never going to be hugely important to their schemes. At best, she made some documents that made it easier for them to launder money and cross the border." I shrugged, even though it was hard to downplay. I didn't love her brush with the criminal world, but I understood, sort of, why she'd gone there.

The FBI man nodded slowly. "I can see how it looks that way. Of course, I could also point out that she admitted crimes to a federal agent. That's not something that we take lightly. It was one thing to consider immunity when there was some reciprocity. But now?"

"Seriously?" I frowned. This was the worst-case scenario I'd been hoping we could avoid. "You want to prosecute her, even though it won't make a tiny bit of difference to the Ortegas? To prove what point?"

"Crimes were committed. Justice must be served."

I pressed my lips together. I was a family lawyer, primarily, but I had friends who dealt with criminal. I was reasonably certain there wasn't much of a case here. If he pushed, seriously pushed, there might be fines or probation involved in whatever plea deal got worked out. We'd handle that as it came. "I see."

I reached for the documents and slid them back into their envelope. Then I stood. "I guess we'll wait to hear from your attorneys."

I started toward the door.

"Mr. Lee."

I paused and turned.

"There might be other options." He gestured for me to return to the table.

I stepped closer. The shop wasn't crowded, but his raised voice when he called my name had a few heads turning. There was no need to entertain the masses. "I believe we'll explore those with counsel."

He sighed. "You're sure about that?"

"I'm sure that the people who referred us to you wouldn't have dreamed that you'd take this hard line given the circumstances."

He winced.

I nodded. "So yes. You can have your attorneys contact me and I should have the name of our counsel by then. She won't do time."

I could see Special Agent Orbison's wheels turning as he considered my words. He had to know I was right. Of course, there was a small possibility I was wrong—sometimes the government decided they needed to make an example of people. But a good attorney could hopefully keep that from happening.

I had enough favors to call in that I should be able to secure the best.

Finally, he sighed again. "I guess we'll see."

I nodded briskly and headed for the door, glad that I'd convinced Faith to go to work and skip this meeting. Megan would have understood, definitely, but Faith had been torn about missing her second day on the job.

Hopefully, by the time I had to lay it out for her, I'd have the name of our criminal defense attorney in hand and a reasonable explanation of the path forward.

I sorted through the names of lawyers I knew as I walked to my car, unsure of exactly where to start. I immediately ruled out my former firm. They had great lawyers; it wasn't that. I'd referred cases to them when I hadn't felt able to provide the kind of service the client needed. At the same time, I didn't feel like delving into the whole thing with them. None of them were believers. Or, at least, they didn't let their faith get in the way of their practice. And maybe that was what we needed—but it wasn't what I wanted.

Ultimately, it had factored into my decision to strike out on my own.

The thought solidified into a direction.

I climbed behind the wheel, pulled the door shut, and set my phone in its mount before turning on the engine. I didn't go anywhere, but instead scrolled through my contacts until I found the name I was looking for and hit dial. It rang twice before it was answered.

"Allison Reid."

I smiled at the brisk, no-nonsense tone of her answer. "Hi, Allison, this is Tristan Lee. We met at a Christian Legal Society event probably two years ago now. I doubt you remember me."

"Was that the dessert fundraiser for international legal aid?"

I chuckled. "Or maybe you do remember. Yes, that was the one."

"Phil and I always remember meeting promising members of the next generation of Christian lawyers. What can I do for you?"

I took a deep breath, then explained the situation as thoroughly—but concisely—as I could. "So I guess the bottom line is, it seems like we're going to need a criminal defense attorney who has experience with the feds. And I was hoping that would either be you, or you would know the right person for us to contact."

"Hm." Allison blew out a breath. "I'd love to take this on, but I don't have as much federal experience as others I know. On the other hand, what we could do is start with me, and if it looks like we need a heavier hitter, bring on a co-counsel. I have a couple of names in mind that I can reach out to with your permission."

"Absolutely. That would be fantastic. Thank you."

"Not a problem. Is this the best number for you?"

"Yeah, it's my cell."

"Great. I'm going to text you a link. It'll take you to the firm's new-client paperwork. Go ahead and fill that out and then you're free to pass on my information to whoever contacts you from the FBI. I'm going to reach out now, just to get a feel for how they think this is going to go down. There might be a motion I can start crafting now so it's ready as soon as they make contact."

The tightness in my chest eased as her confident and calm words filled the car. "That sounds perfect. I appreciate this."

"Glad to help. The paperwork outlines our fee scale as well as giving information on needs-based adjustments—"

"We're fine there. That's not a problem. I can send you a retainer electronically if you give me those details."

"It's in the paperwork."

"Okay. I'll get started on that as soon as I'm back in the office."

Allison laughed. "Why are lawyers never at their desks?"

"It's a question." I chuckled. It was a valid one, at that. I did a lot of phone calling from my car. "Thanks again."

"Talk soon."

I ended the call, took a moment to breathe a quick prayer of thanks, then buckled my seat belt and headed back toward the office.

Since we'd met in Fairfax, not Old Town, I had a bit of a drive. Of course there was traffic. There was always traffic. Maybe if I'd chosen the back roads it wouldn't have been as bad, but the Beltway was a more direct route and it felt faster, even when it was backed up around the interchange with I-95. Didn't seem like anything they did there really alleviated the congestion that came with the mixing and merging of three big interstates. At least they tried?

I finally got to my exit and made my way through the still somewhat clogged streets of Alexandria and then Old Town until I got to the building that housed my office.

I parked and hurried in.

"Good morning, Mr. Lee." Arlene glanced away from her computer and picked up a small stack of papers from her desk. "Here are your messages. Don't you have court this afternoon?"

I shook my head. "Sorry, I meant to update the calendar. Mediation finally came through. I guess once he realized we were content to appear before a judge, he backed down. I have a few things to write up, but at least it's looking like we can settle things without it getting uglier."

"I'll update your calendar. Are you going to be taking new clients?"

I paused. With this case nearly settled, I had room in my schedule. At the same time, the uncertainty of the situation with Faith and the FBI might be a big demand on my time. "I'll have to look at each one individually. I probably don't have time for something complex just now."

She frowned slightly before schooling her expression.

"What?"

"It's not my business."

I laughed. "Come on, Arlene."

"Well, I just don't know how you plan to keep your practice solvent without cases." She crossed her arms. "I have bills to pay."

"Your salary isn't in danger, I promise. Even if the practice had money problems—which we don't—I have personal savings that can cover us both for a while if needed." It was an understatement, but I'd never felt the need to fill Arlene in on all the specifics. If she dug around online about me, she'd find an article or two that mentioned the b-word. Knowing her, she had that information. She wasn't one to sit around idly when she had questions. But at this point, if she wanted to know, she'd have to ask directly.

"All right." She offered a slight smile. "Let me know if I can do anything to help."

"I will. Thanks, Arlene." I raised the messages in a sort of wave and headed back to my office. I unlocked it, flipped on the lights, and went to sit behind the desk. I started my computer and scanned the slips of paper.

Nothing urgent.

When my machine booted, I connected to the text messages

on my phone—and how cool was that ability?—and clicked the link Allison had sent while I'd been driving.

I spent the next thirty minutes filling out the paperwork online and setting up the payment process for her. When I was finished, I double-checked the contact information I had stored for her in my phone so I was sure to give the proper details to whoever reached out from the FBI.

There was a big part of me praying that this was all just a bluff on Special Agent Orbison's part. When I'd reached out to Christopher Ward at Robinson Enterprises on Scott's recommendation, and he'd funneled me over to his sister, Rebecca, both had assured me that Orbison wasn't an uptight, prosecute-at-all-costs kind of guy. Maybe they'd been wrong? Maybe he had a lot more riding on this than he had on whatever had concerned the Wards?

There was no way to know.

Should I reach out to them and ask? I dismissed the idea as soon as it came to me. What would be the point? They couldn't do anything. And I didn't really want them to. Faith and I would weather this together and, God willing, it would make us stronger as a couple and in our individual walks with Him.

I checked the time. I had several hours before I needed to pick up my parents at the airport and plenty of work here to occupy that time. And none of it was going to get done if I just sat here thinking about the "what-ifs."

Before I dove in, I shot Faith a quick text letting her know I loved her. She still wasn't sure how to deal with that, but I'd take it slow and show her I was serious. I was in this with her, for better or for worse, just like I'd promised all those years ago.

20

FAITH

"Go home." Megan crossed her arms and tapped her foot as she stared at me. "I've got this."

"But—"

"Pshhh." Megan flicked her fingers at me. "I don't know why you're stalling, but you've more than covered your shift and it's time for you to go home to your husband. You should be glad you can! Mine has to come here and hang out if he wants to see me in the evenings."

"So let me close and *you* go home." I grinned. It was the perfect solution. I could avoid seeing Tristan's parents for one more day—surely they'd be exhausted after two days of international travel—and his parents wouldn't be awake when I had to face sleeping in Tristan's room for the first time.

"What's going on?" Megan leaned against the checkout counter.

I sighed and my shoulders slumped. "Tristan's parents are in town."

"Okay? You've met them before, right?"

"Sure, when I was in high school." Not when I'd been married to their son.

"I'm lost. Which, I'll grant you could be because I'm exhausted, but I don't think that's it."

I glommed onto her words. "Why are you exhausted? Actually, you look pale. Are you coming down with something?"

Megan sighed and scrubbed her hands over her face. "Let's go sit."

I looked around the empty bookstore, shrugged, and followed her to the couches. "Is it always this quiet on weeknights?"

"Depends. But yes, mostly." Megan frowned.

"You've got to do the coffee bar. Even if you brought in small bakery snacks instead of worrying about any sort of large menu, that would bring in more people. You know this, right?"

"I guess. I just feel like I'd be betraying the other coffee and food options on the street."

I scoffed. "There's plenty of business to go around. You need people to buy books. If they can come in, get a yummy drink, and sit for a bit, they're going to be more likely to do that instead of ordering online."

Megan groaned. "You and Cody should get together. He keeps telling me the same things. I guess you're both right. I'll spend some time figuring it out."

"That was easy. You were already mostly there, weren't you?"

She shrugged. "I'm too tired to fight."

"And that's because..." I studied her. She really was pale. And a little green around the gills. Plus tired? I pursed my lips. I could think of one thing that might do that. I leaned forward. "Are you pregnant?"

"What? No. Of course not." Megan flopped back against the couch. "Probably. I'm too scared to take a test."

"What? Why? It's a good thing, right?"

"I don't want to steal any of Kayla's thunder. And...I guess after freaking out about it for the last month or so, I'm scared it's not really real."

I hesitated. Maybe I could see what she was saying. Sort of. "I think everyone will be happy for you. And I suspect—granted this is going solely on how I think Jenna would respond, since I know her a little better than any of the others—they'd be annoyed with you for worrying about it."

Megan snorted out a laugh. "You're probably right. Ugh."

"So. Pregnancy test. Do you have one? I can run down to the pharmacy and get one if not."

She sat up. "You're bossy. Also, you were going home, remember?"

"This feels more important."

"Ha. No." Megan pointed at me. "Nice try though, I'll give you that. Unless you tell me Tristan's parents were horrible people when you were a teenager, you know you need to go home and greet them."

I groaned. I could say the words, but they weren't horrible and no one who knew Tristan would believe otherwise, because I was sure he gushed about them to anyone who would listen. They were the embodiment of good people. Just like their son.

"Exactly." Megan grinned like the Cheshire Cat. "Go home."

"Fine. I'll go home. *If* you promise to take a test and then text me the results. It can be before or after you tell Cody, I don't care about that. But no more of this pretending it'll go away because you don't feel like dealing with it." I bit my lip. "I can promise you, that never works out the way you want it to."

Megan chuckled. "Deal. Now go. I'll see you tomorrow."

I stood. "Night."

I gathered my things from the back room and offered another wave as I exited the bookstore. The walk home was a nice stretch for my legs, although my feet reminded me that I'd been on them for a good bit of the day. Now that the mess with the Ortegas was behind me, I delighted in being able to walk the streets without looking over my shoulders. For all that they were bad people, no one disobeyed Manuel Ortega's orders. He'd told them to lay off, so they would.

The temperatures were cooling as the sun set and I made a mental note to start bringing a sweater.

Or to get a new car.

No. Driving to work when it was a decently walkable distance was dumb. Although rain and winter might convince me otherwise, I wasn't there yet. Maybe a bicycle?

I'd talk to Tristan and see what he thought.

My steps slowed as I neared Tristan's condo building. My stomach clenched. Angie had been so kind on the phone. So excited to hear that we were married. So welcoming. But what if it had been an act? What if they were upstairs, waiting to pounce and demand that I exit Tristan's life for good?

I'd do it.

No question.

If they asked me to leave, I would. Because they'd be well within their rights to do so. I'd been nothing but trouble for them since the first time they invited me to church with them. And while I would always be grateful that they did, I owed them enough that I'd walk away.

Even if it killed me.

With growing dread, I passed through the lobby and pressed the button for the elevator. A couple returning from work, hands intertwined, laughed their way over and waited with me. The smile I gave them felt tight.

Finally, the elevator arrived and we climbed in. I pressed the button for Tristan's floor then scooted to the back wall. The laughing couple was a handful of floors below me, and their presence made the trip up seem to take forever.

At last, they got off, and I closed my eyes in the silence as the car traveled to the top floor. I tried to still the thundering-doom music that played in my head, but failed. My steps dragged the final feet to the condo door, and I fumbled the keys.

I pushed open the door, and lilting Irish music and the hearty scent of something rich and meaty poured out to greet me.

I smiled in spite of myself. It was just like Tristan's house growing up—filled with color and laughter and music and meals that hadn't come from the frozen aisles in the grocery store.

I closed the door behind me and paused to take off my shoes and set down my things. I checked that my phone was in my pocket, then took a deep breath and headed down the hallway toward the kitchen and living area.

"There you are!" Angie tapped a wooden spoon against a big silver pot before resting it across the top, wiping her hands on the apron she wore, and hurrying across to wrap me in a tight hug. "Oh honey, it's so good to see you."

I stiffened, then forced myself to relax and return the hug. "Hi, Mrs. Lee."

She leaned back and fixed me with a stern eye.

I winced. "Angie."

"Better." She patted my cheek then stepped back and studied me. "You look amazing. All grown up and gorgeous with it."

My face burned.

"You're embarrassing her, Ang," Mr. Lee—Steve—called from where he sat on the couch. He patted the cushion beside him. "Come sit and tell me about the bookstore you're helping run."

"Oh. I just work there. I'm not running anything." I glanced around for Tristan, but didn't see him. With no escape, I made my way to the couch and sat. "But I like it there."

"You always liked books." He winked at me and everything

inside me warmed. "I remember you used to take off with my leather-bound classics."

"You knew about that?" I could feel the blush crawling back onto my cheeks. "I thought I was being sneaky."

He laughed and patted my knee. "I know. And I figured it made it more fun for both of us. Always did want to ask why you took Dickens time and time again, though."

"*A Tale of Two Cities*." It was one of the reasons I'd always wanted to go to Paris.

"Ah." Steve nodded and sent me a look of understanding. "I always liked that one, too. Romance, intrigue. Redemption."

I swallowed as the final lines of the book floated through my mind. I nodded, but my throat was too tight to speak.

"Tell me about the bookstore." Steve settled back into the sofa.

"There's not a lot to tell. It's just a smallish store. Megan— she's the owner—is married to one of Tristan's friends. Although I guess she's a friend of his in her own right as she's the sister of a different friend." I'd been able to pick up that much from listening to conversations here and there in the six weeks I'd been here. "I like her. She's very resistant to change."

"Ha. Aren't we all? Why do you say that?" Steve shifted so he could watch me more easily.

"The store is struggling. I sold two books today. Megan said that's not unusual. She does better on weekends because she's started hosting local authors and she's carrying books for independently published authors as well, which helps. But other than books, there's no draw for people to come in and browse." I frowned. That made it sound like books weren't a draw in and of themselves. And for some people they totally were. But not for others.

"She needs a café or something. Toys for kids? Story hour?"

I nodded. "Her husband has been on her about the coffee

corner for more than a year, sounds like. But she doesn't want to damage the business of the shop down the street."

"Noble. But coffee is coffee. I doubt very much there's not enough business for both of them."

I grinned at him. "That's what I told her. She said she'd think about it more seriously."

"Helping run. I stand by my previous statement." Steve nudged me with his elbow. He lowered his voice. "How are you? Really?"

I couldn't have explained why my eyes filled if my life depended on it.

"Hey. I'm sorry." Steve slipped his arm around my shoulder and pulled me into a half-hug. "You don't have to tell me."

I swiped at my eyes and shook my head. "No. It's fine. I'm fine. I don't know why—"

"Because from what Tristan says, you've had a rough go of it for a long time. And now that's over. It's natural for your body to need to vent some of those feelings that you've been squishing down."

I sniffled and tried to glare at him. "I don't squish down my emotions."

Angie snorted in the kitchen.

Steve looked over. "Something you'd like to add to our private conversation?"

Angie laughed. "You can't have a private conversation in an open concept floor plan. You know this. I know this. Pretty sure Faith knows it, too."

"She's not wrong."

Steve shook his head. "Fine, fine. Spit it out, Ang."

"Faith knows what I meant." She shot me a pointed look.

I sighed. "Fine. Okay? Yes, I keep my emotions to myself. I don't think that's necessarily a bad thing."

"Oh, but honey, you're wrong." Angie pointed the wooden

spoon at me. "It's not healthy, for one, and it means people around you can't help out."

I winced. The second reason was the primary reason I did it. My parents had always turned emotions into a high-stakes game, and I was always the loser.

Angie nodded. "You're not there anymore. You have Tristan. And us. And, if I'm hearing what you're not saying, Megan, too. Plus the rest of Tristan's friends, because they're a great group."

"It's hard." I snapped my mouth shut on the rest of the sentence. That was enough. The Lees knew enough about my life to know anything I was thinking of adding.

"I know it." Steve rubbed my shoulder. "But you need to learn how to lean. Tristan's got broad shoulders for a reason, and not just because it helps him look nice in a fancy suit."

My cheeks heated again at the gleam in Steve's eyes.

"Steve, stop. We promised we weren't going to pry."

I cleared my throat. "Where is Tristan?"

"Didn't I say? Oh my goodness, I get so scatterbrained sometimes." Angie rolled her eyes. "He ran out to get some bread to go with this soup. The wimpy slices of mass-produced so-called whole wheat he has languishing in his fridge will not do justice to my culinary prowess."

Steve laughed. "She's humble, my wife."

"And you love her for it." I grinned. I'd always envied Tristan his parents. They loved each other so visibly. And they had fun together, too. I think, under everything, they were the kind of friends to one another that made a solid bedrock foundation that could weather any storm.

I wanted that.

When I heard a key in the lock, I turned my head to peer down the hallway. I spotted Tristan with two paper bags. He set one down on the little table by the door, kicked off his shoes, and turned the deadbolt.

Something in my chest clinched.

Maybe I had it already.

Tristan looked up and his eyes met mine. Everything about his seemed to brighten. He hurried down the hall and dropped the bag he still held on the island. "Bakery bread, as requested."

Angie walked to the bag, opened it, and looked in. "Tristan Lee."

"What?" His face was the picture of impish innocence.

Angie reached in and pulled out a clear bag of sliced wheat sandwich bread. "You know this isn't what I meant. The mass-produced part of the commentary wasn't my issue."

"It wasn't? You should've been more specific. They had a really nice-looking sourdough boule that I would have bought instead if I'd known."

Angie propped her hands on her hips and scowled at him.

Steve started to chuckle.

Tristan fought to keep a straight face.

I just shook my head.

"Go get it." Angie pointed toward the door.

Tristan made a show of his shoulders slumping. "All right, but it means dinner's going to be that much further off."

Angie just pointed again.

"You're really sending me back out into the cold? For bread?" Tristan gave an exaggerated shiver and started to shuffle toward the hallway.

Angie looked at the sliced bread with disdain. "Is this really all you brought?"

"Why?" Tristan stopped and glanced back at his mom.

She groaned. "Fine. It'll do. The soup is ready, so we might as well eat. I'm sorry, Faith, that it has to be served with...this." Angie flicked the top of the bag with her fingers.

"It's all right." I stood. "Let me get bowls down."

"No, Mom. If it's that important, I'll go back out." Tristan started down the hallway. "Don't worry about—oh, hey, what's this?"

He came back with the other paper bag. "Maybe I did get that sourdough."

Angie shook the wooden spoon in his face before taking the bag and peering in. "Much better. Maybe I don't have to disown you after all. Sliced wheat bread."

The last was a mutter under her breath and I had to turn away not to laugh. Even the sliced bread looked yummier than the grocery store bread in the fridge. I'd enjoy it for sandwiches at lunch.

Tristan rubbed my arm as he stepped past me to get the bowls. I hurried to the silverware drawer for spoons and a ladle while Angie sliced thick slabs of sourdough.

In minutes, we were all back in the living room with dishes balanced on our laps. Steve said a quick, but thorough, and in no way perfunctory, blessing.

"You need a dining room table." Angie looked around the space. "There's room for something small."

Tristan shrugged. "It's been mostly just me, so the island works. Even with Faith here now, there's just two of us."

"And when the guys come over?" Angie shot him a pointed look.

"It's pizza and chips while we play poker. I get a folding table out for that." Tristan set his soup down on the coffee table. "I can get that out if you want."

"No. This is fine. It's just very...bachelor." Angie's gaze flitted to me. "And you're not one."

I tried to school my expression, but I couldn't help feeling condemned. "It's my fault he's been living like one, though."

"That's not what I meant." Angie reached over to touch my hand. "No one's assigning blame. I'm looking for an excuse to go shopping."

"That's truth right there." Steve took a bite of soup. "We don't need any more furniture, so she's always on the hunt for someone who does."

"I can just order something from Ikea..." Tristan trailed off at the bland stare Angie sent his way. "Or not."

None of them might be assigning blame, but I was. I didn't know how to stop it, either. I was to blame. For all of this. Tristan had married me because I needed help. And, okay, he said he was in love with me even then, and I was trying to believe that, but who got married hoping someone would end up falling in love with them? That was like something out of the eighteen hundreds with arranged marriages so the farm could get bigger. And then, of course, I'd run off. Let's see them avoid assigning me that blame. Because who else would be responsible?

Nobody, that was who.

I sighed.

"What's wrong?" Angie frowned. "I'm overstepping, aren't I? Maybe you and I can furniture shop together. This is your home, after all, not mine. I'd love to make a little table and chairs your wedding gift, though."

I froze. I hadn't meant to sigh aloud. I cleared my throat. "Oh. Um."

I glanced at Tristan. He just raised his eyebrows and waited.

Awesome. So helpful. "Sure. I'd like that?"

"We'll go tomorrow after you're finished at work." Angie didn't seem to care that my response had been the furthest thing from sure as possible. But then, that was how she'd always been. She could be a bit of a steamroller, but no one noticed until afterward, because she was so sweet and gentle about it. "I'll come meet you at the bookstore. There has to be a furniture store in Old Town, right?"

I honestly had no idea. "I'll do some searching and figure it out."

"Perfect." Angie scooped the last of her small bowl of soup into her mouth, then stood.

"Don't even think about the dishes, Mom. You made dinner. I'll clean up." Tristan held out his hand for her bowl.

She sent him a dazzling smile. "I knew I raised you right. And tonight I'm so tired I'm not even going to argue. If the rest of you don't mind, I'm going to head to bed."

"I'm right behind you, Ang." Steve used the last of his bread to wipe the inside of his bowl. With a wink, he handed the dish to Tristan. "You won't even need to wash that one."

"Thanks, Dad. I think I'll do it anyway. Just for fun."

Steve laughed and stood. "Suit yourself. See you two in the morning."

"Good night." I leaned forward and put my bowl on the coffee table.

"Are you done?" Tristan eyed my half-eaten soup.

I nodded. "I can help with the cleanup."

"I won't say no." He stood and carried the dishes over to the island and set them down. "But first, come here."

He opened his arms and I found myself walking into them and wrapping my arms around his waist.

"I missed you today."

His words made me smile. I snuggled my head into his shoulder. "You're strange."

He chuckled.

"I'm not wrong. You saw me this morning. Normal people don't spend all day with their spouse." Not that there had been much normal about any aspect of our relationship. Ever. But still.

Tristan shrugged. "I've never wanted to be normal."

I tipped my head back so I could see him and smiled. His eyes met mine and he eased his head closer. My breath caught. Would he finally kiss me? We'd had so many moments when it would have made sense—in my mind at least—but I wanted—needed—him to be the one to make the move.

Tristan rested his forehead on mine.

"Can I get—oh, sorry." Steve winced as we both stepped back and turned to face him. "Really sorry. I just wanted a glass of water for the nightstand. Sometimes three a.m. comes and I need a little sip of something."

"Sure, Dad." Tristan moved into the kitchen and got down a glass. He filled it from the water dispenser in the door of the fridge and held it out. "Night."

"Night. As you were." Steve chuckled and disappeared toward the bedrooms.

I carried the empty dishes from the island to the sink, then returned to grab mine and tip the remaining soup back into the big pot on the stove. I cleared my throat to mask the disappointment that weighed on me. "What should I use to store the leftovers?"

Tristan came over to peer into the pot. His eyebrows lifted. "She doesn't know how to make a small pot of soup, does she?"

"Soup's always better when it's made in bulk." Years of cooking for one had proven that to me. The first couple of times when I'd tried to just make enough for one or two meals, the soup had been so bland, I'd given up and stuck with canned soup going forward.

"You have a point." Tristan flashed a smile before squatting to open a lower cabinet and pull out three Chinese soup take-away containers. "We can probably freeze some of it in these."

"I imagine so." I took the containers and started the process of emptying the pot into the containers while Tristan rinsed the dishes and loaded them into the dishwasher. The silence was broken only by the clinking of spoons and running water. It was comfortable. And still somehow slightly awkward.

"I met with Special Agent Orbison today."

I paused briefly in ladling, then continued. I'd forgotten. "Right. You said you would. How did it go?"

"Honestly? Not as well as I expected. He made some noises about filing charges."

"What?" I dropped the ladle into the pot and it clanged against the side. "I'll leave. You don't need to be tied to a felon for the rest of your life. Wouldn't that just be an amazing look for you? Billionaire attorney married to a woman in federal prison."

"Hey." Tristan reached for my flailing hands and grabbed them. He held them tightly in his warm grasp even as I tried to pull away. "That's not going to happen."

"You can't say that. You can't know that." I shook my head feverishly. "I'm nothing but trouble. I'm like...Typhoid Mary."

Tristan's lips twitched.

"Don't you dare laugh." I hissed under my breath. "You know it's true."

"I know no such thing." Tristan stood calmly until I stopped tugging on him. "Here's what I do know. I know that Orbison is ticked off that his plan didn't work. I know he threatened legal action. I know I reached out to a well-respected criminal defense attorney—"

My panicked gasp made him pause.

He squeezed my hands and continued, "And she is reasonably certain he's all bluster. But if—or when—the fed attorneys reach out, I'll point them to her and she'll handle it."

"Tristan."

He shook his head and squeezed my hands again. "*We'll* handle this. And I will do what it takes to ensure you don't end up in any sort of federal prison. Even if they're offering the kind that people jokingly refer to as country clubs. Got it?"

I couldn't look away from his gaze, and my objections died on my lips. I wanted to believe him too strongly to force the words out, even though I knew, deep down, that he couldn't promise any of these things. I still wanted to believe that he could.

He tugged me close again and wrapped his strong arms around me. I could feel his confidence in the embrace and I yearned to be able to absorb even the tiniest sliver of it for myself. What I wanted to do was curl into a ball, shut my eyes, and pretend none of this was real. It was a skill I'd perfected as a child, and maybe I was out of practice now, but I had a feeling it'd come back pretty easily.

Tristan's hand moved up and down slowly on my back. Gradually, without really recognizing it, I relaxed. His lips were next to my ear and the breath of his words made me shiver almost as much as the words themselves. "We'll get through this together. I love you. I'm not letting you go."

21

TRISTAN

I lay awake in bed, staring at the ceiling, reminding myself that it wasn't time to get up yet. It wasn't close to time. I couldn't even pass it off as rising early to get in a workout before heading to the office.

Nobody worked out at three twenty-seven a.m.

I'd probably dozed here and there for an hour? Maybe two? But it was all in little snatches of sleep that did more harm than good.

I turned my head to the side and let my gaze rest on the reason for my sleeplessness.

Faith.

She was curled on her side, almost on the edge of the bed, facing away from me. From her slow, even breathing, I believed she truly slept. And so I worked to be still so I didn't wake her.

One of us ought to start the day rested.

Going to bed hadn't been as awkward as I'd feared it would be. She'd come out of the bathroom in a long-sleeved T-shirt and cotton pants. Her hair braided. Her toes were painted a bright pink.

I couldn't have explained to anyone why those pink toes

made my mouth water. I never considered myself a man with a thing for feet.

Maybe it was just her feet.

Because they were part of her.

She'd climbed into bed without saying a word, rolled over, and closed her eyes. After a moment, I'd turned out the light and started counting the seconds as they ticked the night away.

I'd considered—and discarded—the idea of scooting over so we could spoon. She had seemed fine with my hugs in the kitchen, but here, in my bedroom? In bed? It seemed a lot more intimate. And she wasn't awake to tell me if it was okay.

I couldn't decide if that would help me sleep or just make it even more impossible.

Probably the latter.

The covers rustled and Faith rolled over. Her voice was slurred with drowsiness. "You think loud."

"I'm sorry."

"S'okay." She reached up and rubbed her eyes. "What's wrong?"

I shook my head. "Nothing."

Her sigh explained without words that she didn't believe me for a minute.

I smiled in spite of myself. "It's hard to sleep with you right there."

"Did I take your side?" She started to sit up. "We can switch."

"It's not that. And no, you didn't. It's you." I swallowed as her expression turned to confusion.

"I can sleep on the floor?"

I reached out and took her hand. "I'd rather you didn't."

"K?" She yawned hugely.

"Go back to sleep, honey."

Her lips quirked up at the corners and her eyes drifted closed. She shimmied closer until her head was pillowed on my shoulder. I shifted to get more comfortable and she burrowed in.

On the one hand, this was much, much better.

On the other? So much worse.

She slid her arm up my torso until her hand came to rest over my heart. Her fingers curled slightly. I rested my cheek on the top of her head and closed my eyes. I still might not sleep, but at least now she wasn't so far away.

I drifted in and out, spending my conscious moments praying for God to work in our situation. I had to believe He'd brought Faith back to me on purpose. Not to take her away again, but so that we could be together forever.

My phone alarm woke me from a brief snooze. I reached over with one arm to turn it off, fully prepared to try to roll over and sleep for real, but Faith shifted, then stretched, then scooted to sit up.

"What time is it?"

The side of my body where she'd snuggled was cold now. I wanted to pull her back and snuggle under the covers with her. But there was no way she was ready for that. For that matter, I probably wasn't either. We might have been married for fourteen years, but we were still new to this idea of making it real.

"Seven." I sat up and tossed my legs over the side of the bed, then stood. Better to get up and face the day than to sit there with her, letting my mind wander. "What time do you have to be at work?"

"Megan wants to watch me open to make sure I know what I'm doing, so nine thirty. Ish."

I nodded. "You'll be off at five?"

"Yeah. That okay?"

"Absolutely. Mom wanted to come by, remember, and go furniture shopping?"

"Right." Faith wrinkled her nose. "Just a little table, right?"

"You can get whatever you think we need. If you want to replace anything, do it. I'm not attached to any of the stuff in the condo. And I've had it all at least five years. Probably closer to ten on some of it."

"I don't...I like what you have."

"We." I looked at her. "We have it. Which means it should reflect you, too."

"Okay."

She didn't look convinced, but I absolutely couldn't get into that conversation until after a gallon of coffee and the world's hottest shower. "I'm going to go make coffee if you want the first shower."

"Okay."

I frowned at her. "Are you all right?"

"Yeah. I'm just...adjusting."

I chuckled. "Fair enough. I'll bring you coffee if it's ready before you are."

"Thanks." She still hadn't moved. But then, I didn't remember her as a bouncy, early morning person.

She wasn't a grump. She didn't grunt or growl her way through the morning. But she hadn't been one to spring out of bed with a smile and a song.

I almost laughed. Neither did I. Nor did anyone I knew.

I made sure the bedroom door latched behind me and yawned as I made my way to the kitchen. The coffee pot's gurgle and rich aroma reached me as I stepped in.

"Morning, my baby." Mom looked over from where she waited for the coffee. She was wearing the same pale green terrycloth robe she'd worn in the mornings for as long as I could remember. It couldn't possibly be the same one, but she apparently replaced it with an identical twin whenever it wore out. She studied my face. "You slept poorly."

"It happens." I glanced at the coffee. "Is that ready?"

"Just about. Go sit down and I'll bring you some."

"Thanks." I made my way around the island and sat. "Dad's not up yet?"

"Nope. He's still in there snoring like a lumberjack." Mom laughed as she got down a second mug. "Honestly, this time I'm going to force the issue and make him do a sleep study. A CPAP would have to be better to listen to than that noise."

I smiled. Mom had been threatening Dad with that for at least the last five years. "I'm surprised you haven't already followed through on it."

"Oh, well. He gets stubborn. Sometimes you have to pick your battles."

I understood that.

Mom set a mug of coffee in front of me. "You haven't changed how you take it, have you?"

"Nope." I blew across the top and sipped. "Mmm. Perfect. Thank you."

She patted my cheek and came around to sit beside me. "Why didn't you sleep well?"

I shook my head. As much as I loved my mother, I wasn't getting into that with her. There were some conversations that just didn't need to take place with a parent. Especially not once you passed thirty. "How'd you sleep?"

"Fine. Other than the times I woke up wanting to smother your father with his pillow." She grinned and sipped her coffee. "I think I might drag him downtown today to the Museum of the Bible. It's new since we were here last and it seems like a good place to spend the day."

"It's nice. I went down one afternoon after a client meeting in DC. I didn't get to see everything, but I liked what parts I did. I'm told the restaurant on the top floor is amazing." Most people said it was expensive but amazing, but I'd get Dad to let me pay for it, so Mom didn't need to worry about that. I could pay their admission, too. "Let me get a car to take you down. That way you don't have to deal with the subway. And if you change your mind and want to see something else, the driver can scoot you around."

"Tristan, you don't have to—"

"I know that." I held up a finger. "I want to. It's been too long since we made a visit happen. My fault. I let myself get busy."

"We stay busy, too." Mom rested her hand on top of mine. "But your father would tell me to just say thank you, so I will. I wish you could come with us."

"Me, too." And I probably could, if I shifted some things around. But I wanted to be in the office and available if the feds got in touch. I also had a little client work that I needed to do. I wasn't behind, yet, but I didn't want to get there. Regardless of the upheaval going on in my personal life right now, my clients deserved my best. So that was what they'd get. "You'll still head to the bookstore around five to get Faith and look for a little table?"

"Of course. Maybe your driver can hang out with us for that, too? I found a few places that we could walk to, but I don't think they'd have the kind of furniture you're looking for."

"I haven't been looking for furniture." I shot her a grin.

Mom poked my arm. "Watch it, buster. You know exactly what I mean."

"I do. I appreciate you taking this on."

She laughed. "Like it's a hardship to spend someone else's money?"

"I thought you were buying this as a gift?"

"I am. I'm spending your dad's money."

"Ah. This is where I don't point out that it's your money too, right?"

"Right."

"Could I convince you to let me pay for it?" Because at the

end of the day, I had plenty of money for furniture and while my parents did okay, they were retired and spent a lot of their time doing mission work. That wasn't something known for setting people up to be well off.

"We'll see. I can manage it for the initial purchase. If you feel like you have to reimburse us, I probably won't fight too hard."

My eyebrows shot up. I hadn't expected her to give in easily. Or at all. "Are you two doing okay?"

Mom wiggled a hand back and forth. "God provides."

"But?"

She glanced toward the hall, then back at me. "Your father's health isn't as good as he makes out. He's had a few little episodes with his heart."

I grabbed Mom's arm. "What?"

"Not attacks. There's an electrical defect, apparently. It's mostly handled with a beta blocker, but if he gets too stressed or his allergies get out of whack, it gets bad again. We might be stuck in the States for the foreseeable future."

"Oh, Mom." That was a blow for them both. They'd been planning for a retirement spent in missions for as long as I could remember. They'd never felt that God wanted them to change course and go out on the field while I was still at home— it had always been retirement. Now? It must feel like the rug had been pulled out from under them.

"We're adjusting. And honestly? I think this situation with Faith is a good reminder that we might not have spent our lives with the far-flung unreached people, but we shared Christ wherever we were." She sighed. "It matters."

"It does." I dropped my head on her shoulder for a moment.

Dad strolled into the kitchen and his eyebrows shot up. "You making time with my girl?"

"Always." I kissed Mom's cheek and slid off my seat at the

island. "I'm going to make Faith a cup of coffee and take it to her. Mom's got your day all planned out. She can fill you in."

"She usually does." Dad's laugh carried me through the process of fixing Faith's coffee and heading toward the bedrooms. I smiled as I heard the cabinet doors opening and closing as Dad hunted around for what he needed.

I paused outside my—our—bedroom door. Should I knock? I glanced back toward the kitchen. Mom and Dad couldn't see me from here, but they might hear me if I was too loud. And that was still better than walking in on Faith before she was ready for me to come in.

I tapped quietly.

"Yeah?"

It wasn't the most helpful response, but I'd go with it. I turned the knob and pushed the coffee through first. "I brought you coffee."

"You can come in."

I opened the door the rest of the way. Dressed in casual slacks and a sweater, Faith squeezed her wet hair with a towel. "Your coffee, madame."

She laughed. "Lifesaver."

"I do what I can." I shut the door behind me and took the mug across to her. "You look really nice."

Her cheeks pinked. "Thanks. Megan said casual, but it feels like jeans might be a little underwhelming."

"I get that. I can do jeans on days when I don't have clients scheduled, but there could be walk-ins, all kinds of things. So I dress the part."

She sipped and closed her eyes as she breathed out. "This is perfect."

So are you. The words were on the tip of my tongue, but I held them back. I couldn't gauge her response to them and I didn't want to set us back further than we already were.

"Mom and Dad are up and in the kitchen. I don't think it would take much to talk Mom into eggs or pancakes if you were so inclined."

"Can she do French toast?"

I nodded. "She can."

"Then I might see what I can do. We have that fancy wheat bread and everything."

I laughed. "I wouldn't say no to a slice or two if you ask. But I want to grab a shower if you're finished in there?"

"Okay. Let me grab my hairdryer. I can finish out here." Faith set her coffee down on the nightstand and hurried into the bathroom. She was back out quickly, holding her hairdryer and makeup bag. "All yours."

I took a minute to grab clothes out of the closet and take them in with me. It seemed like we were being extra careful with one another today, so I didn't want to risk her still being in the room if I came out in a towel.

I made quick work of the shower and getting dressed. Even still, when I left the steamy bathroom, the bed was made and the door stood ajar. Faith had hung her towel on the bathroom doorknob, so I took a moment to hang it on a rack then followed the sound of laughter and clinking forks to the kitchen.

"Look at you, all spiffed up for a day of arguing with people." Dad glanced over from his plate of French toast with a grin. He shifted to look at Faith. "Always knew he'd make a good lawyer. He had an argument and objection for everything."

"Hey." I pointed my finger at Dad. "Careful, old man."

"Old? Who're you calling old?" Dad scowled at me.

"You." I grinned, then crossed to kiss Mom's cheek. "Did you make me any?"

"I'll do it now. I wasn't sure how long you'd be. I was just telling Faith about how you used to shower for close to an hour when you were a teenager."

"Mom." Heat crawled up my neck. Maybe having them around wasn't such a good idea, after all.

"And the time I came up to see what was taking so long and you were sitting on the floor in your underwear reading a book, having completely forgotten you started the shower. Remember that?" Dad slapped his knee as he began to guffaw.

I scrubbed a hand over my face. "When are you two leaving again?"

Faith chuckled. "They need to stay. I'm reasonably certain I wouldn't get any of these stories out of you."

"For good reason. There is zero need for you to know about that." Less than zero. I could remember it perfectly well, if I wanted to. And I did not.

"I don't know. It's good to realize you weren't always perfect. Sometimes I wonder." Faith stood and crossed to me. She took my hand and gave it a squeeze. "You know all my embarrassing stories. This feels fair."

I sighed. Maybe she had a point. But I didn't have to like it.

I plowed through three pieces of French toast while Mom, Dad, and Faith told stories and joked around. Usually at my expense. I tried to grin and roll with it, but I was starting to worry that Faith was going to realize she could do a lot better than me.

Finally, when the dishes were cleared and the dishwasher loaded, Mom and Dad went back to their room to get ready for the day. I took a minute to line up a driver for them, then gathered my things.

"I should probably head to work. You're okay with them without me?" I held Faith's gaze.

"I am. They're great. I'd forgotten just how much I used to envy you your parents." She took my hand. "You'll let me know if anything happens, right?"

"Absolutely." I leaned forward and pressed a quick kiss to her forehead. "Have a good one."

I wasn't positive, but I thought I saw a flash of disappointment in Faith's expression. That was good, wasn't it? I knew I needed to wait until she was on the same page with me when it came to being physical. The problem, of course, was how to tell.

Maybe she'd end up telling me herself.

22

FAITH

"I really think I should just go home." I edged toward the bookstore door. "I don't want to intrude."

Megan propped her hands on her hips and glowered at me. "Does it sound like you'll be intruding?"

"Well—"

"No. Exactly. In fact, you've been invited multiple times by multiple people. So shut it, get away from the door, and tell me if you want Italian or Tacos."

I hunched my shoulders. "You're mean."

"Can be." Megan pointed to the couches. "Only when my friends are being stupid."

I held my hands up and gave in. "Fine."

"Good." Megan checked the time on her phone. "The rest of the girls should be here any minute. We can order as soon as they get here and as soon as you decide what it is we're ordering."

"Italian."

"Good choice." Megan flashed a grin.

"You really have girls' night every Friday in your bookstore?

That doesn't...I don't know, scare away customers?" I flopped onto the end of one couch and dug my phone out of my pocket.

"It hasn't so far. In fact, sometimes I think we get more traffic on Friday nights because we've got people sitting here having fun. And it's visible from the window. Of course tonight, you're all going to be helping me decorate for Halloween. I'm a little behind in getting all the spooky decor out."

My eyebrows lifted. "I didn't realize we decorated for Halloween."

Megan pointed to various spots in the store where we'd been setting up seasonal book highlights. "Why wouldn't we? We have book themes. There should be decorations. Plus the kiddos come trick or treating down the shops and I like for them to have some ambience."

Okay. That made sense. "It's just the tenth. You're really behind?"

"I usually aim to decorate the last week of September. That's still later than all the other stores, but long enough that it builds some excitement. Orange and black come down on November first and are replaced with fall and Thanksgiving orange and yellows, complete with turkeys and cornucopias. Then Christmas comes out on Black Friday if there's time."

"All right. I guess I didn't realize it was a thing for stores. I think of it more for like, I don't know, elementary school classrooms." And that sounded like a putdown. Given the narrow-eyed glare Megan shot my way, she took it as one. "Sorry."

"You're forgiven this time. But you probably have to do the spiders now."

I started to ask, then decided not to. As long as the spiders weren't real, I could probably deal with it.

The bell over the door chimed and Megan greeted the customer—a mother with a toddler by the hand and another in a stroller.

I tapped on my phone and opened a text message.

> Are you sure I can't just hang out at home by myself?

> Positive. The girls are fun. You'll have a good time.

> *YOU MAKE A LOT OF PROMISES.*

> *I CAN BAIL ON THE GUYS IF YOU WANT TO HANG OUT. DO YOU REALLY NOT WANT TO JOIN GIRLS' NIGHT?*

I winced. I wasn't trying to get Tristan to give up his evening out. His parents had left that morning and I knew having them for a little over a week had been a lot for him. He'd enjoyed it. As had I, honestly, but there hadn't been time for anything other than making their visit pleasant. Besides, since I'd been on the scene, Tristan's time with his guy friends had been sorely depleted.

> No. You go with the guys. I'll stay and do my best.

> *JUST HAVE FUN. OKAY?*

> *SEE YOU LATER AT HOME.*

I clicked off my phone and tucked it under my leg. So much for getting out of this. And maybe I didn't really want to. I liked Megan. I liked Jenna—at least I had in Paris. Was it possible she'd acted differently because we were on a trip together? Anything was possible. But I didn't get the vibe that she was anything other than who she was. I'd liked Whitney when we met. So really, there was no reason to worry. Sunny and Kayla were probably just as great as the rest of them.

Now I just had to hope they decided to like me. Would they do it for Tristan's sake?

Megan rang up a small stack of books for the mother and her kids and waved them out the door with a smile. A couple of minutes after that, Jenna bustled in on a gust of wind.

"Oof. It's getting chilly. Maybe we'll actually have fall sometime before winter." She shrugged out of her jacket, draped it over the back of a chair, then sat. "What's dinner?"

"Italian." Megan joined us in the seating area and perched on the arm of the sofa. "You know we'll still have a heat wave in two weeks, right? Maybe we'll get some cool between now and then, but it's almost always in the high eighties at Halloween."

"I know you're right, but a girl can dream." Jenna shrugged and glanced over at me before jerking her thumb at Megan. "How is it working for this one?"

"It's fine. I like working here."

"Here, sure." Jenna grinned. "It's books. What's not to love. But cranky pants over there has to be hard to work for."

"Mostly I see her when it's shift change."

"Hey!" Megan frowned at me. "I'm not cranky."

I muffled a laugh.

"All evidence to the contrary." Jenna muttered.

"Look, you. Both of you—"

The bell over the door cut off whatever was coming next. Whitney and a very pregnant Kayla came in together.

"Tell these two to stop picking on me."

Kayla eyed the chairs and opted for one of the firmer armchairs. "What did you do to make them pick on you?"

"She's being cranky." Jenna pulled a face. "I'm sure you'll get to experience it here in a minute."

"I'm. Not. Cranky." Megan stomped her foot.

Whitney started to laugh. "Wow. Someone needs a nap. Here I thought I left tantrums at home with Scott."

Megan crossed her arms.

"Are you okay, Megan? That's not like you." Kayla leaned forward. "You know we're teasing, right?"

"I do." Megan huffed out a breath. "And I know I'm cranky. I'm queasy and exhausted and just...pregnant."

"What?" Whitney bounced out of her seat, clapping her hands. She dragged Megan into a sort of hopping-dancing hug. "That's fantastic! Congratulations."

"What's the party?" Sunshine came in through the door. "Sorry I'm late. There was confusion about who was in charge of the shop tonight—we ended up just closing. We're going to need to figure Friday nights out."

"Megan's expecting." Kayla grinned. "She's cranky and spilled the beans."

"Really?" Sunshine's smile grew. "That's great. Now I'll have two babies to spoil."

"Maybe we won't have to fight over Kayla's after all." Whitney turned to Sunshine offering a fist for a bump.

I was glad that Megan had spilled her concerns to me earlier or I never would have followed the conversation. And, like I imagined, neither of the two she worried about were upset. Or, if they were, they kept it from her and would deal with it in their own time. Which was just what friends should do.

Sunny plunked down beside me on the couch. "Faith, right?"

"Yeah. Hi. I don't think we've actually met."

"Probably not. But I've heard all the things. Wes likes news. That's his word. I call it what it is, gossip."

I laughed. Maybe Tristan was right. Maybe I was going to end up enjoying this group of women. I just didn't have a lot of experience with friend groups, so my general expectation was negative. "I like a good scoop as much as the next person, although I guess that's probably something I should be working on. There's that whole thing in the Bible about it."

"Yeah. I keep reminding Wes of that. He says since he does actually pray about things and he doesn't pass it around willy-nilly that it's different. I'm not so sure. But I guess it's really between him and the Holy Spirit." Sunny shrugged. "Did we decide on dinner already?"

"Italian. But I don't know what that translates to in terms of finding a menu to look at." I eyed Sunny. "Maybe you do?"

"I do." She pulled out her phone and I was shortly looking at the menu for a nearby Italian place.

It all sounded good. "I might just have to close my eyes and point."

"Right? Can't go wrong, honestly, but I do like their baked ziti a lot." Sunny took her phone back. "You're working here with Megan, right? How are you enjoying the retail world?"

"I like it. I did some retail and fast food when I was a teen, so it's not completely unfamiliar. And I like books." I shrugged. Maybe it wasn't a dream job, but right now, I didn't have any idea what a dream job would be.

"Do you scuba?"

I blinked. "Like diving under the ocean? No. That holds zero interest."

Sunny laughed. "Don't tell Wes, he'll take it as a personal challenge."

I shuddered. I wasn't a big fan of swimming in a chlorinated pool where I could see the bottom. I didn't have any idea what scuba diving would be like, but it sounded horrible.

"All right, ladies. Give me your orders, I'm going to put it in." Megan raised her voice over the chatter. "Some of us are hungry."

"Hear hear." Kayla chimed in. "I want the eggplant parm. And the garlic knots."

"Okay. Faith?" Megan looked at me.

"Baked ziti." She kept looking at me. "That's it. Just the ziti. Unless the ziti is terrible. But Sunny—"

"Stop. It's great. Carry on." Megan continued around the group collecting orders.

Sunny also got the ziti but she added fried calamari to her order. Whitney also added an appetizer. By the time everyone was done, I was surprised at the quantity of food we were going to have. They couldn't possibly be planning to eat it all, could they?

Maybe they all got up and went running every morning. For like twenty miles.

Or they didn't eat like this very often.

Or...who knew? It was going to be interesting to find out.

"Excellent. With that out of the way, who is ready for wedding drama?" Jenna was sitting on the floor, leaning back against the sofa. "Because boy, oh boy. I have wedding drama."

"Uh-oh." Kayla chewed her lip. "What happened."

"My venue canceled on me." Jenna tossed her arms in the air. "They just called up and were like, 'Oh hey, by the way, you can't have your wedding here anymore even though you've paid for it.'"

"You're getting a refund at least, right?" Whitney frowned. "I don't think they can do that. You have a contract."

"A fact I pointed out. Which is why I'm getting a refund plus an inconvenience fee because I also mentioned that if I wasn't satisfied with their care of the situation they'd be hearing from my attorney." Jenna raked a hand through her hair. "I wouldn't actually sue them but I'm so mad. What am I supposed to do? How do you find a wedding venue two and a half months before a wedding? And oh by the way, make sure all your other vendors can move to that venue. Pretty sure they're not going to be able to."

"You were getting married at a winery near Charlottesville, right?" Kayla absently ran a hand over her belly.

"That was the plan. It was perfect, too. Everything has been planned to coordinate with the setting and I just—"

"Take a breath." Kayla cut her off. "I might have an idea. Remember when the women at church were looking at having a women's retreat at Peacock Hill, but then it didn't pan out because the speaker they wanted to bring in couldn't make it?"

"Vaguely." Jenna glanced around. "Anyone?"

Whitney raised her hand. "I do."

"I don't." I smiled.

Everyone laughed and a little of the tension in the air eased.

"Funny." Kayla grinned. "Anyway, I know they do weddings there, too. Why not see if they're available?"

"That's a great idea. And honestly, Cody and I got the venue for their big Christmas thing not too much ahead of it last year. It can be done." Megan reached over and patted Jenna's shoulder. "We'll help."

"Thanks." Jenna had her head down and she was tapping at her phone. After a moment, she flipped it around. "Is this the place?"

I twisted so I could see the website. Obviously, I wouldn't know one way or the other, but I was curious. The gorgeous, stately mansion that took up most of the screen was impressive. When the photo slid to the next, revealing lush gardens and bubbling fountains, I reached for my own phone.

A quick search pulled up the site that I'd half-heard Kayla confirm as the correct one. I tapped on the gallery. "Wow. This place is incredible."

Sunny leaned over to look. "Ooh. Of course, it's not going to have the lush gardens on New Year's Eve, but I bet it's out in the country enough that you'll be able to see the stars."

Jenna put down her phone and flipped it over. "All right. I

filled out their contact form. I guess we'll see what we see. I can't use the church—I already called. The youth are having a big lock-in for New Year's."

"I thought they were going to a rec center and renting it out." Whitney frowned.

"Apparently that changed. No idea why."

Kayla snorted. "I bet I know why. Some of those moms hover so well, I'm surprised they don't fly helicopters for the Army. I'm sure they decided the rec center was too dangerous. Or the boys and girls might find corners to behave inappropriately."

"Like they can't do that at church." My hand flew up to cover my mouth. "Sorry. I don't know the kids at your church. They might be great."

"They're a mix." Whitney shrugged. "And you're not wrong. The ones who are determined to find a way to get in trouble are going to do that no matter where the event is held. Some moms just don't want to believe it. You didn't want to get married at the church anyway."

"No." Jenna sighed. "But I do want to get married and at this point I don't know how that's going to happen. Unless we elope, I guess."

"You could get married at your house. The stairway would make a great grand entrance. You could get married right in front of the door. Chairs on either side."

Jenna wrinkled her nose at Megan. "I guess. Do I really want to have to clean up my own house after my own wedding, though? It's not ideal. And we'd have to restrict the guest list. Which might end up meaning uninviting people who've already been invited. That feels like a bad plan. But it's something to keep in mind if we need to."

Megan glanced at her phone then back up. "Food's five minutes out."

"Good. I'm starved." Sunny patted her stomach. "Plus, once

we're all eating, we can grill Faith and get the full scoop on her secret marriage to Tristan."

"What? No. There's no scoop." I shook my head. I'd been enjoying the evening so far, but if this was going to turn into grilling me? I was taking my ziti and hitting the road.

Megan laughed. "There has to be some scoop. Tristan's this mysterious lawyer who doesn't talk about stuff."

"Duh? Lawyer?" I looked at each of the faces, hoping to find one that wasn't the picture of curiosity. "I thought we were decorating the bookstore for Halloween."

"Oh, yeah?" Whitney perked up. "I always love helping with that. You're late this year."

Megan chuckled. "A little, yeah. It's been busy. Not the store —that's the same as always—but life."

"This will happen." Whitney stood and hurried toward the door. I watched her push it open for a young man carrying two large shopping bags with pictures of pasta all over them. I couldn't hear what Whitney said, but she was obviously charming and funny, because the guy laughed and his cheeks turned pink.

"Food's here. Let's eat." Whitney set the bags down on the low table in the center of the seating area. "Grilling optional, although we would love to get to know you. Not in a creepy way, but in an 'our husbands are all friends so we want to be friends, too' way."

Sunny jabbed an elbow in my side. "I have it on good authority that these ladies are like the Borg."

"The Borg?" It took me a minute. "From the space show?"

Jenna shot me a horrified look. "The space show? You did not just call *Star Trek* 'the space show.'"

"That's its name. *Star Trak*." I nodded, glad to be saved from having to think about it for the rest of the night.

"Trek." Jenna enunciated it clearly. "Star. Trek. You, my

friend, are going to be watching a lot of TV with me in the near future. The space show, indeed."

"Sorry." Sunny leaned close, her voice low. "I would have warned you if I knew you weren't a fan. On the flip side, it's kind of interesting. Mostly."

Jenna frowned at Sunny. "You know I can hear you, right?"

Sunny just offered an overly bright smile.

I reached for the container of food that Megan held out. "Thanks. So, since I don't get the Borg reference, want to just share it so it makes sense?"

Jenna sighed. "Resistance is futile."

23

TRISTAN

"You have a call on line one, Mr. Lee." Arlene disconnected the intercom as soon as she finished delivering her statement.

I pressed the line one button and picked up the handset. "Tristan Lee."

"Good afternoon, Mr. Lee, this is Bradley Forrester. I've been assigned the case being brought against you and Faith Clarke by the FBI."

It shouldn't have surprised me. Special Agent Orbison didn't seem like a man who was going to give up easily. Even if it was a bluff, it had always seemed likely that I'd be talking to an attorney. That was why I'd called Allison right away. "Hello. If you give me your contact details, I'll pass them along to my attorney and she'll get in touch."

"Your what?"

"My attorney."

Bradley cleared his throat. "I was under the impression you were an attorney yourself."

"I am. But surely you know the old adage about having a fool for a client." I smiled slightly. Would Bradley see the humor? He worked for the government, so it was unlikely, but I'd met a few federal lawyers who would have.

"Ah. Well, I'm not sure it's necessary. There are just a few little things to clear up. It would be easier, certainly, if we could handle them between ourselves."

I fought a laugh. "Do you have a pen and paper handy?"

"I do."

"Great. Allison Reid. Here's her number." I read the digits off the email I'd quickly pulled up. Then went ahead and offered her email address, just in case. "I'm sure she'll be happy to hear from you. I'll give her a quick call right now so she'll know to expect it. Have a great day."

I ended the call on Bradley's stuttering, then switched lines, and dialed Allison.

"Allison Reid."

"Hi, Allison. It's Tristan Lee."

"Uh-oh."

"Yeah. Just got off the phone with a man named Bradley Forrester. I gave him your details, but he didn't read them back, so I'm not sure how long it'll take for him to get in touch." I hadn't given him the chance to read them back, but it was probably better to let Allison find that out on her own.

She scoffed. "I know Brad. He knows how to get a hold of me. He won't want to, but he can."

I chuckled at the smirk in her voice. "I take it you've gotten the upper hand on him a few times?"

"I have. He's a good guy, just very by-the-book. That makes him great as a government employee, but it also means he doesn't see the ridiculousness sometimes." She sighed. "I can probably talk him out of taking this all the way, though. I guess it depends on what instructions he's been given."

"He seemed surprised that I had counsel. Really wanted to, and I quote, clear this up between the two of us."

"Hm."

My eyebrows lifted. "What's that mean?"

"Not sure. Sounds like he had some kind of deal already in mind. One he doesn't want a whole bunch of people knowing about. He wouldn't have come up with that on his own, though. It would have come from whoever got a case going in the first place."

I nodded, thinking. Orbison would have been the one to get Forrester involved. He was probably pushing for me to still take on the undercover agent as a client. That would give the agent more legitimacy and possibly get the feds in the door. On the flip side, at this point if I did it and Ortega ever found out, not only would I have the cartel gunning for me, it would be very bad for my career. I couldn't be the lawyer who took on clients that were a direct threat to another client. It was why one firm couldn't represent both sides of any case.

"You're quiet."

"Yeah, sorry. I think I know what it is, but I'll let him tell you. If I'm right, though? I can't do it. If that means this gets ugly, then that's what it means."

Allison cleared her throat. "What don't I know?"

"I don't want to get into specifics in case I'm wrong. Let's just say it probably has to do with something that would be a direct conflict with another one of my clients, so privilege comes into play as well."

"Well. This should be fun." Something in the background began to beep. She chuckled. "That's probably Bradley. I'll be in touch."

The call ended and I lowered the handset back to its cradle before taking a deep breath and holding it. I counted to six, then let it out as slowly as I could. It didn't do much to slow my racing heart. So I tried again.

And again.

The fourth time finally seemed to help. At least, it quieted the noise in my mind enough that I could sort of pray. I found myself grateful, yet again, for the reminder in the Bible that when we didn't have words, the Holy Spirit would intercede for us. I needed that right now.

I didn't want to let Faith know, but I also knew better than to keep it to myself until the end of the day. I picked up my cell and tapped her contact.

It rang twice before she answered. "Hey."

"Hey yourself."

She laughed and the sound finished off the de-stressing that deep breathing had started. "Slow day for you, too?"

"Not really? I just got off the phone with a federal attorney."

"Oh." Faith blew out a breath. "Hang on a sec."

After a few seconds, she came back. "Sorry about that. I ducked into the break room."

"You're not alone there, right?"

"No. Megan's still hanging out the whole day. I thought the point of hiring me was so she didn't have to work every possible hour, but so far, she's here not long after I open and just hangs out. Well, that's not completely true. She does office work and some of the stuff that she says she was getting behind on. Anyway, she took the front for a few minutes for me. So tell me."

I took a second to filter through everything Faith had said and analyze the tone. She didn't seem annoyed by Megan being there, so I'd leave it alone. It'd be nice for Faith to make friends with the rest of the group on her own. I wanted her to fit in. To meld, like so far everyone had. So this was good. I cleared my throat and summarized the calls. "So, all told, Allison has it under control, but it may not go away as quickly as I'd hoped."

"Okay. Don't get mad."

"Faith. You know nothing good ever comes after a statement like that." I pinched the bridge of my nose.

"No. I know. And I also pretty much know this is a dumb idea, but I have to say it."

I shut my eyes. "Okay?"

"Should I leave? Just go? It would fix all of this for you. And okay, sure, I'd still have the Ortegas to deal with but they were never your problem in the first place. I hate that they are, now. I can walk away if you need me to."

Her words stabbed like a hundred little knives into my soul. "You can?"

"If you need me to."

"That's not what I want." I wanted her to want to stay. Would we ever get there, or should I give in and cut my losses? I'd thought—hoped—that the time we'd spent sharing my room would have helped her see what it could be like. Honestly, my parents had only left because they said, and I'd agreed, that things were looking up.

"It's not what I want, either." She paused. "Did you think it was?"

I paused. "Yeah, actually. You keep offering. So..."

"I'm sorry. That's not what I'm trying to do. I want to make your life easier. I...care about you."

Some of the tightness in my chest that had been building eased. "My life is easier, and better, with you in it."

She laughed. "That seems impossible, but it's a nice thing to say. Thank you. You're really not worried about this?"

I hadn't said that. At all. The truth was that I *was* worried. But I also knew worrying wasn't going to change anything. Was it better to be honest about that? Honest was always the right choice, according to my parents. Their marriage had lasted a long time. "I'm worried. But I'm trusting that God is going to work things out. Or I'm trying to, at least. We've taken the right steps. We're praying for Him to make it clear what the next steps are. That's all we can do."

"Okay. You're right. It's hard."

"Yeah. It is." I leaned back in my desk chair. "What time do you get off tonight?"

"Six."

"I'll swing by and pick you up. Let's go out to eat." Saying it made it sound even better. In fact, maybe I'd see if I could get us a table somewhere fancier than the places in town.

"That sounds nice. But not Italian, okay? We did that on Friday, with the girls, and I may never look at baked ziti again."

I chuckled. The portions at the Italian place in town were notoriously huge. I always reminded myself to take half home. Because they were also delicious, and I wanted to finish the plate, even though it left me hurting. "Steak?"

"I like steak."

"I'll get us a reservation."

"Reservation?" Her voice took on a twinge of panic. "I'm not dressed for—"

"Don't freak out. I'll handle it." If it meant I had to buy her something to change into and take it with me, well that was just fine. In fact, it might be fun to do. She'd enjoyed shopping in Paris, but hadn't really bought much. Just two outfits. Even then, she'd dithered because of the price tags. "Trust me?"

"More than anyone in my life."

My lips curved. "I'll take it. See you tonight. I love you."

"You too. Bye."

The call ended and I frowned at my phone. You too?

I sighed and dropped my cell on the desk. Maybe it was better than nothing, but it sure wasn't the declaration of love I'd been hoping for since...well, basically since Faith had walked back into my life.

Every night, I held my breath as we neared bedtime, wondering if tonight would be the night Faith chose to go back to the guest room. So far, she hadn't. I hadn't gone in and changed the sheets or anything yet, either. Part of me didn't want to, in case that made it easier for her to leave.

And I really liked having her with me.

Even if she scooted as close to the edge as she could reach without falling off.

Usually, in the middle of the night, she rolled closer and I woke with her in my arms. It took all the self-control I possessed to ease away and out of bed without waking her the way I figured most husbands dreamed of waking their wives. But we weren't there yet.

Please, God, let there be a "yet" at the end of the sentence.

I took comfort in the fact that, subconsciously at least, she wanted to be near me. Besides, she'd said she cared.

And "you too."

I sighed. Maybe it was progress, but it was slow. Patience was hard.

I dragged my attention back to work. I had clients and they deserved my best, regardless of whatever turmoil existed in my personal life.

About an hour before I'd normally end the day, I shut down my computer, locked my files, and grabbed the things I needed to take home. I checked that my office door was locked before heading into the reception area.

"Heading out early?"

I nodded. "I thought I'd take my wife into DC for dinner tonight."

"Your wife?" Arlene blinked several times as she assimilated that information. "Congratulations."

"Thanks. Um. I guess I should give you the long story some-time." I offered a sheepish smile.

Arlene waved it off. "Your business is your business."

"This is more than that, and I'm sorry I haven't kept you in the loop. Her name is Faith and I'll bring her by to say hi sometime soon. Promise." I watched her face and relaxed when she finally nodded, her posture unbending slightly.

"I'd like that. Have a good evening."

"Thanks. If you want to head home, too, you're welcome to lock up and do that."

Arlene checked the time. "I might. Maybe in twenty minutes or so. Thank you. Have a good evening."

"You too." The echo of Faith's words made me wince. Hopefully, she hadn't meant them in the same, breezy casual way I'd just used them. That had been more of a verbal placeholder out of politeness than anything else.

Oh boy. What if Faith thought I'd said something like "see you later" or "have a good one" and so she'd simply responded by default with "you too"? What if that had been reflex rather than inching closer to telling me she loved me back?

I called the restaurant I had in mind from the car. The fact that it was Tuesday worked in our favor and I was able to score a reservation without too much fuss. I never liked to pull the "do you know who I am" bit, and I was grateful that I hadn't needed to.

I probably wouldn't have, honestly. But sometimes I thought about how much easier things might go if I did.

Leaving early meant traffic was lighter. I got home in good time and was able to zip up to the condo to change out of the casual outfit I'd worn to work for a desk day into a suit. The rest of the guys tended to whine about dressing up, but I didn't mind it. Maybe that was from the years at the firm, where suit and tie was the outfit of the day every day. There was no casual anything at the big firms around here.

Even before the money, I'd made the investment in higher quality—and therefore comfortable—suits. That was the key to not hating every minute.

I went into the closet and eyed the section where Faith had

hung her clothes. The outfits I'd gotten her in Paris were neatly stored in the hanging bags that the store had provided with the purchase. I unzipped each one a little so I could tell which was which, then grabbed the hangers for the dark-rose option. I had a tie that would coordinate. And I'd loved it on her when she'd tried it on.

I eyed her small collection of shoes and winced before grabbing a pair that I thought would work. If not, hopefully I'd get points for trying.

I glanced at the time and hurried to finish getting ready. In under five minutes, I was heading back to the elevators and through the parking garage to the car. Another five and I pulled into a sweet spot just one shop down from the bookstore.

I grabbed the hanging bag from the trunk and strode to the store, my steps slowing as I took in the Halloween decorations that filled the front window. Nothing scary. Just campy and fun. Playful spiders with googly eyes and laughing mummies telling knock-knock jokes.

I grinned and pulled open the door, making the bell chime.

"Hey there, stranger." Megan looked up from the book she was reading behind the register. "Been a while since you stopped by."

"Sorry." I fought the urge to hunch my shoulders. Megan knew I preferred to read on my Kindle. Or even my phone. Paper books were fine, but they took up space and they cost more and, unless it was a reference book or something that held a lot of nostalgia, I was much more likely to go the e-book route these days.

"Pfft." She waved it away. "I don't think you could single-handedly save the store."

"Save it? It's that bad?" I looked around again. There were no customers in sight. But it was a Tuesday evening. How busy were bookstores supposed to be?

Megan waggled her hand from side to side. "Cody thinks putting in a coffee bar will help."

"Haven't you been talking about that for a while?"

Megan groaned. "Yes. But I'm scared. I keep going back and forth."

"You should just do it. What do you have to lose?" I looked around the bookstore again. It couldn't get emptier. And Cody would be willing to invest to keep it afloat, if that was what Megan wanted, until the coffee idea had a chance for a good trial. "I thought the local author things were helping."

"They were. Are." She sighed. "Kind of. My problem is that I've been working with local authors who aren't big names. And I haven't been able to catch the eye of the big publishing companies to lure any of the authors who would actually draw a big crowd."

"Have you written them directly to ask?" I didn't know a lot about the publishing world. Or, well, anything, but writing was one of those professions that I often saw lumped into "starving artist" territory.

"No. Do you think it would matter?"

I shrugged. "It's like the coffee thing. What do you have to lose?"

"I guess that's a point. You want to write them for me?"

I laughed. "No. But I happen to know you have a new employee who's actually really good at written communication and was, at one point, interested in marketing. She never got the degree she talked about in high school, but I bet she studied on her own."

Megan's eyebrows lifted. "You mean Faith."

I nodded.

"Why wouldn't she tell me that?"

I didn't know quite how to answer. I knew why—but it felt like talking out of turn to explain. "She's had it rough."

"That's not really—" Megan broke off as Faith came out of the back room.

"Hi." Faith brightened. "I thought I heard your voice."

"I was a little early." I offered the hanging bag of clothes. "I thought you could wear this if you wanted."

Faith peeked in and grinned. "Sure. I'll go change."

Megan waited until Faith closed the back-room door then smirked. "You two are so cute."

"Like puppies."

She laughed. "Pretty much. You really think she could help with getting more notice around here?"

"I do. And I think she'd love to be asked. She'll probably try to deflect at first, though. Be persistent."

Megan nodded. "I've noticed that tendency. All right. I guess I need to pull the trigger on the permits. I've had them saved as drafts for a while. Cody keeps asking about it. What if it doesn't work?"

"Then you'll know for sure?" I leaned on the counter. "Do you really only do things when you're guaranteed an outcome?"

"No." She nodded. "Point taken. Thanks."

"Anytime." We chatted about nothing of consequence while I waited for Faith to change. It didn't take her long to emerge, wearing her French outfit and carrying the hanging bag. "Ready?"

"I am. Do I get a hint about where we're headed?"

"Do you want a hint or just the name of the place?"

Faith laughed. "The name. Definitely."

"Hell's Kitchen."

Her eyes widened and her face radiated excitement. "Really? You're not pulling my leg?"

"I am not. They just opened downtown not long ago. I remember you used to be a big fan of the show."

"Still am." Faith bounced up and down on her toes, then, in a rush, pressed a kiss to my cheek. "Best. Ever."

I laughed and offered my hand. Hopefully, she wouldn't leave me hanging under Megan's watchful eye.

She didn't.

Faith's fingers wove through mine and she squeezed. She glanced at Megan. "I'll see you tomorrow?"

Megan nodded. "Probably not until the afternoon. I think you've got it under control."

"Yeah?"

"Yeah." Megan wiggled her fingers at us. "Go have fun."

"Bye." I kept Faith's hand in mine as I pushed open the door and waited for her to go through. Her reaction to our destination was better than I'd anticipated.

It gave me hope.

24

FAITH

The barista slid the large, teal mug across the counter to me, and I glanced down, then grinned. "Foam art, too?"

The girl nodded. "It's okay?"

"I love it. Maybe it's a tad early for Christmas, but probably not. And honestly, if I got a latte with a fancy Christmas tree in the foam in July, I'd probably still be impressed." I took a second to frame an arty—at least I hoped it was arty—photo of the latte for the store's social media, then picked up the mug and sipped. "Especially when it tastes this good. Nice job, Carrie."

Carrie stopped twisting her fingers together and swiped a hand across her forehead in an exaggerated expression of relief. "Whew. Do you think Megan will agree?"

"She'd be crazy not to. And she's not crazy. You're a find."

Carrie laughed. "Well my mom always says that, but I'll tell you, I was beginning to doubt I'd ever find a job that agreed. My friends all say I'm crazy for turning down the big chain position, but I like working the coffee machines and getting to interact with customers. I think this is going to be ideal. And since my fiancé is good with it, I think I'm in the clear."

"Sounds like it. When are you getting married?" I sipped the coffee again. Megan really had done a great job in the last month getting the coffee and snack bar set up in the back corner of the bookstore. Finding Carrie to man the thing was nothing short of a miracle. And the last month had made me much more willing to believe that God actually cared about the little things in our lives. That probably counted as another miracle.

"We haven't set a date yet. He just proposed last week. He said he was trying to wait until Thanksgiving, but he couldn't take it." Carrie's laugh filled the space and she held out the rock sparkling on her left hand. "I can't say I mind."

I admired her ring. "It's lovely. Congratulations."

"Thanks. I imagine we'll wait until he finishes school in the spring. I graduated over the summer and he's still at Mason." Carrie wet a rag and began wiping down the counter.

"Will you stay in the area?"

"Oh, absolutely. Both our families are here and he's already got a job lined up with a software company in Arlington. My parents said we could rent their basement until we find something affordable, which is huge. The housing prices around here are nuts and neither of us was excited about adding a huge commute if we could avoid it. He gets along great with my folks, though, so it should be fine."

She reminded me of me and Tristan. If my life hadn't been quite so terrible when we got married. And if I'd made smarter choices. I sighed quietly. I'd been overwhelmed with regret about the what-ifs more and more since Tristan had taken me to dinner at Hell's Kitchen. I didn't deserve him—never had—and yet, he seemed content. Happy, even.

"Sounds like you've got a great plan in place."

Carrie beamed.

The bell on the door jingled and I turned.

"Hey. I'm not late." Jenna hustled over to the café space and looked around. "This is amazing. You got this done in what, a month? You're going to be ready for Black Friday shoppers?"

I nodded. "We're officially in operation as of today. That gives us—well, Carrie mostly—a week to work out any kinks. But if everything else is as fantastic as this latte, I don't think there are going to be kinks."

"Ooh. Can I have one?" Jenna's eyebrows lifted. "And we're eating here tonight, right? With the girls? Rather than ordering something else in?"

"I think so. Since Megan found a caterer to provide food offerings every day, it seems like we should take advantage of it. Especially since I think we have to toss everything that isn't eaten each day." I frowned. That seemed wasteful. But after some back-and-forth, Megan hadn't wanted to put in a full kitchen and have someone making food on-site, which meant we also didn't have a lot of food storage space.

"Not all of it." Carrie glanced over her shoulder from where she worked on Jenna's drink. "We have the fridge in the staff area that we plan to use as much as we can. But yeah, that's why we run the risk of selling out right now. We need to work out quantities. The caterer says she can do mid-afternoon deliveries if needed."

I nodded. That was good.

It took only another minute for Jenna's latte to be ready. This time, the foam art looked like an open book.

"Oh, nice." Jenna picked up the drink and sipped. "Yum."

"Thanks." Carrie glanced at me. "I think that'll be my go-to for drinks when we don't have something seasonal going on."

"I like it. I think Megan will, too."

Jenna looked around. "Where is Megan?"

"She should be here soon, I imagine. She's been letting me hold down the fort most days on my own. She comes in around now and works until close. I keep trying to get her to alternate or something, but she says Cody enjoys coming by and hanging out after work, so she doesn't mind." I shrugged. It wasn't my place to tell someone they were doing it wrong when it came to their marriage. If it was working for them, then it was probably all good.

"Hm." Jenna sipped her drink and stepped to the side so she could view the contents of the bakery case better.

I stepped back and looked as well. I'd had a sandwich for lunch. Carrie was coming in right at noon and working until close for now, although I'd made a mental note to talk to Megan about the possibility of tweaking it some. In my mind, it would be better for her to work eleven to two, take a break for a few hours, then come back and work four to seven or so. The chance of someone coming in and wanting a coffee or snack at three or nine was slim. And the snacks could easily be managed by whoever was working the rest of the store. The fancy coffee? Probably not.

Then again, we didn't have a lot of early customers, so maybe this was the better schedule even with the afternoon lull.

Jenna tapped the case and looked at me. "Have you tried the quinoa salad? It looks good."

I glanced at it and wrinkled my nose. "I will admit to being a little scared of the word quinoa."

Jenna snickered. "Don't be a baby."

"Hey."

Jenna just shook her head. "I'll have that and one of the croissants."

"I guess you're hungry?"

"Always." Jenna shrugged. "And if the rest of the girls are going to take their sweet time getting here, I'm going to eat. You should join me."

Before I could make some kind of excuse to delay, my stomach gurgled loudly.

Jenna laughed.

"All right, all right." I eyed the quinoa salad. It did look good —other than the small beady stuff, which was probably the quinoa. But maybe I'd like it. "I'll try the same."

"Do you want to taste the salad first?" Carrie plated Jenna's order and set it on the counter. "I have tasting spoons."

"No. I'll live on the edge. Can you add a double chocolate chunk cookie to mine though? Just in case." If the salad wasn't a win, the cookie and croissant would be enough to get me through until I got home. Tristan and I had ordered Chinese last night, and I knew for a fact that there were pot stickers in the fridge waiting for me.

Carrie plated my food, rang up Jenna, and then me. I tapped my phone to the credit card reader to pay, appreciating again that Megan wasn't scared of technology so I didn't have to go into the back room, dig out my wallet, and pay that way.

"Should we sit at a table or over at the couches?" Jenna held her tray of food.

"Couches." I took my food and started that way.

The door jingled again and Megan came in, followed closely by Whitney, Kayla, and Sunny. My eyebrows lifted.

"Did we miss a memo?" Jenna settled on the couch and set her tray on the low coffee table.

"No. We ran into each other on the street." Megan waved that off. "Oh good! You're trying the food. How is it?"

"Don't know yet, but the lattes are amazing. Plus the foam art is on point." Jenna ripped one end off of her croissant and popped it into her mouth. "Bread's good, too."

I chuckled as I took my seat. I was getting more comfortable with this group of women, but there was part of me that wanted to hold back. Probably the same part that kept me holding back from Tristan, too. Dumb. I wasn't going to think about it now, though. Right now? I was going to enjoy my food and listen to this group of friends talk about their lives and handle any customers who might wander into the bookstore on a Friday night.

It only took a few minutes for the rest of the group to get their food and join us at the couches. There were lots of yummy noises as people took their first bites. I finally worked up my courage to try the quinoa salad and...it wasn't horrible.

I didn't see myself wanting it on any kind of regular schedule, but I could eat it tonight without it being a "choke it down" scenario. So I'd take it. But I also couldn't stop a wistful side-eye at the roast beef sandwich that Whitney had chosen.

"Okay. This is fantastic. Why didn't you add a café sooner?" Kayla pointed her fork at Megan. "Prices are amazing. Food's great. You're going to be a smash."

"You don't know that." Megan hunched her shoulders. "I agree that it's tasty, but people have to come in here to know that."

"We're starting to get more browsers since we started up the Instagram page." I cleared my throat. "When you're sure about the café being ready, I'll work food photos in. I've already taken some."

"Do it. In fact," Megan frowned at the coffee table where we'd all put our food. She gestured to it. "Can you do something with this to give the idea that it's okay to come, eat, and hang out for a little bit with friends?"

I nodded. "Of course."

I studied the table then stood. I took away the trays and moved things around a little, arranging forks so they looked more like the owner had just stepped away. When it was more pleasing to my eye, I adjusted my position and took a couple of shots.

"Can we eat now? Some of us are hungry." Kayla laughed as she rubbed her baby bump. "I cannot wait for Christmas."

"Or earlier. You know babies come when they want." Whitney's gaze held a tiny glint of sadness. "And honestly, you're not the only one looking forward to this. I can't wait to hold him. Or her. Tell me again why you refuse to do a gender reveal?"

"Because they're ridiculous?" Kayla rolled her eyes.

"Okay, you don't have to do a big party, but you could at least find out." Whitney bit into her sandwich.

"We will. When the baby's born. Surprise!" Kayla made jazz hands.

Whitney snorted. "Are you narrowing down names?"

"Oh my gosh." Kayla turned to Megan. "Did you know your brother is a nightmare?"

Megan's eyebrows lifted. "You were his best friend how long and didn't figure that out?"

"I never talked to him about naming children, strangely enough."

Megan laughed. "What's he doing?"

Kayla reached for her chicken salad sandwich and took a bite. She held up a finger as she chewed. When she had swallowed, she wiped a corner of her mouth then said, "He says he has to see the baby before he'll agree on a name."

"Oh. Well, that makes sense." Megan nodded. "I thought he was doing something dumb."

"What?" Kayla's mouth hung open. "You don't seriously support this madness."

Kayla's gaze darted around the group. "Please tell me you all don't think this is reasonable."

"Meh." Jenna shrugged. "I can kind of see where he's coming from. How do you know if the baby is a Joshua until you see him? Maybe he looks like a Fred."

"If he looks like a Fred, you're better off naming him Joshua and hoping he grows into the name." I slapped my hand over my mouth. "Sorry. That was supposed to stay inside."

"All this time, and I didn't realize you had snarky in you." Whitney nodded slowly. "You definitely fit in. I'm glad."

Sunshine chuckled. "Pretty sure I didn't look like Sunshine. Not sure I do yet. And still, here we are. A name's a name. Just choose some, put them on a list, and tell Austin to choose from them after he sees the kid. Everyone wins."

Megan shot a finger at Sunshine. "Perfect solution."

Kayla frowned. "Jenna?"

"I plead the fifth."

"No. No way. Do none of you understand that I need to know what the names are going to be?" Kayla set her food down and crossed her arms.

"Why the names and not the gender?" I didn't understand at all how she was okay with leaving the gender a surprise until birth but wanted to nail down two complete names beforehand. "Wouldn't it be smarter, if you're all gung-ho about the name, to know what kind of names to choose? Unless you're going neutral there. Which you could be, I guess. Robin. Pat."

Jenna snorted and coffee leaked out of her nose. "Ugh. Not when I'm drinking."

I laughed. "Sorry."

"We aren't naming the baby Pat. Or Robin." Kayla scowled at me. "Maybe I need new friends."

Megan mouthed the word "hormones" and I fought a laugh.

"Don't think I don't know what you just did." Kayla smacked Megan's arm. "Austin is all about blaming my reasonable requests on hormones these days, too. Also? You, of all people, should talk."

"Hmm. Like what requests?" Whitney took the last bite of her sandwich. "I think we need an example to see if they're reasonable."

"Cheese fries. I can't be held responsible for needing cheese fries at all hours of the day, can I?" Kayla's eyes brimmed with tears. "And he gets them, I'll give him that, but I know he's making fun of me."

"Pretty sure he's not." Megan rubbed Kayla's leg. "When did you last get good sleep?"

"Nine months ago." Kayla's response was a watery mumble as she wiped at her eyes. "I know I'm ridiculous. I do."

"It's okay. I'll be there before you know it." Megan leaned back in her seat. "I'll take it over the constant nausea though."

Ugh. Was everyone going to start sharing pregnancy stories now? Although, really only Kayla and Megan could. To my knowledge, none of the rest of us had any experience to offer.

"You say that now." Kayla sighed heavily. "Sorry, girls. Now you see why I'm ready for the baby to be here. Let's change the subject. Has everyone figured out what they're bringing to Thanksgiving yet?"

I listened as the conversation turned to a heated discussion of required versus optional Thanksgiving dishes. I slipped my phone out of my pocket and texted Tristan.

> Are we doing Thanksgiving with your friends?

I didn't expect him to answer right away. The guys were all over at his—our—condo playing poker tonight. My phone buzzed almost immediately.

> I meant to talk to you about that. They're all flying down to Wes's island on Wednesday. The main house is finished and he wanted to show it off. You want to go?

I bit my lip and clicked off my phone. I didn't know how to answer the question. Part of me did. I liked Tristan's friends. And they seemed to be okay with me. He'd get annoyed with me for phrasing it that way, insisting that there was no "seem to be" involved. But it was a hard habit to shake.

"You're coming, right?" Sunshine's voice was low.

I hadn't noticed her move closer. I lifted a shoulder. "Not sure. This is the first I've heard. I don't know what Megan's plans are for the store. Closed Thursday, obviously, but she really needs to be open on Friday. There's enough retail on this street that she'll miss out on a lot if it's not open. Especially since I thought that was going to be the café hard launch. She probably needs me?"

"I think everyone but me and Wes are planning on flying back Thursday evening. Wes just wants to show off the house and take everyone through his plans in person for turning the island into a scuba destination. We're only staying an extra day. Maybe two. Not long enough for any of us to dive, anyway." Sunshine sighed. "Unfortunately."

"How come?" I'd never been diving, so I trusted that there were reasons, but I couldn't imagine what they were.

"Decompression sickness. You really shouldn't fly for a full twenty-four hours after diving. I always try to wait thirty-six. Wes is the same. There's just no point in risking it. Especially when we have such a beautiful place to stay and relax above the water to do it. But I have to say I'm itching to start exploring the reefs around the island more." Sunshine leaned forward and put her empty cup on the coffee table. "And I'm a little homesick."

"Homesick?" I'd pieced together some of Sunshine's history, but obviously I missed something. "I thought it was an island Wes owned? Other people live there?"

She chuckled. "No. Just the Caribbean in general. We were going to try to stop in and see my bestie, Zee, but she's actually going to be stateside for the holiday. My other friends are also busy. It happens. Heck, it happened when I lived in the islands. So many people leave to avoid the tourists, if their jobs allow it."

That made sense. "Tristan says the same about DC. He says he starts avoiding the National Mall and that area whenever possible during holidays, spring break, and the summer. Which basically translates to never going downtown, I guess."

Whitney leaned forward, breaking out of the conversational bubble the other women had formed. "I'm that way, too. No way I'm dragging Beckett around to see museums when I have to fight with school groups. You'll learn the rhythms as you get used to the area. Sometimes it's worth braving the crowds. I was so glad we hit the cherry blossom festival last year. I definitely want to do that again this year. The photos of Beckett surrounded by all the delicate pink flowers are precious."

"I've seen photos of the cherry blossoms near the monuments. They're stunning." I made a mental note to ask Tristan if we could plan to go down and see them in person. "Is that in March?"

Whitney waggled a hand from side to side. "Ish. It varies a little every year depending on weather and so forth. They plan the festival, but the trees don't care and bloom whenever. When we're close, you'll hear the status on just about every radio news report."

"I'll keep an ear out."

Kayla tipped her head to the side. "Does that mean you're sticking around?"

I blinked.

"Don't look surprised. Should I not have asked?" Kayla looked between Megan and Whitney.

"Maybe with a little more finesse." Megan hissed under her breath. She shot me an apologetic smile. "But we are all wondering."

"I want to. I just don't know what Tristan really wants. Maybe when we know what's happening with the government lawsuit, I'll have more information." I wasn't going to share that my safety from the Ortegas hinged on being married to Tristan. That wasn't pressure I was going to put on him, either. His need to be a knight on a white charger was too strong, and I didn't want us to stay married simply because I needed saving. Again.

Jenna frowned at me. "Why won't you recognize that he loves you? I saw it in Paris. I thought you did, too."

The weight of all their stares was heavy. So heavy it ought to have pushed me into the ground, and honestly that would have been an amazing relief. I cleared my throat. "Sometimes that's not enough."

Kayla scoffed.

"No." Megan held up a hand. "She's not entirely wrong. Do you love him?"

"I do." There was no point in trying to hedge. I'd been trying to gather the courage to tell Tristan. He'd said it to me. I was a big chicken and had yet to respond in kind. I was holding out hope that maybe if he kissed me it would loosen the words from where they got stuck in my chest, but so far, we shared a bed— chastely—and a few light touches. And that was it.

"Then Kayla's right. You're being ridiculous. Take matters into your own hands. Tell the man you love him and you want your marriage to..." Megan paused and waved her hands around.

"I'm not versed in whatever sign language that is." I raised my eyebrows. "What am I supposed to tell him?"

Megan stuck her tongue out at me. "Fine. It's probably tricky. And yet, I believe you can do it. Start with 'I love you' and go from there. You're already married, so you can just see where it goes."

I sighed. "It'll never work. He hasn't kissed me properly since I came back."

All of the ladies looked shocked.

Sunshine patted my knee. "Maybe he's scared."

I nodded. "Probably. But I don't know how to fix it."

"Can I be blunt?" Jenna shifted so she was facing me.

"Can I stop you?"

She grinned. "Not really."

I closed my eyes. "Yeah, all right. Hit me."

"You ran away back in college, right? Then again after you sought him out here in September. So chances are high that he's waiting to see if you're really going to stay."

I nodded. Jenna had a point. One I'd gotten to on my own, thanks so much. There was just one problem. "I don't know how I prove that I'm not running away again except by not doing it. Which I haven't."

"You need to do something symbolic." Jenna drummed her fingers on her knee. "Like give him a box of sneakers in your size like that one movie with Julia Roberts."

"Ugh. I hated that one." I scowled. "Wait. Do you think I'm like her?"

They were all suspiciously silent. Wow.

Thankfully, the bell above the door jingled. I jumped to my feet.

"Oh, no. You're off the clock." Megan stood and pointed at me. "Sit down in your *Runaway Bride* glory and figure out how to convince Tristan you're staying without being cheesy."

I slumped back into my seat. "Are you girls always like this?"

"This is what friends do. We tell each other the truth." Jenna tipped her head to the side.

Whitney nodded. "Even when the truth is annoying."

Kayla chuckled. "Maybe especially then."

I would have liked to have said something witty and cutting, but I couldn't come up with anything. At the end of the day, they were right. And I owed Tristan that same unadorned honesty.

25

TRISTAN

I was dumping out the vacuum cleaner bin when I heard the door open. "Is that you, Faith?"

"No. It's a robber."

I laughed at the tease in Faith's voice. Sure, it was a dumb question, but it was a reflex. A dumb one, apparently. "Well, I don't have a lot of easily portable things, but you're welcome to whatever you can find."

Faith snickered as she came into the kitchen. "You vacuumed at eleven p.m.?"

"The guys are messy when chips are involved. I don't like to let it sit." I clicked the canister back into the main body of the vacuum and pressed the cord rewind button. "It only takes a minute."

I couldn't decipher the look she gave me. Was it wrong to be tidy? She hadn't complained before, and it wasn't as if the condo magically cleaned itself. I'd caught her doing a chore here or there—but most of them had been me. Which was fine. I was used to it.

I cleared my throat. "Did you have fun?"

Faith opened the fridge and grabbed a can of ginger ale. She popped the top and took several long swallows.

"Uh-oh." I rolled the vacuum over against the wall. I could put it away later. This seemed...serious. I walked to the living room and sat on the couch, then patted the seat beside me. "What happened?"

"It wasn't *bad*." Faith frowned. After a moment, she joined me in the living room, but sat in a chair facing me. "They're very honest."

"They are. The guys are, too. It's something we all value." I tried to figure out where this was going. "Were they unkind?"

"No. Nothing like that. I guess it's just..." Faith trailed off.

I waited, even though it took everything I had not to fill in the silence with a prompt. I really wanted her to like my friends. To fit in with them. Honestly, I'd been hoping this whole time that the ladies and their Friday night gatherings would be another check in the column of pros. One more thing that might convince her to stay.

I wanted her to stay.

I wanted her to love me the way I loved her.

Step one, though? She had to stay.

It felt like hours had passed, but it wasn't actually that long before she continued.

"They said something that got me thinking." She leaned forward and set her soda can on the coffee table. "Have you heard anything from Allison lately? About the case? The FBI?"

The girls had talked about the deal with the FBI? "You know, technically, that's not something we're supposed to be doing a lot of talking about. I guess it's okay with the girls, but I haven't even really filled the guys all the way in."

She shot me a confused glance, then her lips morphed into an O. "No. Sorry. I haven't said anything to them. That's not what

—the thing they said brought the FBI situation to mind. I've been getting good at pretending it doesn't exist."

That made a little more sense. "I have been, too. Allison called today, actually, just to say that she expected to have a resolution on Monday one way or the other."

"Why didn't you call and tell me?"

"I honestly don't know. I was going to, then I got another call from a client and the day kept rolling like that. Before I knew it, I had to hurry to get here before the guys showed up. I'm sorry." I could have added—maybe should have—that I'd spent a lot of years operating solo. Looping her in didn't necessarily come naturally.

She nodded slowly. "Okay. That makes sense. Do you have any idea what she means?"

I shook my head. "Not really. I hope it means that she's convinced them that this suit isn't going to go anywhere. and they need to drop it."

"Do you think it's likely?"

"I have no idea. It's the government, so who knows. They seem to do what they want with no rhyme or reason behind it." I tipped my head to the side. "Can we go back to the girls' night? You don't have to go if you don't want to. I'll just put that out. I can pull the condo out of the rotation for poker so you always have a quiet space to call home on Fridays if that's what you want."

Her eyes lit, then filled. She looked away. "I don't deserve you."

My heart sank. I'd made the offer in good faith, and I'd follow through. But I couldn't envision life without my friends. I'd always thought that if Faith came back, she'd slide seamlessly into the group. The times we'd been together so far, it had all seemed to go well.

"I'll let the guys know. I'm sorry they're not a fit." I swallowed and hoped those words had come out with the cheer I'd been aiming for. There was no need to dump my disappointment on her. We could make new friends. Friends who knew us as a couple. Couldn't we? Maybe if I followed back up with the animal shelter and we really went ahead and rescued a dog, we could meet other dog people and go from there.

"Wait. What?" She frowned at me. "I don't care if you have poker here. Why would I?"

"I thought you were agreeing that you'd like to have the condo free on Friday nights."

Her eyebrows knit together. "When did I say that?"

"I offered it. You got teary and said you didn't deserve me—I disagree, by the way—but didn't that mean you liked the idea?" I rubbed the back of my neck. I was usually pretty good at reading people. It was a skill I worked on. It came in handy for clients and when I had to go to court. But Faith? She was a mystery.

She chuckled. "No. I'm sorry. That's not it at all. I love that you'd offer. That's what I meant. You take care of me. Always. And I don't understand it or deserve it, but I appreciate it."

I leaned forward and reached across the coffee table to grasp her hands. "I love you. That's the why. It's the only reason I need."

Faith took a deep breath, and her gaze locked with mine. "I love you, too."

I closed my eyes as relief coursed through me. "You mean it?"

"I do." She squeezed my hands.

I stood, stepped around the coffee table, and pulled her into my arms.

She laughed. "Tristan!"

I spun, holding her tight. "Does this mean you'll stay for me? Not just because of the Ortegas?"

Faith pushed away slightly. I set her back on the ground. She looked up and met my gaze. "Yeah. That's what I want."

I pulled her close again and rested my cheek on the top of her head. I wanted to kiss her more than anything, but this felt so fragile and new, I didn't want to make her change her mind.

We stood like this, every heartbeat a pulse of joy that I hoped God understood was gratefulness for His work in our lives. I had hoped He would bring us here—but I'd struggled to believe that it wasn't an unreachable end.

Faith eased back. She searched my gaze before clearing her throat. "See the mountains kiss high heaven. And the waves clasp one another; No sister-flower would be forgiven if it disdained its brother; And the sunlight clasps the earth and the moonbeams kiss the sea: What is all this sweet work worth if thou kiss not me?"

I blinked. If she was going to quote poetry, who was I to argue? Throwing caution to the wind, I lowered my lips to hers.

And that was the last conscious thinking either of us did for quite some time.

The next morning, I slipped out of bed, pausing to watch Faith's slow and steady breathing for a moment before heading into the kitchen to start the coffee. I hummed quietly as I puttered around getting the beans ground, filling the water, and pushing the button to brew. Should I scramble some eggs?

I pulled open the fridge and peered inside. I wasn't big on eggs for breakfast. Neither, really, was Faith. But I'd love to do something special to start our first day together where we were both—finally—on the same page.

Could a bowl of cereal do that?

I wrinkled my nose and shut the fridge.

Maybe I could convince her to go out for brunch.

That was a winning idea. The more I thought about it, the happier I was. Then, maybe we could spend the day walking the path along the river. The weather looked nice, for all we were nearing the end of November. The real cold didn't usually come until after Christmas or January. Even then, it didn't stick around forever.

Or we could rent bikes and ride the path down to Mount Vernon. That might be even more fun.

I grabbed my phone off the charger and opened a browser. I'd suggested it before without having all the details hammered out. We'd ended up flying to Paris instead. Today, Paris wasn't a reasonable option. So I needed details.

There weren't a ton of bike rental locations, but there was one within walking distance that would work. I browsed over to the Mount Vernon website to look at the restaurant page. The fancier place—not the food court—had a weekend brunch. I grinned. That sealed it, as far as I was concerned.

If Faith didn't want to bike, we could drive down. Maybe she'd enjoy getting tickets and touring the house and grounds. The gardens wouldn't be anything to speak of at this time of year, but at least it wouldn't also be blisteringly hot and humid like it was in the summer. So much of Mount Vernon was open. No shade. So touring the grounds was a sweat-fest.

My parents still tried to drag me there every time they visited in the summer. At this point, I figured it was purely to see how long it would be before I started to whine. Of course, I could get my revenge with the museum near the entrance. There were so many wonderful movies and short videos to experience, not to mention interactive displays. I could—and did—spend hours there.

Plus? Air conditioning.

The coffee finally finished. I poured two mugs and fixed them to our varying tastes, then carried them down the hall to the bedroom.

Faith slept on.

I set the coffee on the nightstand closest to her side, then leaned down and oh-so-gently pressed my lips to hers.

She sighed and sleepily returned the kiss. Her hand lifted and curved around the back of my neck, drawing me closer.

The coffee had cooled considerably by the time we got to it.

"Good morning." Faith was sitting back against the headboard, cradling her mug. "Thanks for the coffee."

"You're welcome." I sipped my own and couldn't regret the temperature. "What do you think you'd like to do today?"

"Hm. It's Saturday. I don't have work. You don't have work?" She glanced at me.

I shook my head.

"Then we should definitely do something together. Did you have something in mind?" Her eyes sparkled as they met mine.

I cleared my throat. I wasn't going to turn down the invitation she was giving. But also, I kind of liked the brunch plan. "How do you feel about Mount Vernon and brunch?"

"I like brunch." Faith took another long drink of coffee. "Mount Vernon would be cool, too."

"Do you want to bike down there and back?"

"You have bikes? Plural?" She frowned. "Why?"

I laughed. "I don't even have a bike singular. But we can rent some. I found a place not far from here."

She was quiet a moment as she studied me. "You've been thinking about this a while, I guess?"

"While the coffee brewed." Maybe it was a dumb idea. "We can just drive."

"No. I didn't say that. The bike idea is intriguing. What sparked it? I don't remember you being a big bike rider when we were teens."

I shifted, trying to find a comfortable place for my head against the headboard. I didn't do a lot of sitting in bed, and this was why. "I rode as much as the next kid, I think. At least until I could drive."

A small smile played at the corners of her mouth and it was all I could do not to lean over and kiss her again. "You did love your car."

"Still do. To be honest."

"I know."

I set my coffee aside and crossed my arms. "How? How do you know?"

"It's pristine. And the one time I even thought about asking to drink something not water in it, I could feel your disapproval before the words came out." She tipped her mug up before setting it on the night stand.

"I'm not that bad." I scowled. "Since when is wanting a car that's not full of trash a bad thing?"

"It isn't." Faith leaned over and kissed me quickly, then moved out of reach before I could respond. "But you're fussy about your car. Just like you were in high school."

"I object to the term fussy."

"Overruled."

"Oh, ha ha. Look who's so clever."

Faith bounced out of bed. "I do my best. If we're going to Mount Vernon, I want a shower." She paused halfway to the bathroom. "Do you really want to ride bikes?"

I lifted a shoulder. "I don't know. It sounded fun. But we could do that another time. Just ride along the river."

She nodded. "I like that idea better. I'm not sure the last time I was on a bicycle. And I'm not convinced I want to walk around a historical home after rigorous exercise."

People did it all the time. But I could also see her point. And if we did go ahead and tour all the gardens and grounds, we'd be doing a lot of walking. Getting on bikes for a thirteen mile or so trek home after was probably not the best plan. "Fair enough. Go get ready. I'll shower when you're done."

She disappeared into the bathroom. I grabbed my empty coffee mug, slid out of bed and went around to her side to grab that one, then headed back out to the kitchen. I rinsed the mugs and set them in the dishwasher, then walked over to the windows that looked out over the river.

For the first time in a long time, everything in my life felt like it was right.

Neither of us hurried to get ready, so it was well after ten when we made our way out of the condo and down to my car.

My car.

I frowned as I held open the passenger door for Faith.

"What's that look for?" She paused as she was sliding into the seat. "Did you remember you had something else planned? It's okay if we can't do brunch."

"No. Nothing like that. I just realized, we should get you a car."

"I have a car." Faith gestured to the beat-up death trap she'd driven here.

I scoffed. "That hardly qualifies."

"It works. Mostly."

I pointed at her. "Exactly."

She finished getting in and I closed the door, then went around to my side.

"Will you let me get you something else? Something better?" I glanced over at her as I fastened my seat belt. "Please?"

"I don't think I need one. I can walk to the bookstore."

I started the engine and backed out of the spot. "Sure. But it's going to get cold in another couple of weeks. And the summer is hot and muggy. Not to mention rain, sleet, snow."

"You left off gloom of night." She laughed as she said it.

"You kid, but tell me honestly you felt one hundred percent

safe walking home last night after girls' night." I checked both ways, then pulled out of the parking garage and started toward the road that would carry us along the river to Mount Vernon.

Faith stayed silent.

"You're quiet."

She sighed. "You have a point. But my car is really fine. I have money and can fix it up if I need. I also thought about buying a bike, believe it or not."

"I have money, too." I glanced over at her. "Or we could go halfsies."

"Halfsies?"

"What? It's a word."

"It's absolutely not a word." She shook her head. "At least I think I understand what you're getting at. And as awful as you may think me, I guess I'd like that better."

I nodded. "Okay."

"Just like that?"

I shrugged. "Sure. You have money, like you said. Now that the Ortegas are out of the picture, there's no reason you can't access all of it, right? So if you feel better splitting the cost of a car, I'll feel better knowing you're driving something completely reliable."

"Okay." She turned her head and looked past me. "Is that the bike trail?"

"Yeah. It's pretty, isn't it?"

"It's not flat."

I chuckled. "Virginia isn't flat."

"Well, sure. But I just thought...you know what, never mind. I'll simply say I'm extra glad that we aren't biking today. I think I probably need to do a lot of shorter trips and get back in shape."

I glanced over at the trail. "That's fair. We can rent bikes once and make sure we like it. If we do and it's something we're going to do, we can invest in our own. Sound good?"

"It does." She paused. "Since we're making future plans..."

I waited, but she didn't continue. I slowed as we hit the change in speed limit that announced we were nearing the giant roundabout in front of Mount Vernon. "What?"

"Did you ever decide about getting a dog?"

I shook my head. "It's been busy. And honestly, I mostly wanted a dog so I wouldn't be so lonely if you left."

Faith reached over and rested her hand on my leg. "Sorry."

"Don't be. We're good. Right?" I glanced over and frowned slightly at her expression. "Is there something else?"

"Well. We never talked about kids. Not back in high school, at least."

I slowed further and turned into one of the parking lots for the mansion. There were already several cars parked—eager tourists determined to get a head start on the day. Or locals with the same plan we had. George Washington was a draw any time of year, for practically any reason.

I eased the car into an empty spot and parked. "I've always wanted them."

"Okay."

Okay? That was not as encouraging an answer as I'd hoped. "It doesn't have to be tomorrow though. Do *you* want kids?"

Faith winced. "Would you believe I haven't really thought about it? With Megan expecting. And Kayla. Last night, there was a lot of baby talk interspersed in there. Sunny took it all in stride, though she made a few jokes about her age. But honestly, she could probably still have one or two if she wanted. Whitney just kind of hung back, which from what Megan's told me made sense. But Megan didn't say, and I didn't know how to ask, why they don't adopt."

I pushed open my car door and climbed out. Faith got out of her side and joined me as we started toward the entrance. She reached out and took my hand.

I glanced down at our interlaced fingers and smiled. "I don't know. I haven't wanted to push. Scott doesn't offer much information. I figure something like that is private."

"Of course. Sorry. You know I like to have details."

I brushed a kiss to the top of her head. "It's not a bad thing."

We walked across the lot and around to the arched entryway that led to the low-slung brick building where we could purchase tickets. I paid our fees, including snagging two spots on a house tour in about an hour, and we went through into the museum, greeted as all visitors were by a bronze statue of George and Martha. Their hands and noses had been touched and rubbed by so many patrons that they sparkled brightly against the patina of the rest of the sculpture.

Faith dragged me over to stand beside them, then tugged her cell phone free and angled it out in front of us. "Smile."

I laughed and looked into the camera. She'd framed us perfectly with the Washingtons. She took the picture and adjusted the angle for another. At the last second, I shifted and lowered my mouth to hers.

She nudged me in the ribs.

"What? I figure if we're taking selfies now, they ought to be good ones."

She tapped the camera app and pulled up the photo of us kissing.

I nodded. "See? It's perfect."

"I'm not going to argue." Faith turned off her phone and put it back in her pocket. "Come on. Let's go soak up some history."

26

FAITH

"Someone's happy." Megan leaned against the checkout counter and beamed at me. "It's nice to see you can smile for more than three seconds at a time. You had a good weekend, I assume?"

My grin widened and I nodded. "I did. We did. We went to Mount Vernon on Saturday."

"Oh yeah, George and Martha always leave me giddy." Sarcasm dripped off Megan's words and she propped an elbow on the counter and leaned closer. "You don't have to tell me, but I can't promise not to be hurt if you don't."

I laughed. "Subtle."

"Never claimed to be." Megan's gaze drifted over to the café in the back corner of the bookstore. There were a handful of people sitting with drinks reading or chatting. "Why didn't I do that sooner?"

"Fear of change?" I fought the urge to hunch my shoulders under the glare she shot my way. "What? I make a lot of decisions based on a fear of change. Or I did. I'm going to stop. Looks like you are, too."

"You know what? You're right. I am. We are. This was good.

And even if it doesn't work out long term, I'm glad that I took the chance."

I sifted through the words, then nodded. "Exactly. Although I'm banking on long term."

"I get the feeling you're talking about Tristan and not coffee."

"Guilty." I sighed happily. "After Friday night, when everyone was so mean to me—"

"Hey." Megan interjected. "We aren't mean."

I made a humming sound. "Anyway, it made me and Tristan talk—for real—and put all our cards on the table. Speaking of which, why don't the ladies play poker with the men? I like poker."

Megan laughed. "That is a can of worms we have all tried to open and then given up on. But there's nothing stopping us from breaking out the cards when we're hanging out."

"We should. Then we can organize a co-ed night and clean their clocks."

Megan shook her head. "You think we would? I know Cody's pretty good. I haven't actually ever played poker."

"For real?" I brushed away her objection. "I'll teach you. It's easy."

Megan looked skeptical. "Back to you and Tristan. What does having those cards out mean? Be specific."

I shook my head, chuckling. "It means we're married. And we're going to stay that way. And not because of outside forces, but because we want to."

I could tell Megan wanted to ask about the outside forces, but I was saved from having to dodge by a customer and her armful of books. The look Megan sent as she headed back to the office worried me slightly. I'd need to ask Tristan what we were telling his—our—friends about the whole Ortega thing.

And that would all be easier if we had closure on the legal end of things.

I pushed the thoughts away and smiled at the woman. "Did you find everything all right?"

"I did. I don't know how I missed this place before! And to use the Stephen King quote in the name of the store is so clever." She beamed and set the stack of books down. "I'll be back. Probably tomorrow, honestly, because the coffee is amazing. And the brownies. Although I can't eat those every day or I'll be waddling inside of a week. The local and indie authors section is so fun—I'll be sharing that with some friends."

I grinned and rang up the books, letting the woman prattle on. She didn't seem to need more than an occasional nod or grunt of agreement, and that was easy enough to provide. Even better? She didn't blink at the final total—just tapped her credit card to the machine while she continued to gush.

"I put a calendar of store events in the bag. We have author readings and signings often, as well as some fun events for kids. And there will be sales starting Friday going through Christmas that you won't want to miss." I slid the bag of books across to her. "Thanks for coming in."

"Thank you!" She peeked in the bag, grinned, and then headed for the door.

I had just enough time to shoot Tristan a text asking about how much I could say to Megan before another customer approached with a pile of books.

Between the steady stream of customers and going through the shelves to straighten books and note what needed restocking, the rest of my afternoon passed quickly. For once, I was actually anxious to leave on time. To go home.

How long had it been since I'd had a real home? One I was excited to get to?

Too long.

I knocked on the office door before entering to grab my stuff. "I'm off."

Megan looked up from the computer and frowned. "Already?"

Her gaze darted to the clock on the wall.

"Yeah. It's time. But business was good today. I think the café is going to be a winner. I left restocking notes for shelves that are looking bare if I couldn't find anything in storage that would go there. When did you last do inventory?"

Megan winced. "I'm behind. I'll bump it up on the list if I have downtime tonight."

"Okay. If there's a way for me to help, let me know." I gathered my things. "Have a good night."

"You too." Megan lifted a hand before returning her attention to the computer.

I pulled the door to the office closed behind me and did a quick scan of the store. It wasn't crowded and the few people left seemed happy to be engrossed in their coffee and treats. Hopefully, Megan would come out before anyone needed help.

If things kept up this way, she was really going to need to think about another full-time employee. She needed to be focused on the business details, not trying to do it all. I wasn't sure if I had the rapport with her to mention that, but I'd think about it.

I exited the store and started down the sidewalk toward home. There was a wet chill in the air that hadn't been there this morning. The sun had set—thanks daylight savings—and a wrinkle of unease settled in my gut.

Maybe I did need a car. Or at least to start driving the one I had. Tristan was right, though. It wasn't super reliable. Which meant maybe tonight we could do some looking online to see what I might want to buy. I was definitely going to pay half. That was nonnegotiable. I'd prefer to pay it all, but I didn't want it enough to have a big fight with Tristan about it.

He was a billionaire.

I still couldn't wrap my mind around that fully. Not even after the trip to Paris and the luxury boutique hotel. The money I made paled in comparison to that. But I could afford a car. And I was going to keep my job at the bookstore for as long as Megan let me. I didn't want to be a kept woman.

I never had.

But maybe I'd think about going to college. Now that I wasn't trying to stay off anyone's radar, I could do anything.

I paused at the corner and watched the traffic. The street-lights kept everything bright, and there were crowds heading out to hit the nightlife even on a weeknight. But still, nerves twisted in my belly. I was being ridiculous.

How many nights had I walked this route without any issue? Often, it was even later than now, when rush hour traffic still clogged the streets with tired commuters heading home.

The light changed and I stepped into the crosswalk.

A car blazed through the red light. The driver of the first car off the line now that his light was green leaned on his horn. I had just enough time to register the noise before a blast of pain and a sense of flying.

Then? Nothing.

THERE WAS an elephant sitting on my chest.

And my hand hurt.

Beep...beep...beep

Was it dark? I grunted and the pressure on my chest eased some even as the constriction of my hand increased.

"Faith?"

I knew that voice. I struggled to open my eyes. "Ngh."

"Shh." Tristan clenched my hand—how had he managed that—and leaned in to kiss my forehead. "I'll call the nurse."

"Wha—" I paused, cleared my throat, and tried again. "What happened? Did I...did I get hit by a car?"

That couldn't be right, could it?

Tristan's expression turned stony. "You did. Thankfully, the car that almost got hit first saw what happened and kept them from driving away. Which they were trying to do."

My eyebrows lifted. "Who would do that?"

I tugged my hand free and stretched my fingers.

Tristan blanched. "I'm sorry. I've been so worried. You've been out about three hours."

"Is that bad?" If I knew anything about car accidents and head injuries, I couldn't come up with it right now. And that might be bad. Or it could just mean that I'd been hit by a car.

"The doctors said it's normal. Do you hurt? I really can call the nurse." Tristan hovered—and wasn't that ridiculous—indecisively.

I took a minute to listen to my body. I couldn't say I felt like getting up and dancing, but I wasn't actively hurting. I glanced down the bed and noticed the absence of casts. "Nothing broken? How is that possible?"

"God. That's all I can say. You should be in worse shape. They thought you'd have a spinal injury, but the swelling is already going down and they've ruled it out. You're going to stay here tonight. Just to be sure."

"Oh but—"

"No. Don't even try. I'm staying with you. And you're staying here."

I frowned. If I was okay, shouldn't I be able to go home? I was going to object again when I truly zeroed in on Tristan's face. I'd never seen him this pale and drawn. Though he'd come close the night he convinced me to marry him as a solution to my problems.

The fight left me. "Okay."

"Good. Thank you." He swallowed and lowered his head to our clasped hands. "I was so scared."

"I'm sorry."

He looked up. "Don't be. This isn't on you. Remember that."

"I didn't mean—" Anything I would have added was cut off by Tristan's kiss. Though it was gentle, he was able to convey his worry and relief more clearly than I'd imagined possible. It left me feeling relieved.

And cherished.

But then, Tristan had always made me feel cherished.

Maybe that was why I had such a hard time believing in us. I'd never had someone care for me like that.

"I love you." I cleared my throat as my eyes filled.

His lips curved. "I love you, too."

It's impossible to truly rest in a hospital, so I was glad when, finally, the nurses came the next day to let me know my discharge was in process. Even so, it was another two hours before Tristan was gently loading me into his car and heading us back toward home.

"I think maybe you're right."

He glanced over, his eyes dancing. "I like how this is going."

I slapped his arm lightly, then winced. Maybe I wasn't quite up to quick movements like that. For all I hadn't broken anything, I was sore in places I didn't know I had.

"What am I right about?"

I sighed. "I should drive to the bookstore. And my car is probably not reliable enough. So will you help me buy a new car? But nothing flashy, okay? Just reliable. Maybe electric? Or hybrid? I'm not driving far, so there's no real need to break the bank on gas."

"Wes had a Tesla for a while. He liked it. Maybe we should do that."

"Why'd he get rid of it?" If he liked it, why would he not still have it? It didn't inspire confidence.

Tristan laughed. "Because Wes changes cars almost as often as he changes socks. He donated it to a struggling single mom—because he also does stuff like that—and then got something else. But I can't remember what it was that time."

I tried again to wrap my head around being that free with money. "Billionaires are weird."

"Hey." Tristan shot me a mock scowl, then shrugged. "Wes was like that before. At least now he's not having to worry about lease terms. Anyway, if you like the Tesla idea, there's a showroom in Arlington. It's sort of on the way home. Or we can go another time."

I thought for a moment. "Can we just go home?"

"Of course. There's no hurry. And if you want to wait and look around at other options, I can drive you to and from work. My work is flexible."

I glanced at him and smiled as my heart filled with love. "I'd like that."

I let my eyes drift closed and woke again when Tristan took my hand. "We're home. Can you make it inside? I could probably carry you."

"I'm fine. Just tired. And achy. But the car cat nap was exactly what I needed." To prove it, I pushed open my car door and stepped out. Maybe my muscles complained some, but moving felt more good than bad.

Tristan took my hand when I reached him and we walked slowly to the elevators. He leaned forward and pushed the call button.

"Mr. Lee? Ms. Clarke?"

We turned.

Special Agent Orbison stood by an open car door. He raised his hands. "Could we speak?"

Tristan let go of my hand, shifted until he was partially in front of me, and crossed his arms. "If you have something to say, you should be speaking to our attorney."

"I have permission from Ms. Reid to approach you. She said she was going to get in touch to let you know."

Tristan frowned, but he reached into his pocket and drew out his phone. He tapped at the screen then tipped it so I could see the text from Allison. "Okay. Speak."

"Could we—"

"No." Tristan cut the man off. "You've caused us a lot of problems, and my wife is just getting home from the hospital and needs to rest."

Special Agent Orbison sighed, but he nodded. "All right. The FBI would like to officially apologize for the inconvenience they've caused. We've dropped all legal proceedings and have launched an internal investigation surrounding some of the actions that were undertaken."

I waited.

The FBI man didn't seem to be in a hurry to say anything else. Nor did Tristan.

I eased out from behind Tristan. "That's it?"

Special Agent Orbison had the grace to look chagrined. "Unfortunately, that's all I'm officially allowed to say. Unofficially...well, Special Agent Blake was working a sideline with the Russian mafia. He was hoping to get in with the Ortegas to broker information to the Russians. And the FBI. When you pulled out, he saw his chance to win disappear. I guess he'd made some promises that the Russians were definitely going to collect on. I'm still not clear why he thought murdering Ms. Clarke would fix anything. I'm not sure he could explain himself. He was desperate and stupid. And the FBI missed all of this. I missed it. Which makes me culpable as well. I'm sorry."

I mulled those words and looked at Tristan. "You're saying Special Agent Blake ran me down?"

Special Agent Orbison looked pained, but his nod belied his next words. "I'm not officially saying that."

Tristan snorted.

"I'm so, so sorry. I trust my people. I feel like I have no choice but to do that. And usually they don't let me down." The FBI man's shoulders slumped. "Usually."

After a moment, Tristan nodded. "So we're clear?"

"Yes. With our apologies. Official. And my own, besides. I realize none of that makes up for the turmoil that we added to." The man actually looked like he cared.

I slipped my hand into Tristan's. Maybe I should be angrier than I was about it, but if it meant an end to all of the drama, I was okay with letting it go. "It's all right. Thank you for coming to tell us in person. You could have easily let the lawyers handle it."

Special Agent Orbison's smile flashed briefly, then disappeared. "That was the agency's recommendation. I felt I owed you more than that. I wish you both the best."

We stood by the elevator and watched as he climbed back in his car and drove off.

I sagged against Tristan.

He slid his arm around my waist. "Are you okay?"

"I'm tired and I'm ready for us to go home. Our home."

Tristan looked down at me and the love in his eyes made my breath catch. I definitely needed rest. But maybe after that, well, there were some beautiful perks to being married to the love of your life.

EPILOGUE

Tristan

New Year's Eve

The main floor of Peacock Hill was awash in gold and silver balloons, twinkling lights, and gleaming wood. Noah had looked as though he was going to swallow his tongue when Jenna came down the impressive staircase toward him earlier in the evening during the short but moving wedding ceremony.

And now?

I picked up two glasses of champagne from the table where it flowed from a fountain and servers filled flutes to load trays, then scanned the crowd for my wife.

My wife.

Since November, Faith and I had been getting used to living together. We worked well as a team—except when we didn't. I smiled. I didn't mind fighting with her when necessary. Making up was awfully fun, too.

My parents assured us that it was normal growing pains.

And I was ready to believe them. We were learning to put God first in our relationship, and we were going to be okay.

I finally spotted her and nearly laughed as I started in her direction. Of course she was sitting by Kayla, cooing over the baby.

"There you are." Faith glanced up with shining eyes. She took the flute. "Thank you."

"It's almost midnight." I looked back out at the crowd where servers were passing through with trays of a variety of beverages to welcome in the new year. "I didn't want to miss being with you for the countdown."

"You two are so cute." Kayla beamed at us as she shifted the sleeping baby and stood. "I'm going to take that as a hint to find Austin. I don't want to miss my New Year's kiss."

Faith laughed and stood. She eased closer and I slipped my arm around her waist, loving the feel of her snuggled up close.

"It was a beautiful wedding." Faith sighed.

I glanced down. Had that been a happy noise or wistful? "Do you wish we'd done something like this? We can, you know. Mom would love nothing more than to do up something big to celebrate our marriage."

"Oh, no." Faith shook her head firmly. "No. I was simply appreciating this. The venue was amazing, and the planner—Sean, I think?—was able to do so much in a short period of time after Jenna's initial plans tanked. The end result was beautiful."

I looked around and spotted each of my best friends. I nodded toward the center of the foyer where Scott and Whitney stood. Their son, Beckett, nestled in Scott's arms with his head resting on Scott's shoulder. Jenna and Noah were making their way through the crowd in the same direction. Jenna glowed in her Parisian gown, and Noah gave off the pride of the happiest man in the world.

"Let's go join the gang." I nudged Faith toward the foyer.

Kayla had found Austin—and apparently a place to put the baby down—and the two of them walked with Wes and Sunny, laughing their way across the foyer. And finally, Megan and Cody snagged flutes off a tray and completed the circle just as we arrived.

I raised my champagne and looked around at the faces of my friends. "To the best group of friends a guy could have and the women who make us all better."

Laughing, everyone clinked their glasses together and took a sip.

Over the DJ's sound system, the wedding planner spoke, "Ladies and Gentlemen, it's nearly time. Everyone raise your glass and count down with me. Ten..."

I joined in with my friends, my heart full. "Three. Two. One. Happy New Year!"

I spun Faith into an embrace and lowered my mouth to hers, only peripherally conscious that my friends were doing the same with their wives.

I took a moment to whisper a prayer of thanksgiving to God for my friends. My family.

And my Faith.

ACKNOWLEDGMENTS

This book is truly a work of miraculous grace.

I had plans for this book to be out so much sooner. But life. I'm so grateful to Jesus for getting me to the end of the story eventually.

I'm also grateful - every day - for you. The reader. Because you give books life beyond the walls of my imagination. And while I would probably still write even if no one read, I get more joy knowing that people have enjoyed time in the world I created.

Thanks are owed to my husband and kids. Thank you for making space for me to write. For not minding when I'm preoccupied as I dig out plot holes or disappear for "just a few minutes" that turn into something longer.

Thanks to my editor, Lesley McDaniel, who takes the time to explain all the rules that I mess up, even knowing that I'm going to mess them up again in the next book. I do try to learn. I promise.

Thank you to my writing squad. You ladies are amazing and I'm so grateful to call you friends.

Finally, thanks to my sister, who went home to be with Jesus in February, while I was a few chapters away from finishing the book. My sister and my mom were the two loudest cheerleaders for my writing. They encouraged me to write long before I ever dreamed of publishing. And without their support, I doubt very much that I would have had the courage to start. Or continue. Life without you here is taking a lot of getting used to.

WANT A FREE BOOK?

If you enjoyed this book and would like to read another of my books for free, you can get a free e-book simply by signing up for my newsletter on my website.

BUY DIRECT FROM ELIZABETH MADDREY

The 'Operation Romance' Series

Operation Mistletoe

Operation Valentine

Operation Fireworks

Operation Back-to-School

Postcards

The Baxter Family Bakery Series

Loaves & Wishes

Muffins & Moonbeams

Cookies & Candlelight

Donuts & Daydreams

The 'Taste of Romance' Series

A Splash of Substance

A Pinch of Promise

A Dash of Daring

A Handful of Hope

A Tidbit of Trust

The 'Remnants' Series

Faith Departed

Hope Deferred

Love Defined

The 'Grant Us Grace' Series

Wisdom to Know

Courage to Change

Serenity to Accept

Pathway to Peace

Joint Venture

For the most recent listing of all my books, please visit my website.

OTHER BOOKS BY ELIZABETH MADDREY

Billionaire Next Door

The Billionaire's Nanny

The Billionaire's Best Friend

The Billionaire's Secret Crush

The Billionaire's Backup

The Billionaire's Teacher

The Billionaire's Wife

Postcards, A Novel

So You Want to Be a Billionaire

So You Want a Second Chance

So You Love to Hate Your Boss

So You Love Your Best Friend's Sister

So You Have My Secret Baby

So You Need a Fake Relationship

So You Forgot You Love Me

Hope Ranch Series

Hope for Christmas

Hope for Tomorrow

Hope for Love

Hope for Freedom

Hope for Family

Hope at Last

Peacock Hill Romance Series

A Heart Restored

A Heart Reclaimed

A Heart Realigned

A Heart Redirected

A Heart Rearranged

A Heart Reconsidered

Arcadia Valley Romance – Baxter Family Bakery Series

Loaves & Wishes

Muffins & Moonbeams

Cookies & Candlelight

Donuts & Daydreams

The 'Operation Romance' Series

Operation Mistletoe

Operation Valentine

Operation Fireworks

Operation Back-to-School

The 'Taste of Romance' Series

A Splash of Substance

A Pinch of Promise

A Dash of Daring

A Handful of Hope

A Tidbit of Trust

The 'Grant Us Grace' Series

Wisdom to Know

Courage to Change

Serenity to Accept

Pathway to Peace

Joint Venture

The 'Remnants' Series:

Faith Departed

Hope Deferred

Love Defined

Stand alone novellas

Kinsale Kisses: An Irish Romance

Luna Rosa (part of A Tuscan Legacy)

For the most recent listing of all my books, please visit my website.

ABOUT THE AUTHOR

USA Today bestselling author Elizabeth Maddrey is a semi-reformed computer geek and homeschooling mother of two who lives in the suburbs of Washington D.C. When she isn't writing, Elizabeth is a voracious consumer of books. She loves to write about Christians who struggle through their lives, dealing with sin and receiving God's grace on their way to their own romantic happily ever after.

facebook.com/ElizabethMaddrey

instagram.com/ElizabethMaddrey

amazon.com/Elizabeth-Maddrey/e/B00A11QGME

bookbub.com/authors/elizabeth-maddrey

youtube.com/@ElizabethMaddreyAuthor